LIGHT & SHADOW

a novel

by

Charles M. Hunter

ISBN: 978-1-7777235-8-3

For requests and/or additional information, contact:
scarletmere7@mail.com

Wendy

"Our greatest glory is not in never failing,
but in rising every time we fail."

~ Confucius

Prologue

In the dark depths of the Earth, in a place no mortal could exist, stands a sealed ebony sarcophagus wrapped in bonds of silver light. Trapped within a maddening prison, the undying spirit of he who was once a man had been cast into the darkness of the underworld, condemned to spend eternity in turmoil and isolation, as one who cannot be reasoned with nor destroyed must be.

After witnessing the destruction and sinking of a great city into the sea, and seeing the absorption of soul energy belonging to thousands of fleeing innocents, it was Marquis, the man seen as the greatest of Lythia's Sacred Knights, whose weapon of silver light was the one to cast a monstrous foe back into the underworld, having led a party of five of the Goddess' bravest to take on the Demon of Darkness, each of them wielding a weapon of great power to aid them in their stand against annihilation.

The weapons of power bestowed upon the Knights had each been sought to favor an Element – the forces in existence that possess the innate quality of supporting life. Brought into being by the strength of Lythia's will, the Divine Spirit of each Element was imbued into a Relic: an artifact through which great power could be focused and wielded. *The Divine Relics.* Instruments of astonishing, near-limitless power that, when fully linked with their human counterparts, together become capable of the greatest and most astonishing feats imaginable.

Countering the unpredictable, raw nature of the Elements, was the aforementioned *link;* a metaphysical bonding that allowed the host to tap directly into abilities and traits that were otherwise unattainable and unknowable, all the while providing a vessel for the Spirit to directly act and speak through, giving birth to a new form of emerging consciousness as a result. *Elemental Life.* Non-corporeal beings, who although required a human host to be actively sentient, could nonetheless retain the experiences and knowledge of each and every past link, recalling memory from across the Ages, often in gaps of many centuries when circumstance prevented consistent awakening.

With the body of a human host inevitably succumbing to time itself, the Relic would as well grow cold and enter into regression, returning to a state of unconsciousness until conditions allowed for either its re-genesis or its reawakening, the former of which involved prerequisite conditions of difficulty if the prospective host was of a bloodline unrelated to the previous bearer. On those occasions of inertia which became more and more common with widespread knowledge of their existence fading from civilizations, still, they passively existed in the endless time of the present, awaiting the moment they would be once again called upon to serve their true purpose.

Over half of a Galactic Year, the full phase spanning nearly twenty-six-thousand years on Earth, each of the Divine Relics became known at different times and by entirely different cultures in various geographic locations, and known only to a select few individuals.

From present day, going backward in time, the first mysterious and deadly Relic was given the name *Starsword* in mid 20th century America. A century prior, a re-genesis in the far off country of Japan earned it the name *Raemueru* before its host was compelled to cross the ocean, all the way to the United States of America via ship in order to complete her one and only mission. A reawakening by a blood relative in England in the 1400's called its fiery and secretive nature, *Ignisbrand,* and it carried the memory remnants of many others prior. Originally given the name *Lünaflara* by the Ancients, circa 14,000 B.C., the feminine-leaning Spirit of Divine Fire was bonded to a Relic containing the power of a compressed star. As initially blinding as the brightest break of dawn, it had at its burning core a scarlet red, indestructible gemstone in the shape of a brilliant blade that would be summoned through the Source Field of the Galaxy by the living Goddess of the Ancient World, Lythia, herself. Utilizing her Astral Form to project her consciousness as pure energy soaring through the cosmos, and by nothing more than chance and curiosity, she suddenly ceased her high-velocity travel, halting herself in the vacuum of space to form a metaphysical body with which to see and feel, having become enamored by the multicolored radiance of a single star; one star out of a galaxy of stars, emitting violent bursts of solar flares in shades of red, pink and white, expanding and collapsing like the clockwork of a steady breath. Something was there. Entering the star's corona, an experience felt to be blinding even to her Earthbound self in meditation, she began to perceive a formed object within the core, lying in the untouched oblivion of a gravity well, shaped by heat, pressure and time. Upon draining her psychic stamina to succeed in willing the collapse of the star, its boundless energy compressed into the bladed gemstone at its heart, and thereafter, the Divine One, Goddess of Light, found cause to search out the cosmos for other candidates, each worthy enough to contain a portion of her will and the unfathomable power she reined-in, though she reigned over none by choice.

The second Divine Relic came to be that of a Great Spear bearing the Spirit of Air. The Pierced Lightning; *Vüntihast*, the Storm King, came to command the power of the wind and skies. The masculine-leaning elemental weapon acted as a lightning rod that, together with its wielder, could summon and absorb electric energy directly from the Source Field, the unseen, binding force of the universe, storing it for a violent release through contact with its deadly tip, electrocuting and disintegrating its most unfortunate enemy. When spun at a rapid rate, it unleashed a fierce torrent of wind with all the force of a hurricane, capable of sending even the largest and sturdiest adversary flying.

The third Relic was bonded to the Spirit of Earth. Twin Gaia was purposely constructed by the finest smiths of the Ancient World as a two-sided, two-handed weapon of formidable masculine might, and was only wielded by two men over a 16,000 year period. Awakening the least often of its brothers and sisters, it featured a curved ebony blade on one side, ornately patterned in touches of silver, coated in hardened, unbreakable Ether that allowed it to cleave man and beast alike in two. The other bore a compressed ebony war hammer that could not only smash through the toughest of armor, but bestowed upon its symbiont the strength and ability to fell a mountainside, quaking the ground for miles in every direction. Woe to the foes of the Sleeping Giant, *Terrameta.*

The Aquae Glacium represented the fourth and fifth, and were initially the last of the Relics that were to be bonded with the Spirit of an Element. Differing from the others in several ways, they were recovered from an abyss at the furthest edge of the galaxy, found together as a pair of bracers left over from an untold civilization, lost in a frozen wasteland for eons. One was of a dark, metallic blue. The other of a frosty white. The Goddess then proceeded straight away in enchanting the first with a feminine spirit representing water and the flow of time. The other was bonded to a masculine spirit of intense cold and isolation, representing the absence of time. Able to be utilized individually, they certainly were, however the Goddess' true goal in seeking them out was to combine two complementary Elements into a more deadly force, as well as a great force for protection. Brought into close proximity, Enchanted Ice in the form of whatever the wielder conjured in their mind would appear from out of the Source Field as a hardened crystalline, existing until disenchanted through an intended or otherwise loss of concentration, offering endless creative possibility through a most versatile and elegant harmony of Human, Element and Relic.

Yet there would exist two others.

Chapter 1

Drowned Dreams

July 19th, 1967 – 15:00 hours.

John Donovan, Junior was starting his fifth beer as indicated by the four empty bottles on the bar top just to his left. With talk of how God must be laughing at him, he continued to drink as if his words were a mere prelude to further mouthfuls. Hearing the sound of a pen tapping on an open notebook was an instant reminder of the impatience of the classically beautiful, intelligent blonde seated to his immediate right.

"Start at the beginning," the woman requested, in a rather charming, refined accent.

"Where are you from again? And what are you writing?"

"London," she responded. "I told you, I'm a freelance journalist."

"Well, sure thing, pretty l-lady," John said, slurring his words just a little. "I'll tell you whatever it is you wanna know. I can picture everything like it all happened yesterday," he recollected, "but June 29th of last year..." he said, pausing his speech to take a swig of beer, "...that was the day she drowned in Scarletmere. Hey, that rhymes," he commented, before taking yet another drink of his favorite amber brew.

"...Well, go on," the writer told him, as she adjusted the small, stylish, rectangular eyeglasses she wore, wishing for them to rest higher up on the bridge of her nose.

"Well, Kimberly," he continued, using the opportunity during a slight shift in the direction of his bar stool to attempt to touch the Englishwoman's softly painted, blue fingernails, "I was in charge of the camp. Still am, kinda, n-not that it really matters anymore."

"Ms. Hunter," she corrected him, while moving her hand away from his, revealing only the slightest irritation through a forced grin that was intended to keep him on the hook for a little while longer.

"Now, what about the bodies that were found at the shore? Do you think what they say is true? Is the ghost of Scarletmere real?"

The camp owner's son had already begun to shake his head at the absurdity of the questions being asked, but still, the writer persisted.

"One of the old guys in town said he saw a young girl in a tattered white dress, walking on the water in the moonlight," she informed him. "What do you make of that?"

"I don't know," John replied, in a tone of annoyance, considering the impossible nature of it all. "Inebriation?" he guessed, while acknowledging the bottle in his hand as a possible explanation for the absurd. "Look, I'm not sure how this got so blown out of proportion, or who started *that* crazy rumor, but a girl drowned in the Mere and that's all. There's no ghost, no spirit, and nothing supernatural is going on. I mean, come on, you can't possibly believe in that sort of thing," he said, and scoffed to mock those that did as he lifted his beer toward his mouth, producing a low enough sound that told of its near emptiness. "Get real."

"Well, I..." Kimberly began to reply.

"As for who killed my friends, well, the Sheriff has him behind bars," the young man added, interrupting her response.

"But, do you believe he's guilty?" she truly wondered. "Because, as I understand it, several people who met him last year as he passed through town have all said that he couldn't have done it. They witnessed him leave town, going west on foot only to return days after the murders took place."

"Exactly," John said, as he pointed a finger into the air. "The Sheriff found him at the shore concealing a red, blood-stained sword. I mean, come on, a *sword.* What else are you going to do with a sword but use it to kill someone?"

Already aware of the erroneous reported details, the eyes of the writer rolled with disgust for untruths. "Yes, I inquired about that since it was mentioned in the paper, and do you know what I was told?" she rhetorically asked, causing the eyes of the young man next to her to roll out of annoyance. "I was told that there was nothing at all found on the sword. No blood and no fingerprints means no evidence."

"Well, I hadn't heard that," it was admitted, as the young man rested his chin on his hands, set over top of his beer.

"It seems to me the Sheriff is holding that man with less than circumstantial evidence," Kimberly quite boldly stated.

"The Sheriff told me in person that it's what he saw," John insisted. "It was a dark red blade, stained with blood. He knew something strange was going on and made the arrest. You know, I remember seeing a sword last year, but it damn sure wasn't red," he said in recollection. "But, I do remember seeing...something. A bright, red light," he recalled, while zoning out and staring straight forward until he gave his head a shake and returned to the active moment in time.

"Any idea what it was?"

"I dunno," he responded, having dismissed the recalled image of the bizarre event from his mind. "Might've been a flash of lightning. It was gone as quick as it appeared. I remember it was storming, though. The rain was heavy that night. It was hard for me to see."

Regardless of what she personally believed, Kimberly jotted the information down before saying, "I heard from one of the Deputies that the bodies were drained and weighed next to nothing, and that there were no stab or slash wounds that would be consistent with that type of weapon," she was sure to throw in.

"Believe what you want," John told her, not at all caring about her suggestive opinions. "There's nothing else I can tell you, except that when he suddenly left last summer, fleeing the scene," he speculated out of spite, "it was soon after the camp was set on fire."

"You don't think it was the girl's mother or father?" the informed journalist made certain to ask. "They were reported missing, after all."

John couldn't help but think about both of them. How Bennett had helped him with repairs at the camp, how the tall, burly man talked about finally beating his alcoholism, and how much he really missed his wife and daughter. Flashes of Leona's warm smile, her flowing auburn hair, and thoughts of the best pie he had ever tasted – so vivid he could practically smell the way the kitchen smelled that night.

"You know," he soon responded, putting off the finishing of his drink, "at one point I thought I was sure about what happened, but the more I think about it the more I don't know *what* to believe, so you just go ahead and think whatever the hell you want," he told her, while staring forward at the bottles of alcohol lining the shelves of the wall behind the bar. "I'll tell you what I *can't* believe, though."

"Yeah, and what's that?" Kimberly asked, as she closed her notebook in preparation to leave, seeing that there was nothing more to be gained from speaking with a man wallowing in an alcohol-fueled self-pity combined with an arrogance of disbelief.

"That anyone would want to write articles about this sort of thing," he replied, wiggling an empty beer bottle while trying to make eye contact with the bartender. "A person like that would have to be a little on the other side of normal."

"Thanks for the vote of confidence, but I've always found *normal* just a little too *boring,"* the writer responded, while donning a light jacket. "In this country, I'd still like to believe, as much as I *hate* that word, that you're still innocent until proven guilty. A wise man once said that all it takes for the triumph of evil is for good men to do nothing, so if you know something that might help establish reasonable doubt, and whether you believe him or not, don't you think that you have an obligation to come forward?"

Ignoring her guilt trip, John successfully signaled to the female bartender cleaning glasses at the far end for yet another round.

"John?" Kimberly eventually said, after waiting for a response that never came.

"Mr. Donovan," he corrected, before guzzling half of a freshly opened beer that the bartender placed in front of him.

"I'm convinced there's a story dying to be told here, even if you're unable, or perhaps unwilling to open your eyes to see it," Kimberly said, just before taking her leave of the spiteful man.

"You don't *have* enough to write a story," he countered, raising his voice slightly, as the blonde writer made her way across the dimly lit bar toward the exit. "There *isn't* enough!"

With that statement, the writer stopped in her tracks and turned her head to the side, looking back toward the bar with the aid of just one eye bearing an irritated gaze. After a moment of meditative composure, she decided to respond calmly before making her exit. "You didn't think I came all the way from England just to interview *you,* did you?"

With that said, the bar door opened and closed, leaving just three people inside.

"Women," John muttered.

Instantly realizing what he had just said out loud, he looked down the bar toward the female bartender, who had her hands on her hips and a look of disgust on her face.

"Sorry, Marlene."

A lone old man seated at a table across from the bar counter, having overheard a good portion of an interesting and amusing conversation, could only shake his head in disbelief as he looked down at a newspaper and took a drink from a glass of whiskey.

~

The thirty-three-year-old writer stepped out into the drizzling rain and descended a flight of stairs that led away from the entrance to the bar, above which there was a sign illuminated as *AR* due to a burnt out letter *B*. Hastily approaching three vehicles that were next to each other in the small parking lot, she quickly got into the oldest and smallest one in the group – a Volkswagen Beetle. After the engine turned over several times, it finally started, and with the expression of the driver having been unchanged in the process, it seemed to the only one watching her that it was to be expected.

Sighing heavily, Kimberly tossed her notebook onto the passenger seat and was about to pull away from the building when she decidedly shifted the transmission into neutral, engaging the hand brake, as well, just to keep the car from rolling. She then flicked a switch on the dash that activated the dome light on the ceiling, and with the additional light, a messy, disorganized interior was suddenly illuminated. There were dozens of newspaper clippings in various shapes and sizes strewn about, requiring the driver to twist around in her seat in order to reach into the back for the ones on her mind. A gathered-together pile was soon rested against the steering wheel, enabling her to clearly see the text. The first one in the group read:

Scarletmere Shore; Two Bodies Discovered

On the morning of June 30th, the bodies of Camp Scarletmere counselors Shane & Maggie Brewer were discovered washed up on the shoreline. The Sheriff's Department ordered the immediate evacuation and shutdown of the camp, and for the second year in a *row, Camp Scarletmere will remain closed. Perhaps just as unsettling is the fact that 13 year old Lydia Looms drowned in the mere exactly one year prior to this tragic event, stirring up ghostly rumors and talk of old stories involving the mere and its rather ominous, all but forgotten history.*

The first newspaper clipping was moved to the back of the pile, revealing a black and white photo of a young, dark haired girl on the next, with burn scars that marred the right half of an otherwise lovely face. The name printed underneath the picture read: ***Lydia Looms.*** The left of the page featured the article:

Tragedy At Camp Scarletmere

The Sheriff's Department has come under much scrutiny in the public eye recently, as a statement regarding the death of young Lydia Looms was released only yesterday. The thirteen year old girl had apparently fallen into the mere, and being a poor swimmer, subsequently drowned over three weeks ago. Both the father and mother of the deceased have been declared missing in the aftermath of this terrible tragedy. Speculation as to the reason for the delay have persisted in the wake of the announcement, and the general consensus among the townsfolk is that the financial interest in keeping the incident a secret, if only until the end of the summer, took priority in the eyes of the camp owners.

The writer then moved the second clipping to the back of the pile. The third was somewhat larger and featured another photo, the headline of which read:

Suspect In Scarletmere Double Homicide Arrested!

The photo on the left was of a dark-skinned man in a cowboy hat being escorted by a Sheriff's Deputy. The article alongside it read:

Suspect identified as Marcus Walther, a non-resident of Scarletmere County. Not much is known about this shady-looking character dressed completely in black attire, as according to the Sheriff's Department, he has chosen to invoke his right to remain silent in not speaking a word since being placed under arrest. Several strange items and weapons were found hidden on his person, including a loaded magnum revolver, a supply of hand-loaded ammunition, a large serrated hunting knife, a vial of water with a cross etched into the glass, a cloth bag containing a quarter pound of *salt, a small container of lighter fluid, matches, several cigars, and last but certainly not least, a very sharp and rather unique sword. Suffice it to say, things could not be worse for the young man. The townsfolk, however, seem entirely divided concerning the guilt of Mr. Walther, as many people have come forward indicating their doubt as to his involvement in the murder of Shane & Maggie Brewer, whose bodies were found washed ashore at Camp Scarletmere just weeks ago on the morning of June 30th. Many of the elderly residents in town instead place the blame for the deaths where they have always placed them, and that is on the nature of the mere itself.*

With the information from the newspaper articles swirling around in her mind, Kimberly set her collection down onto the passenger seat, released the parking brake, shifted into first gear, turned the windshield wipers on to combat the light rain and pulled out onto a paved road. Heading north below a gray sky, she soon passed by a highway sign displaying mileage to the next few towns, only one of which managed to capture her focus: Scarletmere – 189 Miles.

The rain grew heavier as she drove, and three uneventful hours later, Kimberly turned her sky blue VW into the very first gas station at the edge of town and pulled up to the pumps. Waiting there for the service attendant, she flipped a switch on the dash that activated the dome light and quickly looked over a map to confirm her next driving route. Feeling tired, she yawned and closed her eyes as she rested her head back against the seat, when suddenly there was a loud double knock on the driver's side window. Mildly startled, she opened her eyes in immediate reaction only to discover a dog-faced, aging man staring back at her from the other side of the glass. *Probably looking for booze money,* she thought to herself, before rolling the window down just enough to avoid getting wet.

"Yes? Can I help you, sir?"

"Isn't that supposed to be my line?" the old man responded, in a raspy voice that could hardly cut through the sound of the falling rain.

"Excuse me?"

"Fill her up?" he clarified.

"Oh, *I'm* sorry," she said, upon realizing that he was in fact the attendant. "I was expecting...um..."

Seeing that he'd embarrassed her, "...a much younger man?" he asked, finishing her sentence for her.

"No, I..." she said, as she rolled her window down a little further.

"No harm, no foul, ma'am," his raspy voice assured her, before he began to set the pump to fill the tank automatically. *"So,"* he said, raising his voice to compensate for the sound of the falling rain, *"you're the one who's been asking questions all over town!"*

"Pardon?!"

"You're the writer," the old attendant said, when he returned to his customer's window, glancing into the car's newspaper-strewn interior – a subtle tactic intended to get her to acknowledge the contents of her messy vehicle so that he could take a longer look without her noticing. "It seems that an intelligent woman such as yourself isn't content to accept what they want her to believe."

"Just what is it that *they* want me to believe?" Kimberly asked, with her interest peaked.

"That the Mere is nothing more than a body of water. But, it ain't. Hasn't been for decades, maybe centuries. So far, no one's been able to completely silence it. Sure, it goes quiet for awhile, lays dormant, but under the light of the full moon, its influence grows. Under rare scarlet moonlight, its influence grows tenfold."

Highly interested in where the conversation was steering, and motivated to get to the bottom of the Scarletmere mystery, the writer opted to use the opportunity to learn more. "You've got my attention, Mister..." she said, awaiting a name.

"Flynn," he responded, in his buttoned up gray raincoat and matching duster hat, displaying a salute so practiced and refined that it seemed to momentarily transform the stature of the aging, dog-faced old man into that of a well-trained soldier. "Master Sergeant 'Lightning' Llewellyn Flynn, U.S. Army, retired."

"That's an interesting name," Kimberly immediately commented.

"A nickname I earned while boxing in the army. I'm not as fast as I used to be, but, it stuck."

"I think I can see why," the instinctive writer said, knowing from the posture of his salute alone that there was much more to the man than his appearance suggested. "I'm Kim. Kimberly Hunter."

"It's a bit dark and rainy out here, Ms. Hunter," the old Sergeant noted, "so how about inviting me into that nice warm car of yours after I top up your tank? We've got a lot to do if we're going to figure this thing out together, but we can start by convincing the Sheriff to drop the charges against the man featured in these articles," he suggested, flashing them a glance, letting her know that he was already aware of the subject matter of the newspaper clippings scattered about the car's messy interior.

"...Get in," she responded, before reaching over to unlock the passenger door, deciding to extend her trust to the ex-soldier who had quickly and unexpectedly acquired knowledge of the contents of her car. *"Why him?!"* she loudly asked, having to shout as Flynn secured the VW's gas cap, desiring the long awaited answer to the question that interested her a great deal more than his uncanny ability to instantly absorb details.

Setting the handle back on the side of the pump, the old Sergeant fast-walked into the open garage of the gas station and disappeared out of sight for a few seconds before he came back out into the rain and proceeded straight around the front of the VW to open up its passenger door. Sliding into the front seat, carefully shutting the door, buckling his seat belt and making himself comfortable, all the while knowing that the blonde-haired driver was staring at him through her rectangular eyeglasses, certainly tested her resolve. "He carries the blood," was the eventual answer he provided to the persistent yet patient Englishwoman – an answer she never would have predicted and, at the time, did not understand.

Chapter 2

American Hero

18:30 hours.

Marcus Walther stood in his jail cell, holding onto the iron bars that had trapped him for days, wishing that he had possession of the lock pick he kept hidden inside of his custom-made trench coat. Of course, it would likely no longer be there. Every object he valued had been withdrawn from the jacket's many hiding places, inventoried, and put into a storage bin in the station's evidence room. The Sheriff had even taken his lucky hat: A worn-in, dusty but cherished item that his father had given him for his seventeenth birthday.

Dispatching the out of shape lawman would have been an easy enough task had he considered the Sheriff a true enemy, but the hunter found himself quite unwilling to harm a man who was only doing what he believed was best to ensure the safety of his County during a murder investigation. The Sheriff, at least from his own perspective, caught his suspect red handed – in a manner of speaking – and the explanations provided to him were either ignored or rejected outright. Ironically, by locking up the mysterious man in a jail cell, he had unwittingly placed the town in far greater danger.

As far as the hunter knew, the only hope that remained for his release was to get off on lack of evidence at his scheduled trial. After all, he had done nearly nothing wrong, and each of the items that he preferred to keep with him at all times, including his brand new magnum revolver, were completely legal in the State where Scarletmere was located. Unfortunately, the one thing the Sheriff *did* have on him was a failure to properly adhere to open-carry regulations for firearms.

"Say, Sheriff?" Walther unexpectedly said, to the heavyset man in uniform seated at a desk across the room. "Is it not about high time I paid my fine and moved on from this here town? I appreciate the hospitality and all, but I did not intend to overstay my welcome."

The Sheriff, entirely uninterested in playing games, continued looking down at his pencil in motion as he completed the day's paperwork. "Sit tight, Walther," he told his prisoner. "You're seeing the judge tomorrow. A jury will decide your fate."

"I have urgent matters to attend to," the jailed man continued, more or less trying to annoy the lawman at that point.

"Urgent matters?"

"Yes," Walther firmly said. "Let me out of here for one week, and I promise I will return to face your judge and jury."

Hearing what he interpreted to be a ludicrous statement, the Sheriff let out a series of deep belly laughs, causing his beer gut to shake up and down. He then got right back to his paperwork with a shake of his head, ignoring what was thought to be an insincere promise.

"Look, every second that I'm in here puts the town in greater—"

Quite suddenly, the door to the hall opened and an aging man with a rough, hardened demeanor, dressed in a gray raincoat with a gray hat, who was immediately followed after by an attractive blonde wearing a pair of rectangular eyeglasses with a blue blouse and black slacks, entered the room and headed straight toward the Sheriff's desk, but not without flashing a glance at the captive prisoner who curiously raised his eyebrows in response.

"I'm not in the mood," the Sheriff said, as he continued to work away, barely looking up to even see who had barged in.

"I'm afraid we'll need a moment of your time," a raspy old voice countered.

"Who's *we?"* the lawman asked, as he began to take interest in the only female in the room, never knowing old *misery Flynn* to be in the company of anyone but himself.

"This is Ms. Kimberly Hunter."

"How do you do, sir?" the polite Englishwoman said, choosing to greet the rather stern-looking, middle aged man by way of a respectful, disarming handshake.

The Sheriff stood to his feet to gently accept the delicate hand being offered to him. "Pleasure to make your acquaintance, Ms. Hunter," he said, smiling and feeling invigorated by her very presence. “Tell me, Flynn,” he said, without so much as glancing away from the attractive blonde, “how is it that you've come to know such a charming woman?”

“Ms. Hunter is a freelance writer,” the old man explained, in his raspy voice. “She has something to show you. Go ahead, my dear.”

“Well, Sheriff,” Kimberly began, while reaching into the leather satchel she carried, “suffice it to say, you've locked up an American hero,” she casually concluded, as she pushed forward an old newspaper clipping for the lawman to read.

The Sheriff looked at her blankly, and then across the large room at his lone prisoner, whose interest in where their conversation was leading had obviously been peaked as he looked on between the bars of his cell. “Well,” the lawman said, stroking his thick mustache, “let's just see what we have here. Washington Herald, Tuesday, October the 24th, 1965. At last the people of Washington, D.C. can breathe a sigh of relief, as Marcus Walther, pictured above, performed an arrest of one Thomas Hayden Payne, a man wanted by both police and FBI in connection with an ongoing trail of gruesome murders. In a momentary interview with Mr. Walther, a man of mixed African-American and Native American descent, he described himself as a bounty hunter of sorts. When asked about his role in the apprehension of such a frightful killer, he stated that, “the killers ought to fear *me*,” adding that he was, “the metaphorical Devil called in to do God's work.” Subsequently, he was to receive a medal from the President, but in the aftermath, could not be located for commendation.”

“Will you let him go?” Flynn wasted no time in asking. “He clearly isn't your man.”

“Well, Mr. Walther,” the Sheriff said, as he began walking across the hall. “It seems that you've done this country a great service, but do you really expect me to just let you go in light of these circumstances? Says here you're a bounty hunter, and I've got two dead right on my own doorstep, so to speak,” he said, referencing the area beyond the Mere as the end of his jurisdiction.

“Let me go so that I can find the one responsible for those murders,” Walther suggested as the better reason.

After a moment of contemplation, the big lawman removed a ring of jingling keys from his belt, located the correct one for the cell door in front of him and decidedly unlocked it. When the door was pulled open, his prisoner looked at him with raised eyebrows and stepped out for the first time in days. “I am free to go?” he inquired, just to be clear.

“Not quite,” the Sheriff replied, as he returned to his desk. “There's still the matter of you failing to observe open-carry regulations for that cannon of yours. The law states that I can confiscate the weapon, but I suppose a hefty fine will suffice. Fifty dollars.”

Hearing the amount, Kimberly began searching through her satchel at the same time that Flynn began searching his pockets, and seeing that they were together trying to come up with the money to pay his fine, Walther felt the need to stop them. “I can pay it myself,” he said. “If you do not mind, Sheriff, I would like to gear up.”

“Here,” the lawman said, before he picked up an empty holster that had been hanging from a hook on the wall and immediately tossed it across the room.

The hunter snatched the incoming item out of the air, gave it a once-over and draped it over his shoulder.

“You know where the rest is,” the Sheriff commented. “If you're a southpaw,” he said, noting the hunter's re-positioning of the holster to his left side, “where you had it before, in your jacket, you were more or less cross-drawing.”

“I will make good use of it,” Walther responded, as he began making his way toward a door marked 'Storage'. “I will return shortly,” he told Flynn and Kimberly, before stepping into the side room.

While gearing up, he ritualistically did an inventory of his equipment in the same way he always did – in his mother's native language – mumbling to himself each item's name as he progressed along, ignoring the fact that an attractive blonde was watching him through the glass in the door, periodically switching between observing and writing in a notebook.

“You might offer the man some privacy,” the Sheriff suggested.

“You don't understand,” Kimberly replied, as she continued to observe the man for a few more seconds. “I've read many articles about this guy. When unexplained deaths occur, or a serial killer is on a rampage, or something supernatural happens, a man fitting his exact description shows up and then disappears without a trace. According to some of the articles, several people came to know him by one name. *Walther."*

"That's because he *is* Walther," Flynn explained.

"How is that possible? The articles go back to the late 19th century. The earliest one, that I just so happen to have a copy of, is dated *1899. Look,"* she said, and slapped down a newspaper cutout onto the Sheriff's desk for them both to read. "It's from a town about sixty miles from here."

"They may bear the same name, Ms. Hunter, but you can rest assured that they are not the same person," Flynn insisted, after looking the article over. "The man who is here among us is one *Marcus* Walther, son of the late Luther Walther, son of the late Jefferson Walther, who is the man mentioned in this article."

"Oh, *I* see," she realized, and immediately began to record the information in her notebook, demonstrating no ego whatsoever in immediately accepting the new information. "So, Walther is his family name. I guess I didn't consider that."

"You believed something supernatural was at work? Giving one man eternal youth?" Flynn asked, scoffing and pretending to make fun of her, to help ensure, for the first time in his life, that the Sheriff was none the wiser to the truth he so often tried to convince him of.

"But, Flynn," Kimberly said, sounding a bit confused, "you were saying the Mere—"

"Nonsense, my dear," he interrupted, flashing the writer a stern gaze when he was sure the Sheriff was busy with his paperwork.

"Oh..." she finally clued in, just before the hunter exited the storage room dressed in his full attire, drawing everyone's attention.

"Is that the description you were imagining?" Flynn asked, nodding in the darkly-dressed man's direction.

"What description?" Walther wondered out loud, as he straightened his favorite cowboy hat and proceeded to hide something beneath the length of his trench coat.

"You dress exactly like him," Kimberly answered.

"Who?"

"Your grandfather," Flynn clarified, as he approached the freed man and handed him Kimberly's newspaper clipping.

Marcus Walther – the sole-surviving Dark Hunter – read the article carefully. His heart and mind, but not his expression, filled with feelings of pride, respect and admiration to be reading such an old article about the man who held legendary status within the ranks of his once flourishing family. The icing on the cake was finding out that the man's description and personal taste very much matched his own.

1899. The man known by many as 'Walther' is a dark-skinned, six-foot-tall man from North Africa, dressed in tasteful black and gray Western attire. According to several people interviewed, this young man is friendly, helpful, approachable, and is seeking out odd jobs in neighboring communities. As well, according to at least one individual from Scarletmere County, troublemakers ought to beware, as Mr. Walther is an honorary Sheriff's Deputy with full arrest powers for his services to the people. Several hooligans have learned, albeit the hard way, that he is not one to be trifled with.

"I last saw your Grandfather in 1947," Flynn confessed, as the article was returned to him and then to its owner, who accepted it and hurried to get her pen moving so that she could record the unexpected information in her notebook. "I was a young, troublesome kid when I first met him. He told me about the history of Scarletmere in a way I'd never heard before. I first took an interest in him when a sudden wind flared up and I caught sight of the unique artifact he carried."

The Dark Hunter's interest had peaked at the opportunity to discuss his grandfather, a man whom he had never met, with another man whom he had never met and yet who seemed to know something about him and his heritage. Upon hearing the term *unique artifact,* however, he found himself quite taken aback. "You knew him?" he calmly inquired of the raspy-voiced older man.

"Correct."

"And you have laid eyes on the artifact that he refused to show even to my father?"

"That's correct," Flynn again confirmed.

"I do not suppose you know what happened to him?" Walther asked, as he placed several bills taken from a roll of cash onto the busy lawman's desk as payment for his fine. "Buy your wife something nice, Sheriff," he took the time to say, while at last taking his leave as a free and clear man, wondering what the lawman's reaction would be when he finally added up the one-hundred dollars left on the corner of his desk.

Flynn, following alongside Kimberly, had been thinking of an appropriate response before answering, "He was here in '47, but I don't know what happened to him after that, because, truth be told, I never saw him again."

"And the artifact you happened to witness?" Walther asked next, as he led the way down the station's main hallway, garnering looks from the station's custodian and a lone deputy who was pouring himself a cup of coffee and had become distracted enough by the group's appearance to accidentally burn himself.

"Took it with him, of course."

"Of course..."

"What's so special about this artifact?" Kimberly interjected, as the trio made their way through the station's front doors and into the drizzling rain of a warm summer evening.

Upon hearing the question, the Dark Hunter came to a stop and felt the flash of distant memory as a boy listening to his father's stories, allowing him to repeat the words of the past. "It used to be nothing more than a custom-made Winchester – a lever-action rifle – but it came to be much more than that," he said, as he stood in the light rain beneath a gray, cloud-filled sky. "I assume one of you has transportation?"

"I do," Kimberly eagerly said, while jingling a small set of keys taken from the pocket of her jacket.

"Where are we going?" Flynn naturally wondered.

The hunter drew in and exhaled a deep breath of fresh air. "On a very important and dangerous mission," he replied, more so to prepare himself than as a statement of warning to the others. "The two of you seem quite open-minded," he acknowledged, in an assessment based on the initiative that got him out of jail. "I am thinking I could use all the help I can get to track her down."

Motioning with her hand, the writer directed the way toward her sky blue '62 VW Beetle, haphazardly parked across two spaces on the other side of two Sheriff's Department cruisers. "Just who is it you're looking for?"

"A young woman who continues to elude me," Walther responded, as they walked toward the rather distinct-looking vehicle. “She is five-foot-nine, cute-faced, has dark, wavy hair, and probably a summer tan by now.”

“Do you know this young woman's name?” Kimberly asked, awaiting a response with her pen pressed to the paper in her notebook.

The Dark Hunter nodded assuredly. “I most certainly do.”

Chapter 3

Ruby and Scarlet

23:30 hours.

Sound asleep in a soft, warm bed, lay a cute-faced young woman with wavy, shoulder length hair. The man with short, naturally curly blonde hair who lay next to her slept shirtless, with his mouth agape to the ceiling, breathing heavily and occasionally mumbling bits of jumbled sentences as the young couple dreamed the night away.

A loud knock at the door was jarring enough to instantly awaken the two lovers.

"What time is it?" the shirtless man asked, as he sat up in bed, rubbing his eyes.

The young woman rolled over and reached up to turn on a bedside lamp. With one open eye, she stared down through her dark hair at the face of a small clock on the nightstand, its trio of hands altogether providing her with unfortunate information. "We've only been asleep for an *hour,"* she complained, before throwing herself back down onto her pillow amid the sound of intermittent knocking – knocking that repeated in sequences of seven.

"Bah," her man said, as he shielded his eyes with his arm and rested his head back down. "It's probably Marcy, locked out again. You get it, Trin'," he said with a yawn. "I'm going back to sleep."

"Fine," she said, before smacking his arm with the back of her hand. "You owe me."

"One foot rub," he lazily responded into his pillow.

"Two," she countered, thereafter taking his steady, uninterrupted breathing to mean his silent capitulation.

The knocking continued on like clockwork, predictably repeating a steady pattern every few seconds as she quickly slid her feet into a pair of fuzzy purple slippers and pulled a rather plain, gray housecoat on over her soft pink negligee. She then made her way out of the bedroom and down the hallway toward the front door, with the sound of the knocking growing louder and louder as she drew nearer and nearer. Moving the small window curtain aside, she stood on her tiptoes and peered through the looking glass at the top, trying to find out who had been brazen enough to wake her in the middle of the night. The eyes she found herself staring into belonged to a dark-skinned man whom she neither expected nor hoped to ever see again. Lowering herself slowly back to a flat-footed position, she paused a moment to consider waking her boyfriend, but in deciding to quietly turn away the unwelcome visitor by herself, she reluctantly opened the door and stepped outside onto the deck.

"Greetings, Ms. Ryder," a deep voice spoke from the darkness. "Imagine. *Me,* finding *you, here.* You must have written to him just like you said you would."

Scowling, the young woman crossed her arms. "What the hell are *you* doing here?" she responded, with a great amount of irritation present in her voice.

"Oh, just stopped by to say hello to an old friend," the voice in the dark responded, and though he certainly knew that she would never believe that as the real reason for his visit, it was still a psychological move that he actually hoped would insert a degree of humor and levity into a difficult situation.

"I know what you want," she very seriously responded, dismissing the unwanted memories that uncontrollably flashed through her mind while trying to zero-in on his hidden location, well aware that his true aim was dead-set in alignment with an ulterior motive, "but, I won't do it. I can't ever go back."

"Fate has chosen you," he insisted, as he at last stepped forward from out of the shadows and into moonlight, trying to coax the defiant young woman gently but assuredly. "No one else can truly wield it," he said, keeping hidden the object of his meaning.

"I'll choose my own fate, thank you very much," she argued, before turning back toward the door in anger.

"Trinity. You *must* come back with me," the voice insisted, throwing caution to the wind, managing to at least halt her in place. "Accept it, or we will *all* die."

"...You know," she soon replied, as tears welled up in her eyes, "every time I look at the moon, now, I can feel her in the back of my mind."

Tilting his head back, the Dark Hunter looked up and to the left, high into the night sky, where a beautiful crescent moon shone among the stars. "And what is it that you feel?"

"...Anger...resentment......darkness," Trinity said, fighting against tears, as she turned to face the darkly-dressed man on her doorstep.

"You *can* do something about it," Walther said, while brushing aside the right tail of his jacket, revealing the instantly recognized hilt of a sheathed long sword resembling a four-pointed star.

"Please," Trinity fearfully reacted, as she pressed her back up against the door to the house, fumbling for the knob a single time, feeling that she needed something to hang onto. *"Y-you...* keep that away from me!"

"It belongs only to you," he persisted, though cautious enough to keep her listening. "It longs to return to your hand. All you have to do is accept what it has to offer. Accept the symbiosis."

"Symbiosis?" she repeated, at the time having no idea what the word meant.

"It *needs* you, and you need *it*, whether you know it or not."

"What can it possibly offer aside from more pain and suffering," she said, responding with a rhetorical question.

"Protection, reliability...courage," he stated as examples. "And that goes for any weapon, really, though few things can compare with *this.* If you open yourself to it, you will possess a great power."

"I...*can't!* I'm...afraid..."

"Must I beg? True fear is coming for *us* if we do *nothing."*

A single tear fell from the left eye of the young woman and was quickly wiped away with the back of her hand. "I know..." she sadly admitted, remaining stationary on the porch in the dark, saying nothing more for the time being.

"Keep it safe from prying eyes," Walther soon instructed, as he presented the Relic in both hands, giving off the false impression that he would leave her alone if she would only agree to take it. "You will at least feel better having it nearby," he casually suggested. "It will be there for you when you need it most."

Even through the blade's black scabbard, a restrained life force, longing to be free again, began to subtly glow a deep shade of red as the young woman hesitantly stepped closer to begrudgingly accept it in both hands, giving her an immediate sense of its contentment. With her fear and trepidation beginning to melt away, she slowly moved her right hand to the bare hilt of the ancient weapon, causing the blade's veiled light to glow more intensely from inside the sheath. Whatever she felt in regard to apprehension had by then dissipated and, from within herself, she felt another consciousness rise to the surface as her eyes rolled over a deep, opaque red.

"Finally," two female voices spoke in unison. *"I thought she might drop me again."*

The Dark Hunter, though slightly taken aback, had long come to terms with everything that had happened and was expected to happen. Still, the Communion of Souls had occurred far quicker than he was expecting. The soul, eternally bound to the sword, was already quite able to speak directly through its counterpart: Trinity, who was, at the time, the only human in existence symbiont with one of the Six.

"And you are..?" Walther could only think to ask.

"Someone has already decided what I am to be called in this era, have they not?" the voices spoke together. *"You may call me Scarlet."*

"And what about *her?"* he next inquired, as he stared into a pair of dark red eyes, no doubt concerned for the young woman's safety.

"The girl? Trinity..." Scarlet noted, in reference to her young symbiont. *"We have an understanding,"* she confidently declared. *"There is a mission to carry out, and so shall it be. She knows that when she touches me,* ***I*** *take over command of this...underdeveloped vessel,"* she decided, after giving her petite, borrowed body a rather judgmental once-over, and then, all at once, the intense red vanished from both sword and eye, and control over a borrowed body was reinstated. The turbulent emotions of a young woman, however, were being secretly guarded and constantly monitored to ensure stability.

"I think I'm gonna be *sick*," Trinity said, right before she arched over the patio railing, holding the sword by the sheath that concealed an indestructible blade so as not to evoke the Fire Spirit a second time.

The feeling will subside. You will grow accustomed to the sensation over time.

"Are you alright?" Walther asked, shortly after going to her side.

"How dare you call me *underdeveloped,"* Trinity said, sounding nauseous but nevertheless having the energy to shake the sword in spite while staring directly at the hilt as if it were a face at which to direct her complaints.

"Trinity," Walther gently said, drawing the young woman's attention away from the weapon, "I wish for you to become my successor."

"Huh? Your what?"

"Protege. Apprentice. *Student."*

Still looking and sounding sickly, not giving the proposed idea much thought, and as well having no clue what acceptance would actually mean for her, Trinity nodded. "O-okay."

The Dark Hunter raised his brow, surprised by her sudden willingness to cooperate. "What say we get out of here and get to work?" he strategically asked.

"Y-yeah," she decided, in the midst of breathing slowly and considering what delay could mean for the future. "We think that would be best for everyone," she added, knowing that even John's life hung in the balance of life and death.

I have faith in you, young one. We will undo what must be undone.

For Trinity, denial of reality was no longer possible, and Scarlet had made it so by knowing what emotions would hinder their purpose from those which they could most benefit. With the hunter's assistance, the young sword-bearer stood upright and took a deep breath. "I'm good," she told him, though it was obvious from her facial expression that she still felt nauseated after a life-changing experience.

"There is a car waiting for us down the street," Walther informed his recently appointed apprentice. "There are two people I will introduce you to who are hoping to lend a hand. One of them is an older fella who learned a little bit from my grandfather. The other is a woman who is a few years older than us – a journalist and researcher who happens to be very sly and eager to learn. I tell you this because I do not wish for her, or anyone else, to know too much. Let her draw her own conclusions."

"We understand," Trinity replied – an acknowledgment that the hunter found interesting, as she apparently did not even realize that she had altered her speech in order to speak on behalf of the sword as well as herself. "Um, she wants to say something to you."

He flashed her a quizzical look, surprised that such a thing was possible without direct contact. "And how is it that you know that?"

She appeared to be thinking about it. "...I don't know..."

"Well, alright," Walther replied, "only, speak quickly this time."

With a simple touch of the weapon's hilt, the sword-bearer's eyes again rolled over a deep red, and the same color that could hardly be contained emanated from within the cloak of its black scabbard.

"Worry not over word of these events spreading, but rather their failure to spread," Scarlet's mysterious and haunting voice corrected. *"The Myrr has existed for thousands of years. Ignorance of its true purpose is the sole reason why so many have fallen victim to its power,"* she said, being rather direct about it. *"We will undoubtedly speak again, Marcus, but the girl is scratching at the surface,"* she confessed, and began to slowly relinquish control with adjusted ease upon finishing her thought, slowly becoming empathetic to the idea of sparing her host from the nausea of a faltering equilibrium.

"Whoa," Trinity said with an exhale, having to clutch the railing of the deck in order to maintain her balance. "I think I'm getting used to it," she claimed, before suddenly angling herself over the patio to once again vomit out of the hunter's sight.

"Do not do that again for awhile," Walther suggested, as he, like a gentleman, held a young woman's shoulder length hair back for her. "Better that you only interpret her meaning."

"Uh huh," the sword-bearer nodded, most agreeably, and spat from her mouth onto the grass as she hung her head in recovery.

After allowing ample time for her to stabilize, the hunter put his arm around the delicate shoulders of his would-be successor, guiding her toward an objective. "How about you go and get changed into something a little more appropriate for our purposes, and then we can get started," he calmly and quite nicely suggested, while walking her back to the door that he would have to open up *for* her. "Be certain and not wake your boyfriend, alright? We have a very important job to do," he stated, encouragingly, in an effort to fill her reorienting mind with nothing but thoughts of their forthcoming mission.

"Yeah..." Trinity said, as she stood facing the open doorway, absentminded of the hunter's wish for her to step into the house until a gentle but firm hand on her back encouraged her to move forward, seeming to have lost all basic understanding of how doors functioned and was learning how they worked, all over again. *"Oh..."*

Just as she was about to shut the door, realizing she had to do *that* on her own, as well, the hunter suddenly stopped it with his hand. *"Say,"* he said, before he quickly glanced around the property and beyond, seeming to be making sure that they weren't being watched. "You still got that nice car?"

~

A few minutes later, Trinity stepped out of the dimly lit bedroom where a snoring man had curiously been determined to be fast asleep. Fully dressed in black slacks with a dark red sweater – an outfit chosen not entirely on her own – she turned the corner down a dark hallway and descended a small flight of stairs, leading to where a closed door blocked her path. Staring at the silver ball attached to it, she slowly grasped the object, turned the knob and gently pushed, with a part of her being delighted to rediscover how it functioned. Then, one foot at a time, she stepped forward into total darkness.

The changing young woman suddenly found herself standing in a different location inside the interior of a garage, having no recollection of her movements while in the dark until an overhead light suddenly came on, presumably by the pulling of the chain still dancing above her head. In the center, backed into the garage, was a parked car with a vanity plate that read, RUBYRED. For a lingering moment her most cherished possession went unrecognized, as if she was laying eyes on it for the very first time, until she acknowledged that a part of her *was* in fact seeing it for the first time. The 57' Chevy 210 had been washed and waxed the previous day, and the light from a single overhead bulb was enough to make the well-tended-to car stand out in brilliant form, so much so that Scarlet's consciousness bubbled to the surface to comment on it.

A curious design. I do not understand why, but, I like this.

Sensing the Fire Spirit's desire to touch the car, Trinity mindlessly obliged and took the time to slowly run her hand over the waxed paint as she passed alongside it, failing to notice the aftereffects of her divine touch. Finding herself in front of a much larger door, she visually scanned all around its rectangular perimeter until her eyes locked onto the handle in the middle, near the bottom. When she lifted the heavy, old door a quarter of the way up, a dark-skinned hand from the other side suddenly appeared underneath and hoisted it the rest of the way in a single effort.

"How are you feeling, now?" Walther asked. "Better?"

"Perfectly fine," she replied, seemingly unfazed by the man's rather sudden reappearance. "Scarlet loves the car," she informed him, while on her way to the driver's side door. "It's her first time seeing one."

"I had forgotten how much *I* liked it," the hunter admitted, as he looked the vehicle over, in admiration. "Still, it is humorous though."

"What is?" Trinity asked, having no idea what he was referring to.

"A sword infatuated with a car," he had to explain.

"Oh," she plainly replied, without so much as cracking a smile. "Yeah, I can see how that would be funny."

"It reminds me of that joke about the blind man teaching the robot how to paint a picture," he remembered, cracking himself up in the process. "It is not entirely wrong, but it *is* incredibly odd."

The sword-bearing young woman stood there beside the car, staring back at the hunter, displaying nothing at all in response to the joke involving a humorous and unlikely image that would normally and quite predictably illicit a reaction from someone.

"Are you...certain you are okay?" he asked, jumping up in the middle of his question to hang off of one of the garage's thick, wooden ceiling beams, going right into a set of pull-ups.

*Can **I** drive it?*

"Seriously, I've never been better," she reassured him, as she pulled open the driver's side door. *"I don't think so,"* she sternly said next, responding to the voice in her mind while in the process of sitting down in the driver's seat.

"Did you say something?"

"Nothing," Trinity called out, raising the pitch of her voice. "Nobody drives this car but me," she then said under low volume, speaking directly to the sword's hilt and cross guard before leaning the sheathed weapon up against the seat, parallel with her left leg.

"Go ahead and drive outta there so I can close this up," Walther said, releasing himself from the exercise he was doing, "but no tricks this time," he added, while bent over at the waist, making brief eye contact with the driver via the reflection in the vehicle's rear view mirror before stepping off to the side, totally unaware that such words would trigger the flash of a memory in the young woman's mind – a painful memory of her younger half-sister – that forced a glowing Scarlet to exercise an even greater degree of control over her host's fragile emotional state.

In the grace of Her fire.

Hearing the soft, fiery words echoing in her mind seemed to erase the pain almost immediately. When the Chevy's engine rumbled to life, the driver began rolling the car forward and out of the garage using only the sweet spot of the clutch to accelerate. When the back end cleared the garage's door, she pressed her left foot to the floor and applied the brake with her right, holding the car in position and in gear as she waited for the darkly-dressed hunter to climb aboard.

"There is a VW parked just down the street at a corner store," Walther said, as he slid into the passenger seat. "A fine vehicle," he said of it, right before pulling the door shut, "but nothing beats the Ruby Red."

Without verbalizing a response, the driver did exactly what was implied by her passenger's chosen words. Traveling a short distance down the street and around the corner, she soon parked and observed the Volkswagen's driver on her right – a blonde woman with rectangular eyeglasses – too busy writing in a notebook to even take notice of the hunter's waving hand as he tried and failed to get her attention. Determining the next available, direct course of action, she opted to rev-up the modified Chevy's steadily rumbling engine to a violent roar in an attempt to acquire the oblivious woman's attention.

"Hey," the Volkswagen's driver acknowledged, as she rolled her window all the way down.

"Kimberly Hunter, meet Trinity Ryder," Walther said, introducing the ladies to one another with a quick gesturing of his hand.

"Hi there," Kimberly nicely said, with her most charming smile being directed at the other driver, whose wavy, shoulder length black hair no doubt complimented the rosy glow of her cheeks despite a serious demeanor.

"Hello," Trinity rigidly responded, with piercing eyes set upon the Englishwoman.

"So, how are *you* involved in all this craziness?" Kimberly asked the younger woman, wasting nearly no time at all in attempting to gather more information for the story she intended to cover.

About to allow Scarlet to voice a response for her, the hunter grabbed the hand of his apprentice and quickly removed it from the sword's hilt. *"Not* here," he said, while placing the young woman's hand back on the steering wheel, holding it there for a good couple of seconds to make sure she understood exactly what he expected of her. "There is a place we are going to travel to," he quickly informed the writer, in a failed attempt to distract her from what she had just witnessed.

"Ah... Did I just see her *eyes* change color?" Kimberly asked, suspiciously, as the Chevy's driver stared forward through the windshield, oddly refusing to make eye contact.

"We will discuss it once we arrive," he offered as a vague response. "Now, what's keeping Flynn?" he inquired, changing the subject and looking toward the store on their collective left.

"Gramps went in to buy me some candy," she answered, as she furiously began sketching in a different book from the one she was previously writing in.

"Candy?" Walther repeated. "You were supposed to buy food."

"We did already," she told him, amid furious strokes of an artist's pencil. "Then we made a bet that he ended up losing."

"What was the bet?" Trinity felt the need to ask, feeling that Scarlet was curious to know the nature of the stakes as well.

Kimberly twice glanced up from her sketchbook, studying Trinity's facial details for a moment each time she did, before resuming her fast-paced drawing technique. "I told him I could recite the name of every state in the union in under a minute. He didn't believe me, and now I'm awaiting the arrival of more candy."

"More candy..." the hunter repeated, figuring that she must have eaten what was already purchased. "What *kind* of candy?" he asked, only because he could think of nothing else to say in the moment.

"I dunno," Kimberly nonchalantly responded, not long after switching over to using a red pencil. *"Voila!"* she suddenly declared, after but a few seconds of thoughtful judgment of her own work.

The drawing she had flipped around to show them depicted her exact view from where she was sitting in the Volkswagen. Though obviously rushed and littered with frantic strokes of graphite pencil, it was nonetheless an impressive piece of art. She had included part of the Chevy's right side, shaded with red pencil, the hunter's facial features and five o'clock shadow in bold, his trench coat and Cassidy crown western hat; all drawn using various degrees of pressure that when skillfully applied to the pencil created different shades of gray all the way down to graphite black when pressed hard enough. Even the store was present in the background beyond the driver's side window. Not least of all, the haunting eyes belonging to the young woman in the driver's seat had especially been included, as they were shaded in a deep, dark red.

"Impressive," Walther acknowledged, as he looked at the drawing being shown to him from but a couple of feet away. "Just do not say or do anything that will get the people around here talking," he requested, while removing a thin, dark brown cigar from one of many interior pockets in the lining of his custom-made coat. "Last thing I need is the Sheriff locking me up again," he added, with the cigar held firmly in place between his lips as he searched his outer pockets for a match, with the young woman on his left watching the search out of the corner of her eye.

"Here comes my candy," Kimberly noted, beginning to shuffle things around to once again make room for a passenger.

Turning her head to the left and looking through her window, a sense of familiarity washed over the young driver of the Ruby Red from the moment she saw an old man complete his descent of the steps that led down from the store's entrance.

You have seen that man once before. The word you used to describe him was---

"Asshole," Trinity said, finishing what Scarlet was about to tell her.

"The hell are you talking about?" Walther said, as he puffed on his cigar and took it out of his mouth. *"Flynn?"* he asked her, upon realizing she was continuously watching the old man's approach. "Have you met?"

"I saw him last year," she answered, with a shake of her head.

"Was this before or after the shutdown?"

"Before," Trinity lightly replied, just as Flynn took notice of the man sitting in the passenger seat of what his gesture suggested was a vehicle that met with his approval.

"Nice set of wheels," he commented, in his usual raspy voice, having come to a stop in the narrow area between the two cars. "Evening, Miss," he said to the Chevy's driver, having to lower his head and lift the brim of his duster hat in order to get a clear view of her. "I quite fancy your ride."

"Hello," Trinity plainly stated, keeping her hands firmly on the steering wheel.

"The sword, too," Flynn added, taking note of the not-so-well-hidden weapon resting alongside the young woman's legs.

How flattering. Tell him thank you.

"Thank you," Trinity said, voicing Scarlet's sentiments for her, and at the same time catching a glimpse of Walther's averted eyes.

"Where are we headed?" Flynn asked the group, as he obliged the writer's impatience in reaching from her car window to rummage through the grocery bag he carried.

"We will lead the way," Walther replied, before moving the cigar held between two fingers back into the corner of his mouth, pinning it firmly between his lips and breathing in to restore its faded ember. "Just follow us," he said, in a slightly muddled voice, while watching the writer unwrap a tootsie roll. "When we arrive, stay put until I give the signal."

"Alright," she agreed, just before biting off a piece of the chocolate candy. "This better be good," she mumbled as she chewed, and tossed the wrapper to the floor of her car knowing that it made no difference whatsoever in regard to cleanliness.

"I can assure you, Ms. Hunter, it will be," it was promised, before the Dark Hunter glanced at the young woman on his left. "It will be," he repeated, between puffs of his cigar.

Still staring forward with her hands firmly on the steering wheel, Trinity responded with a single nod and a subtle smirk, rendering the hunter, alone, a little tense upon witnessing such a dramatic shift in regard to what was either a justified or a naive confidence boost that, for some reason, needed to be restrained when it was previously quite lacking. The darkly-dressed man's reaction seemed to suggest the realization that he, himself, was quite uncertain as to what the two of them, together, actually had in mind, and was beginning to wonder what kind of fire and fury would soon be unleashed upon the world, saving it or destroying it in the process.

In the space between the cars, the old Sergeant, having new mission parameters, quickly made his way around the front of the Volkswagen. "What else did you get me, Gramps?" Kimberly immediately asked as he got in, wasting no time in once again going for the grocery bag set down on the seat between them.

"I'll pass you things as you drive," Flynn told her, taking away the bag and motioning to the fact that the other half of the party was already backing out of the parking space next to them. "Keep up to her," he said, before unwrapping and biting into an egg salad sandwich he purchased, chewing the way an old man in his twilight years might chew. For Llewellyn Flynn, the old Sergeant, those twilight years would not be coming to an end anytime soon.

~

The Dark Hunter tossed the remains of his cigar out of the passenger window and immediately rolled it shut as the Ruby Red picked up speed. "Head northeast toward the Mere," he instructed his apprentice, who seemed to slightly flinch upon hearing it. "When you get to the turnoff, continue north."

"Where are we going?" Trinity asked, just to be sure. "Scarlet wants to know, too."

"To the Looms' house," he stated in reply, as he stealthily observed the young woman's reaction to his response.

"Why?" she asked, after several moments of delay.

"We need a place to rest and to prepare where we will not be disturbed," it was explained. "Where *we* cannot disturb anyone, actually. It should be safe to stay there."

"Safe to stay there," Trinity repeated, as she continued to drive.

"Yes," Walther said, sensing she was misinterpreting his intentions. "We must plan carefully if we are to succeed."

"Scarlet says we *are* the plan," she confidently stated. "There is a dark presence on this planet, and we intend to destroy it."

"Yes, but *how,* exactly?" he asked, attempting to get his point more through to the sentient sword than the young woman behind the wheel. "We cannot afford to be careless," he said, and pulled his cowboy hat down, covering his tired eyes for some rest. "If you are lost in the fight, all hope goes out the window."

That is not entirely accurate.

"You *do* remember how to get there, right?" he inquired of her, before allowing himself to fully relax and drift off.

I can recall anything you have experienced in life, in vivid detail.

"I remember everything," she repeated in her own way, as she drove on into the night, knowing exactly where to go and where to turn, all confirmed by Scarlet's access and occasional flash of her young master's own memory in perfect clarity.

~

Behind the Ruby Red car that was leading the way, the writer drove along in her '62 VW Beetle, chewing away on a piece of red licorice as the old Sergeant comfortably rested his eyes in the passenger seat next to her.

"This is pretty good," Kimberly said, amid her constant chewing. "What kind of licorice is this?"

"It's *red* licorice," Flynn responded, without bothering to open his eyes. "Wake me when we get there."

~

Hours later, Trinity drove straight through the town of Scarletmere to continue northeast toward the Mere itself, with the round headlights of a VW behind her as seen in the rear view mirror. Fifteen minutes later, the two vehicles arrived at the stop sign of a crossroads and, in seeing the red-lettered sign on the other side of the road that read, ***Camp Scarletmere*——>**, the Chevy's driver was immediately engaged in an internal battle with a new part of herself – a fiery spirit within, having a very strong desire for them to travel east, immediately, though it would've meant acting against the wishes of the sleeping Dark Hunter.

Chapter 4

Scarlet's Sanctuary

July 20th, 1967. 03:00 hours.

In the early morning, a large, two and a half-story house slowly came into view as two cars rolled single file over a long, gravel driveway beneath the motionless, overhanging branches of large oak trees. Built almost entirely from a dense, dark wood known as ebony, the Looms' house, known by that name to but a few individuals, had been occupied by the Looms family only days before a tragic incident termed accident had occurred. It had been one year and twenty days since the lifeguard and the hunter last laid eyes on it.

Lydia. That was her name.

"Yes," Trinity confirmed out loud, when she glanced down at the sword next to her leg, though a verbal confirmation was entirely unnecessary. "Wake up, Walther," she said, before smacking her passenger's left leg with her right hand. "We're here."

Startled, the hunter snorted as he jolted awake. "Already?" he asked, before rubbing his eyes to focus himself on their surroundings. "Feels like I slept for five seconds," he said, while glancing around the dark property through the windshield and the passenger window.

"Now what?" the young sword-bearer impatiently asked, as she tapped on the steering wheel with her fingernails while watching her mentor assess the situation.

"I should take a look around," Walther told her, while eyeing the house with untold suspicion. "I am assuming there will be no power, but, as I recall, there is a generator in the back yard. I will see if I can get it running before we go in to search the place."

"Search the place," Trinity strangely repeated, as if struggling with the point of conducting said search.

"Yes," the hunter sharply confirmed, sensing more of what he

understood to be the sentient sword's eternal impatience rather than that of his newly designated apprentice. “To make certain it is safe for our comrades,” he explained, right before hearing a car door slam shut behind them.

“Ms. Hunter!” Flynn harshly called out from the passenger window of the messy VW, in an attempt to summon it's driver back to her seat.

“What's the problem?” Kimberly naively wondered, as the hunter and his sword-bearing apprentice stepped out of the Ruby Red to approach her, with the hunter holding up his hand to indicate to the old Sergeant that he was fine right where he was.

“You must follow my instructions *exactly*,” Walther said, stepping forward to scold the blonde Englishwoman. “Stay in the car with Mr. Flynn where it is safe and do not come out until Scarlet and I return.”

“Scarlet?” Kimberly repeated out of confusion, not failing to notice that the younger woman seemed to be hiding something behind her leg. “I thought her name was Trinity?”

“Y-yes, well...” Walther stammered, and fixed the position of his long coat as a way of coping with his mistake.

“I told you, I'm not afraid,” Kimberly boldly stated.

“You quite likely will be,” he countered, knowing there was almost no chance that she would not be. “Listen,” he calmly said, with his arm around her shoulders, drawing her close at his side, “I understand that you are here to gather information as a journalist, and I respect that, but there is a great deal you do not understand.”

“Then tell me.”

Knowing that simply telling her would not result in acceptance or understanding, he sighed and chose to respond by saying, “Only when I know it is safe.”

“Safe?” she repeated, and adjusted her glasses. “It looks deserted.”

“Possibly,” Walther countered. “This area can be...deceiving,” he decided, while glancing around the property.

Defiantly crossing her arms, “I'm going wherever you go,” the writer stubbornly insisted.

Trinity, sensing Scarlet's frustration and eagerness to get on with their mission, decidedly gripped the exposed hilt of the sheathed sword she carried, causing her eyes to roll over dark red. *“You will do exactly as instructed!"* the sizzling, Goddess-like voice commanded, as she steadily walked forward with the sheathed weapon thrust outwardly, intimidating the uncooperative woman into retreating back to the safety of her car.

Shocked with fear and uttering not a sound, the writer rolled up her window and locked her door while staring into a pair of menacing red eyes that matched her own eye level on the other side of the glass – eyes that when closely examined seem to stretch into a scarlet infinity – before eventually opening her sketchbook to begin drawing the life-changing experience.

"Was that really necessary?" Walther asked, as the instinctive young woman returned to his side, needing to lean on him for support while regaining control of her faculties.

"It worked, didn't it?" she replied. "It's getting easier now. I'll just need a minute."

"Rest in the car and keep an eye out," he instructed as he helped her along. "Once I get the generator up and running, you can assist me with clearing the house."

"Alright," she weakly agreed, as she returned to the driver's seat of what was becoming her second most cherished possession, taking controlled breaths to help restore her stamina.

After closing the door for his tired apprentice, the Dark Hunter began making his way around the eastern corner of the house, en route to the generator shed in the back yard, all the while being highly alert and gripping the hilt of a sheathed hunting knife at the right side of his waist. Arriving in front of the small shed and detecting nothing more than noisy crickets amid the intermittent hooting of a night owl, he quickly pulled aside the thin, sheet metal door, producing a loud and unpleasant scraping sound, immediately igniting a wood match that illuminated the horrific face of a black and blue tribal mask that hung from the ceiling of the enclosed space.

Startled by the frown of the creepy mask he had seen twice before, he quickly executed a one-eighty while drawing his serrated knife and, with heightened senses, glanced around the dark property with his heart beating fast in his chest, awaiting the movement or sound of an ambush. But, nothing jumped out at him. Only the sound of crickets resuming their mating song could be heard in the night after having been silenced from the loud sound of a scraping metal door.

Getting the generator running was easy enough after it sputtered and failed to start on the first few attempts. Adding a half gallon of gasoline found in a nearby jerrycan, pressing the primer a few times and finishing with a couple of strong pull-starts got the rumbling engine going again. The task had even been accomplished in total darkness, as the Dark Hunter had forced himself to utilize his visual memory in combination with his sense of touch, opting to preserve a dwindling supply of matches that were often used to light the campfires that cooked up whatever he happened to hunt for dinner. Then there was the fact that he was working with gasoline and, of course, there were his cigars to consider as well, that although were never inhaled, were thoroughly savored and enjoyed for their flavorful and aromatic qualities.

With his task completed, evidenced by a single backyard light shining over the out-of-control lawn, Walther began making his way around the house, opting to take the western route nearest to Scarlet Forest. Nearing the corner where the backyard light could no longer reach, he gripped the hilt of his blade and continued to walk and look straight ahead of himself, though he would intermittently direct his eyes toward the forest he had been taught never to trust. When he made his way around the southwest corner, heading diagonally across the front lawn toward the driveway, his apprentice took instant notice of him from the driver's seat of the Ruby Red and immediately got out of the car with her counterpart held at her side.

"How did it go?"

"No sweat," the hunter replied, before beckoning with his hand in the direction of the VW, letting the writer and the old Sergeant know that it was alright to get out. "We will all go inside, together," he told his apprentice, as he retrieved a small item hidden in the lining of his cowboy hat.

"What *is* that?" she asked, upon noticing the two-pronged, thin metal item in his hand, before her mentor's next action answered the question for her. "Oh, cool," she plainly said, as she stood to the side, watching him attempt to pick the lock.

"Yes," he agreed, successfully unlocking the door by the time Kimberly and Flynn came to a stop behind him.

"There's no need to be afraid of me. She won't hurt you," the young sword-bearer confessed with a grin, sensing that the writer was keeping her distance while curiously attempting to catch a glimpse of her eyes from an angle.

"In we go," Walther said to the group, taking the lead and flicking on the entryway's light switch just inside the door, making it so that the group could easily see where they were stepping. When they were all inside, "Lock it," he instructed, without looking back, and so Flynn, being last to enter, did exactly that. "Ms. Hunter," he continued, as he stared down the hall where the light met the darkness, "you will accompany me to search the second floor. Mr. Flynn, if you would be so kind as to accompany Ms. Ryder on a search of the ground floor, turning the lights on as you go. Stick together and be sure to check everywhere. Trinity...keep her close," he advised the young woman standing behind him and to his right, flashing an almost undetectable glance down at the artifact she carried. "Move out."

Following the Dark Hunter's instructions and, much to her mentor's surprise, the sword-bearer began leading the way into the house. Turning on the next light switch along the way, a spiderweb covered area at the bottom of the house's grand staircase was suddenly illuminated, presumably covering the length of the entire banister leading up to the second floor. Unfortunately, it was still too dark to see beyond the halfway point.

"Spiders," Trinity commented, stating so only as a matter-of-fact before heading left toward the living room, with the old Sergeant hurrying to catch up to her.

Looking to his immediate right, down the partially lit hallway that led to where he knew the kitchen to be, the hunter's ears suddenly picked up on the sound of scratching, instantly shutting out a series of fond memories that were swirling about in his mind. Scratching. Constant scratching, becoming louder and faster, putting him on high alert that something might attack him at any moment. He soon sighed upon seeing repeating strokes of a pencil and Kimberly's lagging behind, that in the environment of a finely constructed home produced a natural reverb as its Victorian charm was being mapped out on paper. "Follow me, Ms. Hunter," he told the Englishwoman, keeping both sentiment and fear a secret for the time being. "You might want to hold off on doing that in favor of watching your back. You would not want to get yourself killed before learning all of life's little secrets, now, would you?"

As they began to ascend the stairs, the upper staircase and a portion of the second floor hallway were suddenly bathed in light, illuminating more of their surroundings. The living room chandelier had sparked to life, offering a much improved view of the dusty landscape paintings that decorated much of the house. Several spiders scattered in reaction to the unwelcome light, causing Kimberly to shiver in disgust. "Ugh," she said, and decidedly put her sketchbook back into the brown leather satchel that stored her materials. "This place is not what I thought it would be. I know a little about architecture and design, and I can see that the builders used a very dark wood. Something darker than mahogany or walnut. No doubt imported. Even the walls and the staircase," she commented. "It's both haunting and beautiful at the same time."

"That it is," Walther agreed, as he led the way up the stairs, cutting apart the long strands of spiderweb that dangled across their path, making good use of his serrated blade.

Hanging from the ceiling to their left was the abundant-light-producing chandelier, and below it was a fully illuminated living room – its furnishings all protected with bed sheets used as dust covers. Near to the top, the curious writer tried to look over the spider-infested banister to take in the view more completely, but was unwilling to step any closer to it, for obvious creepy-crawly reasons. Down there, the environment seemed warm and inviting – quite the opposite of where they would soon be going.

When the Dark Hunter reached the top of the stairs and slashed at the last and fully formed spiderweb that covered the way forward, he quickly glanced down the east and west hallways. Between the two, the eastern hallway that led toward the master bedroom and master bathroom was of the more illuminated. The second floor's western hallway, that he remembered led to two more bedrooms and the door to the attic, was located behind the upper portion of the living room's north wall, shielded entirely from the light.

Looking to the ceiling of the dark hallway, the writer followed the hunter's gaze when he stopped in place and lit a match that he then held outwardly. Spiderwebs. Nothing like what they had so far endured. Thickly intertwined in vast numbers, there existed far too many to ever count. The eastern hallway, both Walther and Kimberly realized by way of comparison, seemed to be entirely untouched by time.

"We don't have to go down there, do we?" Kimberly quietly asked. "I mean, nobody would be down *there."*

"Nothing *you* can imagine would be down there," Walther corrected in response. "This way," he whispered to her, turning around and setting his sights on the first door of the eastern hallway. "I need you to be watching our backs at all times," he said, as he calmly drew his magnum revolver with his left hand, bringing it up to shoulder level with the blade in his right, making it seem as if they were a single weapon. "That is all you have to do," he told the accompanying writer. "Pay no mind to anything else."

"We aren't leaving?"

"No. Why would we?"

"...Alright," Kimberly said, failing to successfully hide her anxiety.

Grasping the doorknob in front of him, the Dark Hunter opened it as fast as he could in one sudden motion and flicked on the light switch. He then stood there in silence for a moment, listening and aiming his revolver around the dusty, but well-lit bathroom. Quickly and silently, he stepped in and cleared all areas of the spacious room while Kimberly remained at the doorway to keep an eye on what her bold leader termed, *cesspool.*

Finding nothing out of the ordinary, the pair proceeded back out into the hallway, repeating the exact same procedure in the hall closet and master bedroom, the latter of which, Kimberly noticed, had a rather disturbing stain on the hardwood floor. Suspecting that someone had died on that exact spot, she would be sure to include the unsettling detail in her notes, so long as something in the house didn't kill her before she had the chance.

~

Around the time the hunter and the writer were beginning their search of the second floor, the sword-bearing young woman and the old Sergeant were completing their search of the kitchen, the pantry, and the adjacent empty dining room located at the back of the house where the windows faced north into an overgrown back yard. Keeping her deadly counterpart at-the-ready and turning the lights on as she led the way, Trinity found each room's condition to be exactly the way it was just over a year ago, only with the addition of a year's worth of dust accumulation. Discovering nothing out of place, the pair sat down at the dinette to wait for the others to return. Their task, it seemed, was complete.

After a few moments of seated, uncomfortable silence, a thought crossed the old Sergeant's mind. "Shouldn't we check on them?" he asked, voicing his concern.

"We could," Trinity casually replied, as she stared at the table top, flicking her finger against a nearby glass liquor bottle, "but those weren't my instructions."

"I suppose not," Flynn seemed to agree, "but how long will you sit here until you go looking for them, Ms. Scarlet?"

"Now she's demanding that I go," Trinity stated out of annoyance, as she stood up from her seat. "Thanks a lot, old man," she said, and scowled at him as she walked on by, heading straight toward the kitchen door that would take her to the stairs.

"Oh, *now* I remember you," Flynn said, as he followed after her, exiting the kitchen through the swinging, double-hinged door before it settled into place. "Last year," he accurately recalled, with a snap of his thumb and middle finger. "The gas station at the edge of town. That look is unmistakable."

"Took you long enough," she responded. "I knew that I had seen you somewhere before, but *she* knew when and where before *I* did," she confessed, and gave her companion a gentle shake.

"The sword?"

"Yes and no," she strangely confirmed, as she changed direction and began making her way up the staircase to the second floor. "I can hear her in my head when she wants to tell me something. She has direct access to all of my memories."

"Hmm," Flynn said from behind her, sounding interested.

"What?" Trinity asked, wanting the *hmm* clarified.

"Later," he decided, seeing that there were more pressing concerns. "Look there," he suddenly said, pointing across her left shoulder at the ceiling of the second floor hallway. "The webs."

"Yeah," she acknowledged. "So?"

"Where are all the spiders?" he questioned. "The banister was crawling with them not five minutes ago, and now they're *all* gone? Seems unnatural."

He is correct. It is entirely unnatural. Follow the webs, quickly, and locate the others.

"Apparently it *is* unnatural," Trinity confirmed for him, before suddenly evoking the Fire Spirit, forgetting about first unsheathing the weapon, thus destroying the scabbard in a flaming instant. Sword and eye matched in a deep shade of red, and then a hot spark of the purest white violently snapped at the weapon's pointed tip, igniting the ancient blade in a liquid-like fire. Completely unbound and in control of her youthful host, the spirit called Scarlet then proceeded at a brisk but quiet pace, heading down the dark, west hallway, keeping the sword – *herself* – held diagonally at-the-ready as an evenly burning aura defied physics and lit the way forward.

In reaction to the unexpected scene that unfolded before his eyes, the old Sergeant reached around to his back to equip himself with a relic of his own. Armed and at-the-ready, he then followed right behind the fiery swordswoman, intent on finding the other members of the party himself if he had to.

The unlikely trio of sorts headed directly toward the bedroom, specifically the one that Trinity and Scarlet both recognized as Lydia's old room, where the webs on the ceiling converged into an even thicker mass. As they were about to walk in, they unexpectedly found Kimberly backing out of the room in a rather horrified manner.

"Cover your ears!" they all heard, before a loud *boom* echoed through the house.

~

A few minutes prior, the hunter and the writer had together gone down the very same hallway, where they knew the ceiling above them was literally crawling with spiders. Lighting a match to help them see where they were going only seemed to increase the anxiety level even further for the delicate Englishwoman, who was given the unwanted responsibility of igniting additional matches as needed, while the man in front of her dealt with the array of spiderwebs that impeded their progress.

"Do you want to go back?" Walther quietly asked, when the first match went out, leaving the two of them standing in near total darkness. "I can proceed on my own, if you prefer."

"I'm not going *anywhere,"* Kimberly quietly replied, striking another match that popped and sizzled to life. "You've got the gun."

The hunter repeatedly nodded a subtle nod indicative of his complete understanding. "They seem to be coming from that room," he said, as he looked at the ceiling and the concentration of webs leading to a closed door at the end of the hall.

After cutting away the thick webbing that blocked their access, having used one oval-shaped slice to get the job done, the knob was slowly turned and pushed on as the writer lit another match in anticipation of the current flame getting too close to her finely-filed fingernails. The first thing that they both took notice of as they cautiously stepped into a very dark bedroom was a brass candelabra, seen to be resting atop a tall dresser located just inside the door, bearing three used candles that had melted down to within an inch or two. Wasting no time, Kimberly began lighting them as Walther scanned the darkness and tried to focus his eyes on their surroundings. As the strength of the three flames grew in turn, so did the visibility within the room increase. On the single bed, in the far corner where it was darkest, they both took notice of a black mass that was evidently growing in size. The hunter's honed instinct was to ready himself for the unexpected, and so he stood motionless, ready to react to danger. Alarmed by the sheer uncertainty of what she was seeing, the writer's instinct was to quietly step backward out of the room, but what occurred next put a quick stop to her escape plan: The door mysteriously swept shut and locked behind her, even managing to distract the focus of the Dark Hunter, right before the sleeping mass of spiders collectively formed the shape of a most familiar-looking girl, who, in her bed, awoke with a malevolent shriek that pierced the air, immediately rising to begin sauntering toward the intruders who had wandered into the spiders' trap.

"Cover your ears!!" Walther yelled, before firing off a deafening round from the Smith and Wesson M29 at the spiders that took the shape of the girl's head, but no matter where he aimed and fired, splattering spider guts against the wall with each and every pull of the trigger, even more rejoined the horrific horde, taking the place of those just destroyed. When he had fired all six booming rounds and the magnum's cylinder was spent, he began backing away as he emptied, shaking out the empty casings onto the floor. He then began reloading at a rapid rate while the materialized girl, made up entirely of a colony of spiders, lurched forward and prepared to lunge at him in an attempt to overcome him entirely. Thankfully, that was when someone – and something – intervened.

~

A few moments prior, Scarlet had fast-walked her host toward Lydia's bedroom upon hearing the first round of a gun go off. When the door mysteriously closed on her and wouldn't budge on account of the lock being jammed, she used the tip of her sword's red, fiery aura to disintegrate the wooden barrier in an unnatural instant, much to the astonishment of the ex-soldier standing at-the-ready behind her. On the other side, Kimberly, who had been hoping to make a swift exit, suddenly found herself holding a dislodged doorknob that was held onto even as she stood face-to-face with an advancing entity, one that was perhaps even more frightening than the other, and had no other recourse but to back herself into the safest corner to keep clear out of harm's way.

Believing he was about to be consumed by a mass of spiders, some of which were already beginning to scale up the length of his trench coat, the Dark Hunter suddenly found himself under protection, shielded by the ward of a weapon that had transformed into something greater than it was prior. Held between him and the shrieking monstrosity that was forced to back away, the sword produced a radiant inferno within and without the entire length of its double-edged blade, blanketing the room in the color of blood. With millions of micro explosions occurring within, burning gases and destructive energies were forced out and along razor sharp edges, becoming a hot shade of pink when mixed with air. The end result was the visible distortion of a heat wave; strong enough that one could actually feel the oxygen being sucked out of the room, consumed by the sword as fuel for its ancient fire. The Dark Hunter, the old Sergeant and the paralyzed-with-fear writer then watched in dismay as Scarlet slowly advanced on the cowering manifestation that struggled to retain its youthful frame in her divine presence. A deafening shriek in an unpleasant, harsh tone, although matching with the likeness of the creature, was mismatched against the likeness of the young girl it tried to copy, was no doubt a tactic used before a desperate attempt to flee.

"I don't think so," Scarlet's fiery voice responded with attitude and, with added effect, willed the sword's aura to emit a single, violent pulse, painfully discouraging the attempt. *"You are hereby banished!"* she declared, while pointing the tip of her blade at the creature in a threatening and commanding manner, right before it recoiled in preparation to attack. *"Flârâ Crûs!"* she intensely spoke, quickly reacting with a recitation in a long forgotten language as she stepped backward, slashing once vertically and once horizontally, creating a burning cross that moved forward through the spacious bedroom at high velocity, multiplying at just the right moment to trap her enemy in a fiery prison from every direction. Jumping into the air, she brought the magma-like sword violently down upon the isolated, collectively shrieking mass of spiders, causing the trap to flare up and then compress until it all disappeared, disintegrating the contained monster in the process.

The remainder of the spiders on the ceiling and around the room, much to the writer's disgusted and frightful avoidance, were then recalled out of the bedroom in reverse. Crawling backward down the hallway, down the grand staircase and through the entryway, they were withdrawn from the coming sanctity of the Looms' house, squeezing themselves through the cracks at the base of the front door, across the overgrown lawn in the dead of night, and finally disappearing into a dark domain of petrified forest.

Through the window of a slowly darkening red room on the second floor, the sword-bearer looked down on the veiled, moonlit property as her companions gathered together at her back, staring from a respected distance with combined awe and gratitude. They watched as she raised and held her left hand vertically between her closed eyes in meditative concentration and began speaking under low volume in a thought-to-be-forgotten language, causing them to trade glances by candlelight before returning their focus to the young woman who turned around, opened her scarlet eyes and gently thrust the tip of her sword straight down to the floor. In that instant, beginning from all around the perimeter of the house, the energy that had been silently drawn to the exterior suddenly blasted outward, traveling a hundred yards in all directions, battling the darkness of night until it finally dissipated.

"Much gratitude," Walther was the first to say. "I have to admit, she nearly got me."

"Are you alright, Ms. Hunter?" Flynn inquired of the shocked, yet relieved writer, who by that time had formed many questions and thoughts in her mind, though she appeared unable to speak them aloud.

After a silent moment of checking herself over, *"Yeah..?"* Kimberly awkwardly responded, beginning to focus on the fact that Trinity was not only different but that she possessed something truly special and unique in her relationship with the sword, having enough power to destroy a creature as terrifying as anything her imagination could conjure up.

"Is it over or not over?" Flynn asked. "I'm guessing not over."

"That was *not* the Dark Demon," Scarlet replied, as she moved near to the empty bed before allowing Trinity to take control and release her – the sword – from her hand, and for her own good. She immediately collapsed on the bed, and trying to control both her nausea and her sadness, she rested on Lydia's bed, hugging one of her larger plush bears in an effort to normalize her equilibrium and comfort herself.

"I-I don't know what you did," the shocked writer told the group's apparent savior, as she walked across the room to approach the bedside, "but that was incredible."

"Come on, lets get you downstairs," Walther said, as he picked the exhausted young woman up, beginning to head out of the room with her in his arms and the teddy bear in hers.

Feeling her mental connection with her counterpart gradually slipping away, Trinity weakly reached for the out-of-reach weapon that quite harmlessly lay atop Lydia's old bed, having already reverted back to its initial form. “Scarlet...” she mumbled.

Rest. You have done well. This place is now a sanctuary, immune to dark forces. She can no longer reach here, so long as I exist.

“Bring the sword,” Walther instructed, before stepping out into the hallway with his apprentice in his arms.

Rest...

The old Sergeant and the writer, both experiencing feelings of apprehensiveness toward touching the sword, approached the foot of the bed while staring at the rightly named scarlet blade that slowly faded in color as its counterpart was carried further and further away, until only the appearance of silver remained in the dim candlelight.

Rest...

Chapter 5

Moonfire's Gift

07:30 hours.

A young woman found herself awakening to the bold face of a dark-skinned man standing over her. Becoming semi-alert in the middle of a sentence being directed at her, she heard something about gathering for an outdoor training session. Only interested in sleeping, she rolled over onto her pillow, face-first, and pulled the blankets over her head, not at all wishing to even entertain the detestable idea after getting what she knew to be only a few hours of sleep.

Morning.

"Nooo..." Trinity whined, even upon hearing the sweetest sounding voice of her counterpart speaking to her in her mind.

Come on, let's go. I can't do this alone. We've got a job to do.

"...Fine," she soon decided, "but I need to eat," she announced as she sat up, both forgetting and then not really caring that she had taken her blouse and bra off at some point during the night, having felt strangely uncomfortable in them.

"Well, you are in luck," Walther said, having already turned around out of respect for a lady's privacy, not knowing that her words weren't even meant for him. "Kimberly and Flynn are making breakfast," he told her, before heading back out of the room and down the hallway, catching a glimpse of nothing more than her bedhead.

After putting on a baggy sweater to keep warm, Trinity headed into the bathroom across the hall to wash her face. She then tied her hair back into a ponytail with a black scrunchy taken from a drawer, and with Scarlet's predictable suggestion of what color she wanted her to use, she applied some bold, yet tasteful makeup selected from a well-stocked kit. Black eyeliner, dark red eye shadow with lipstick to match, and a hint of blush, too, were among the many items reclaimed after having abandoned them the previous summer.

*I **love** this color.*

"I know you do, sweetheart. Just let me handle this."

You'll need a better method of carrying me around with you.

When both she and Scarlet were satisfied with their shared appearance in the oval-shaped mirror, Trinity went back into the guest bedroom and began rooting around in a chest of drawers until she found a pair of black leather gloves that she tossed at her counterpart – the thirteen-thousand-year-old sword with a crystalline blade far older than even that – set leaning upright against the wall in the corner of the room. Then, feeling nice and refreshed, she began to put together a change of clothes, given that she had access to everything she'd left behind, just over one year prior. It wasn't until she sat on the edge of the bed to pull on a pair of socks that she began to take notice of her better than usual physique, first noticing her athletic calves, then her strong, tight thighs, and so on, until she rediscovered the entirety of her nude self and a rather remarkable transformation that she simply didn't notice in the mirror and under a baggy sweater.

You have finally noticed your improved physical condition.

"What the hell is *this?* What *happened* to me?"

It was achieved while you slept. It was a necessary development in order to eliminate your nausea and prevent your equilibrium from faltering. Think of it as my gift to you.

"I had a nice body, already, but *this..."* she said, while touching her own stomach in admiration, "...this is *great!* I feel twice as strong...and *taller."*

That is because you are.

"Wait 'til John gets a load of *this!"*

Focus. Internalize your thoughts.

Right. So, why was she here last night? Are we at a disadvantage?

Disadvantage? Hardly. I admit, I would have preferred to take her by surprise, but, look on the bright side. Now the demon knows that she can be undone. It is she who will learn what true fear is. I could sense her current level of power and she is of no match for me. She will not enjoy her last day of existence in this era, for she exists now with the knowledge that she is about to be destroyed.

"Alright," Trinity said aloud, as she pulled on a pair of tight, dark

gray slacks that used to be quite loose-fitting.

You know, I'm curious to find out what else I can do.

*You mean, what **I** can do.*

What **we** can do.

...Acceptable.

With that settled, Trinity slid her arms into the sleeves of a white blouse and fastened the buttons, feeling that it felt a little more snug around her bust line than she remembered. She then took a small, black leather jacket with long sleeves and a short back from out of a pink suitcase that was stashed in the closet and put it on over her blouse, having to squeeze into it just a little in order to get it on. Feeling vibrant and strong in her new outfit, she realized that with a good pair of boots and a hat, her appearance would very much resemble that of another.

Well done.

With her clothing and personal hygiene both taken care of, the sword-bearing young woman proceeded out of the bedroom, down the hallway, through the living room where the furniture had been predictably uncovered, past the grand staircase that led to the second floor and straight on toward the kitchen. Hearing voices on the other side, she stopped in place to listen.

"Perhaps she can be saved," she overheard a deep voice say, instantly knowing who it belonged to.

"Are you serious?" a raspy sounding voice responded, one that definitely originated from the retired soldier.

"You don't actually believe that, do you?" a woman's cold voice replied, that she lastly attributed to the serious writer in their company.

Deciding she wasn't really into eavesdropping, the swordswoman opted to push the door open and stroll right on in, causing her mentor to nearly draw his gun out of a failure to immediately recognize the new-and-improved woman who had barged into the kitchen.

"Trinity," Walther said, from a standing position, letting go of his grip on the powerful magnum's stock. "You really look different."

"She sure does," Flynn agreed, as he stared across the kitchen at her, while eating from a bowl of soup on the island counter top.

"You look *great,"* Kimberly complimented from her seat at the dinette, out of pure amazement, having already reached into her satchel to remove her sketchbook. “Hold it right there a minute. Just one minute. Keep the sword at your side, just like that,” she instructed, as she began capturing the scene with rapid strokes of pencil.

“Oh, um...” Trinity said, deciding to comply with the request. “What, like this?”

“Yeah, but turn this way just a little, would you?” was the artist's next instruction, while framing the scene by joining the tips of her thumbs and holding up her index fingers. “There. Yes. Yes, just like that. I have no idea what the hell is going on around here,” she admitted, “but it sure makes for compelling art.”

“What caused this?” Walther had to ask, as he looked up and down at the impressive young woman who no longer seemed quite as young, out of curiosity and a slightness of admiration while encircling her. “How do you feel? Are you well enough?”

“Actually, I'm fine,” she confidently replied, though she would feel a slight blush overtake her due to the attention that her new look invited. “The explanation was that this is a gift.”

“A gift from...” Kimberly assumed, while pointing with the eraser end of her pencil at the weapon in the sword-bearer's gloved left hand.

The sword-bearer raised her eyebrows and gave several short nods of her head to confirm, doing so amid the old Sergeant's slurping of soup and the sound of pencil strokes on paper, otherwise causing the brightly lit kitchen to fall into silence.

“I wanted to ask you,” Walther suddenly said, breaking the silence and changing the subject after sensing a level of discomfort brought on by their collectively intrigued stares, “did you find it odd that the Dark Demon, as you called her, was asleep in her old bed? *Lydia's bed?”*

“What *we* saw,” Trinity began to say, referring to herself and the scarlet sword that she flashed a glance at, “was a colony of spiders, possessed and used to carry out the Dark Demon's will from afar, usually without risk.”

The hunter furrowed his brow. “What do you mean, *usually?”*

“What we did weakened her,” she responded, possessing new, but limited information on the subject of her counterpart's ancient enemy.

"It was a very old recitation."

"How old, exactly?" Kimberly immediately thought to ask.

"Hmm, oh, my," the sword-bearer soon replied, after a moment of thoughtful silence. "It would seem that you've stumped her. Even she doesn't know the answer to that. It's as old as the Ancient language, itself. *Lythian,"* she knew to say, preemptively answering what was sure to be the writer's next question. "That's L-y-t-h-i-a-n," she said, spelling it out for her.

"Ancient...language..." the writer repeated as she wrote down the words. "What did it *do?"* she wondered, uncertain in that moment whether to favor writing or drawing.

"Exactly what you saw," Trinity responded. "The Ancients possessed an advanced knowledge of tone and its effects on the material world. What we call silence, they understood to be the source that binds everything together. They discovered and developed incantations that, when properly recited and directed with intent, can produce results anywhere from subtle and unseen to dramatic and apparent. The one you all saw first restrains and then banishes a corrupting force."

"This...really isn't *you,"* Kimberly acknowledged – a rhetorical statement that Trinity's momentarily lowered eyes confirmed correct.

"Will you use that same recitation on her true form?" Flynn asked, interrupting their back and forth conversation.

"We plan on it."

"Excellent," Walther chimed in, as he smelled one of the cigars withdrawn from the pocket of his jacket, expressing two meanings with but a single word. "Will she be restored?"

"I understand what you desire," the sword-bearer said in realization, quitting her posing posture to take a seat at the dinette, next to the hunter and across from the writer, with Scarlet leaned up between her legs against the chair and the floor, "however, it is not possible. This weapon, that *could* be called a sword, I suppose, is bonded with what they used to call a Divine Spirit. Rough translation, of course, but, that's only one part of it. Really, if I told you what this *really* was, putting the feminine consciousness we're calling *Scarlet* aside, you'd probably faint from the shock, or you just wouldn't believe it. The Ancients named it *Lünaflara.* In English, it best translates to *Moonfire,* though the translation is somewhat misleading. This weapon has been called by many names, I'm told, but *Starsword* seems pretty appropriate, now that I think about it. Its nature is that of extreme heat and combustion, meaning destruction by fire. Sadly, it is not within our power to restore the girl's physical body."

"Most unfortunate," Flynn said from his seat at the island, upon noticing the hunter hanging his head, perhaps upset that he had allowed himself to get his hopes up.

"Divine...Spirit. Moon...fire," Kimberly repeated, trying to record all of the information in her notes. "Is that one word or two?"

From a closed fist, without speaking, Trinity extended an index finger in response and watched the writer make a minor correction.

"As I understand it," Flynn said, in between mouthfuls of soup, "fire can also be used to shape and reform materials, and it sustains life by providing warmth," he added, before raising the next readied spoonful to his mouth.

"It is true that heat sustains life, but that effect is secondary in nature," Trinity explained for her close partner. "On other worlds, there is an absence of life due precisely to extreme temperatures. In order for life to exist, the climate must be relatively stable. When it comes to forging objects, heat only serves to weaken and break down a malleable material so that it can be compressed with force and cooled into a more durable or useful form. For earthly fire to even exist and provide warmth, it must continually consume and destroy oxygen, or it cannot exist beyond the glimpse of a spark. So, you see, her natural state is entirely destructive, even though it is her desire to protect life. There is nothing that can be done to spare those who fall under an unforgiving blade."

There is always something that can be done, the Dark Hunter's memory told him, in an angelic voice that echoed forward from his early childhood, quite nearly bringing a tear to his eye until his focus returned him to the present moment.

"So, there are others like her," was the next thing on the ever-curious mind of the writer.

"Yes and no," Trinity responded.

"Elaborate," Walther immediately requested.

Glancing at her mentor and the old Sergeant behind him, the eyes of the sword-bearer returned to the writer, on account of her being the one to record the information. “There *are* others, but none are much alike,” she explained, in reference to the various physical and spiritual characteristics of her elemental siblings. “They may have a feminine, masculine or neutral quality to them, in one way or another, but that's only from the human perspective since they're clearly of no such gender. I should be clear that I know only what I'm currently allowed to know.”

“Go on,” Kimberly urged, before her pen had even stopped moving.

The sword-bearer glanced at her mentor, who nodded when she appeared to be awaiting his approval to continue to divulge more information that was sure to be written down. “The Elements existed only in a boundless, raw state until they were each bound as a concept to six Relics using blood and voice as catalysts. They knew nothing of consciousness before that time, not in the way that we know it, but they were aware that something was happening to this planet. The intent of their creator, it seems, was to allow human consciousness to wield a power that could stand up to a growing darkness overtaking the land, much like what is beginning to happen in this era. They were presented with a simple choice: Do *something* or do *nothing*. The forces that balance the universe each chose to preserve their existence, and the existence of all things, through symbiosis with one of our kind. It is a choice she made once again, the moment I first made contact with her over a year ago, transmigrated through the source field of reality from her previous location.”

“Fascinating,” Kimberly said, endeavoring to get everything written down, barely even comprehending what was being said. “Who was your creator?” the inquisitive writer thought to ask, without skipping over what she felt was the next most relevant question.

The Divine One.

“Someone who left this planet a long time ago,” Trinity answered, appearing to be saddened by fleeting images of a bygone era, accompanied by Scarlet's own admission of that fact.

“This is turning out to be beyond belief,” said Flynn, before he took a sip from a glass of water to wash his uncommon breakfast down.

"The worst is yet to come," Walther said, issuing them all a grave warning at once. "The mission remains unchanged. When you have all had something to eat, please join me outside. We will discuss our strategy as we prepare to do what we must."

Getting up from his seat at the table, the Dark Hunter immediately headed across the kitchen and through the rarely used door that led into the vacant dining room built along the back of the house, facing north. Through the swinging door, the others watched him continue straight on toward another door, making them all aware of the fact that he was headed to the back yard.

"Something smells good," said Trinity, upon smelling the air.

"Ah, yes, it should be done now," Flynn realized, suddenly getting up from his seat at the island to approach a covered pot on the stove. "You just keep on writing, Missy," he told Kimberly, the moment he detected her getting up to assist him. He then stirred the contents of the pot on the stove before bringing it over to the table along with two ceramic bowls, the silverware already set out, placing it in between the two women. "Beef barley," he informed them. "There's ten more cans in the pantry, so eat as much as you like. By the sound of things, you're going to need your strength," he said, to one of them in particular, before taking his leave of the two women.

"I just can't get over what's going on around here," Kimberly confessed to the young woman across the table. "It's like you've transformed," she aptly suggested. "Can you...do that thing again? You know, when you let her speak directly?" she asked, glancing down at the tabletop to indicate that she meant the unseen scarlet sword resting between her legs. "If it won't hurt you?"

From under the dinette where the writer couldn't see, Trinity, in a manner that, if it weren't for her eyes and voice altering, would have gone undetected, touched the sword's deep red hilt with her bare hand. *"This body is young and resilient,"* dual voices spoke, with one of them having an almost fiery quality to it, in direct response to the writer across from her. *"With the improvements I have made, she will remain free from illness, though she will still need to...eat,"* Scarlet finished saying, just as the opaque red faded from her eyes and the first spoonful of soup reached her welcoming mouth.

"Astonishing," Kimberly said. "Truly astonishing. What's it like?"

"Pretty cool," Trinity replied, with a mouthful of soup.

Opening the screen door that led to the back yard, the old Sergeant found the Dark Hunter standing to his immediate left, puffing on one of his trademark cigars in undisturbed thought. "I'm starting to think we might have the advantage," Flynn said, as he joined the hunter in leaning up against the north end of the house.

"I would not bet on it," Walther soon countered, first needing to exhale the cigar smoke from his mouth. "We must not underestimate her. *It.* Whatever. Despite her confidence, I know that this is an ancient-world demon, completely devoid of human emotion. It knows nothing of fear, of empathy or remorse, except when it comes to exploiting them, and that is precisely what I am concerned about."

"What was it your father told me," Flynn said, furrowing his brow and trying hard to remember the exact wording. "Those who claim to have no fear are neither courageous, nor brave, nor true. They are simply fools, fooling themselves, seeking to fool *you.*"

Immediately recognizing his father's poetic way of speaking, "I am to believe you knew them both?" Walther asked.

"I knew your grandfather. Met him when I was still with the army. Only met your father once. You were probably a year or two old at the time. It was your grandfather who began to teach me what he knew about this area. That was a long time ago, leading all the way up to the summer of 1947. Right after that, your father came to town looking for him. For a moment, I thought it *was* him. When he introduced himself as Walther, I, of course, knew instantly who he was. I told him then what I am telling you, now, that Jefferson had gone east. I remember your father telling me, *no,* stating that he'd already searched over there. He refused to involve me when I offered to assist him, telling him that I had no fear. That was a mistake, as you well know. What happened last night was horrifying, to say the least."

"East," Walther said aloud, as he thought about it. *"East,"* he repeated. "I know what lies in the east. That must be where he went, after all. Through the mirror to the other side...but he never came back...Pops could not find him..." he trailed off, as he expressed his every thought out loud, when suddenly it dawned on him. "That has to be it. He figured it out."

"Figured what out?" Flynn asked, barely restraining his curiosity and from sounding too eager, as he had been secretly counting on the youngest of the Walther family to put together what he, for so many years, could not.

"When you have eliminated all probable solutions, whatever remains, no matter how improbable, must be the truth," he responded, and gently blew away the ashes from the tip of his cigar, revealing and strengthening the glowing ember hiding underneath. "It never occurred to me that Pops might have overlooked something."

"Who should we thank for this one?" the old Sergeant wondered, suspecting that a quote of some kind had been recalled from memory.

"Sherlock Holmes," Walther replied, and with his middle finger poised to strike, flicked away the burning end of his cigar with one powerful stroke, fragmenting the hot ember into a burst of fiery shooting stars.

"What about him?" the sudden voice of the writer asked, entirely as a cover for herself, having heard the fictional detective's name as she stood just inside the doorway, listening in on their conversation.

"A possible, however unlikely contingency," Walther responded. "You are quite inquisitive, Ms. Hunter, and I like that, but keep in mind what curiosity did to the cat."

"What did curiosity do to the cat?" she asked, feigning ignorance of the expression and what it meant.

As he stepped past her, the old Sergeant motioned with his thumb across his neck at the same time that he made a slurping noise, indicating that the cat met an all-too-curious end. Cracking up at the sound that the old man had made, the hunter drew his serrated blade and began alternating between guarding and thrusting as he moved backward toward the door, stopping a few feet out in front of it as he continued his warm-up exercises. Out there on the small, ground-level patio, the retired soldier decidedly sat down in one of two wooden lawn chairs where the writer joined him in settling in, bringing along her satchel that contained her notebooks and an assortment of drawing and writing utensils. A few moments later, the sword-bearer shoved the screen door open and stepped outside, stopping just far enough out of its returning path to avoid being hit by it. After observing her mentor's actions for a short time, she moved to stand directly in front of him with the scarlet sword held in her gloved left hand – the glove being a helpful piece of apparel that allowed her to wield the ancient weapon and retain physical control of her body.

"Let us see what the two of you can do," Walther said to her, as he held his blade outwardly in a mixed defensive and offensive posture, immediately gaining the attention of two others who had been admiring a growing collection of art sketches.

"You intend to use *that?"* she asked, noting that he intended to combat her with only a serrated hunting knife, sizable though it was.

"This is all I need," he casually countered. "I only ask that you refrain from disintegrating my favorite blade."

"No problem, sir."

"I don't know if this is such a good idea," Flynn openly cautioned.

"Please..." the hunter confidently said, assuring the combat veteran that it was no big deal for him. "I wish to know what you are capable of in basic combat," he explained, turning his attention back to his apprentice. "You will not have time to use a recitation without first weakening her. If you cannot disable *me*, providing enough time to do just that, how can you hope to achieve victory?"

"Scarlet...is in agreement," Trinity said, after a moment of pause. "However, we will assume no responsibility if you are injured."

"Fair enough," Walther instantly agreed, before beckoning with his blade that it was time to begin.

"This is intense," Kimberly said to herself, as she positioned her sketchbook in anticipation of drawing the incredible scene that was about to take place.

Without hesitation, the young sword-bearer transferred the ancient weapon into her bare right hand, allowing the Spirit of Fire to act through her once again, evidenced by her opaque red eyes. Keeping the blade under low power, the first thing she did after that involved a quick action to remove the leather glove from her left hand and toss it to the ground. Able to wield the sword in either hand, the entity called Scarlet gripped her hilt, holding herself vertically between her borrowed eyes as she stared beyond the blade and assessed her target, who was none other than the Dark Hunter, himself.

As his opponent lunged forward and slashed horizontally, a thought from the past sprung up in the hunter's mind. *Courage has nothing to do with being unafraid,* he remembered, as he evaded slash after slash and met a vertical strike by blocking with his blade's serrations, matching the still-developing strength of his apprentice and stalling long enough to flash her a grin in close proximity. *Instead, it invites in fear when it comes calling,* the memory continued, as he sidestepped, ducked, and spun out of the way of several potentially lethal blows that Scarlet executed with ever-increasing speed and precision. When he knew that he was nearing the limits of his own evasiveness, he suddenly dropped to one knee, having somewhat twisted it, and held up a hand to indicate that the test was over.

Accepting victory, Scarlet returned control back to Trinity by thrusting herself – that being the Starsword – directly into the ground and letting go, and the moment she did, her mentor sprang up from his ploy and swiftly got behind her, immobilizing her and holding his serrated knife up against her throat.

...and bravely stands firm in the truth that no matter the consequences, it will do what it must to prove its virtue.

“That's enough!” Flynn stated, standing up from the deck chair, continuing to watch the scene that had taken an unexpected turn.

“What are you *doing?!”* Trinity exclaimed, quite immobilized, though she had no intention of struggling against edged steel.

“Showing you *and* her,” Walther said, while eyeing the up-ended sword that appeared to be staring back at them, “that you are not as infallible as you think you are. If your host is lost in battle, you, as well, may forever sleep,” he added, and looked into the frightened eyes of his apprentice before releasing her from his iron grip.

“You could have just said what you were thinking,” Trinity reasoned, as she massaged her throat and checked her hand for blood.

“No,” Walther insisted. “She knows what you know, yes? And clearly, it is not a two-way street. There is no telling what sort of deception this demon will employ to confuse us. Any sympathy resulting in a hesitation, like the one you displayed just now, and our efforts will become futile in an instant. If you fail to destroy her when the moment comes, the entire world may be consumed as a result.”

“The entire *world?”* Kimberly fearfully repeated, having heard something so jarring that it actually managed to stop the busy movement of her pencil.

“Not an exaggeration,” Flynn confirmed for her. “He said that you were going to get more than you bargained for, didn't he?”

“Well, *yeah,”* she agreed, “but, that's unbelievable,” she added, as she began writing the words, *'End of the World',* in her notebook.

“So, if we fail, all hope will be lost!” Flynn summed up for the group. “Is that about right?!”

“I would pretty much say so, yes,” Walther admitted, coming to stand closer to patio. “However, I do have a plan that involves the three of us taking her on at the same time. I assume to exclude you, Ms. Hunter?” he asked, with a slight raise of his voice.

“Assume away,” she replied, as she popped a piece of chewing gum into her mouth. “I'm just here to document this whole thing,” she said, before chomping down on it and getting back to her sketch in progress, at least until the next critical piece of information came to light.

“I should go alone,” Trinity abruptly told her mentor, whose facial expression then seemed to indicate that he was giving her suggestion proper consideration.

“Is this *your* idea, or *hers?”* Flynn asked, with a great deal of suspicion in his tone.

“Not happening,” Walther decided, turning ninety degrees to stare directly into the young woman's dark brown eyes, detecting just a hint of red in them that wasn't there before. “We are going to be bait for you,” he instead told her.

“Are you out of your mind!?” she quickly responded. “She'll kill you without a second thought! What happened last night was nothing!”

“Nothing?” Kimberly fearfully repeated, as horrific images of events from the previous night flashed uncontrollably in her mind.

“Flynn and I will challenge her directly while you remain in waiting,” Walther explained. “We will lure her out with ranged weapons and tactically retreat. As soon as she is a few yards away from the Mere, that will be the time for you to quietly get behind her. Attacking the head or the heart should instantly do the job, giving you the best possible chance to claim victory,” he said, as if appealing to the sword's sense of honor as a warrior.

“She'd really prefer a one-on-one,” Trinity soon confessed,

speaking for her other half, "but it feels like she's in agreement."

"Then it is decided," Walther said, as he put a hand on Trinity's shoulder for encouragement. "You will do fine. Now, put those gloves on and I will show you a thing or two. If you develop skill with the sword on your own, there is no telling how powerful the two of you will become."

This individual seems to have an insight of unerring accuracy toward us. It is true. The more ***you*** *can do, the more* ***I*** *can do, and our combined strength will grow to be more than a mere sum of parts, unlike the Dark Demon, who usurps the souls of mortals to its own twisted ends. To its own* ***end****. Is that irony?*

Yes, Trinity thought in reply, putting on the glove taken from her pocket before taking hold of the hilt that was still sticking up into the air at her waist level. *It's perfect irony,* she thought, before yanking the sword smooth out of the ground, producing a quick, bright flare-up that yielded not a bit of dirt or grass to sully its sharp, deep red blade. She then brought the ancient weapon up and over her shoulder, letting it rest flat across the black leather of her jacket. After accepting the glove for her left hand from her mentor, the two went through various attack, defense and counter-attack drills to expand her range of motion using the sword entirely on her own, all while the old Sergeant and the writer continued to observe the unique entertainment from a distance, content enough with their view to remain in their seats on the ground level patio near the back door of the house.

"Redirect the weight," Walther advised, as his apprentice swung the moderately heavy sword in an X-shaped pattern. "Do not relax on the way up. Instead, use your strength to add force to the blow," he instructed, as he carefully watched to critique her technique. "Good. Very good. *Fluid motion.* Grace with power. Connect your movements so that they create more of a sideways figure eight than an X."

"This is really difficult on my own."

"You will get used to it," he assured her. "Remember, since you have to be in direct contact in order to summon your friend, there may come a time when you will not have her to rely upon. If *that* happens, believe me, you will have to make do with whatever blunt object or makeshift weapon you can get your hands on."

"I hadn't considered that," Trinity admitted, having felt a momentary chill of cold. "Like this?" she asked, before executing the repeated attack pattern in a faster and much more forceful manner.

The Dark Hunter nodded his approval. "A sideways figure eight is also the symbol for infinity," he said, as he continually moved his own blade in the pattern he was describing, standing directly beside his first ever student. "When you intermix a little creativity with that concept," he said, beginning to add in thrusting, crouching, spinning, jumping, and blocking with his serrated knife, "you can attack continually...from a variety of angles...and levels. However, you must always watch for counterattacks, which must be parried, blocked, or avoided entirely. More than that, if you can learn to attack and defend at the exact same time...it is good," he said with a grin, causing Trinity to produce a facial expression that represented disbelief and confusion as she resumed her practice – an expression her mentor removed by swiftly entering her range to block the next practice swing of her sword with the serrations of his blade and, all in the same action, silently drew and aimed his revolver directly at her unguarded midsection. The sword-bearer's attention had been purposely directed upward to the clashing of metal-on-metal. She hadn't noticed the gun barrel pointed at her stomach until the *click-click* of its hammer from below drew her eyes down and then up to meet the hunter's most serious expression. *"Continue,"* he boldly instructed, as he turned and stepped away, leaving her in a stunned silence to practice on her own.

He is highly skilled. We must incorporate his modern techniques.

"Flynn!" Walther called out, as he made his way over to the deck. "What are your armaments, if you do not mind me asking?"

"I still have my Army-issued single-action Colt and a set of throwing knives," the old Sergeant informed him.

The hunter then drew his revolver again – a Smith and Wesson M29 – and entered his close-quarters-combat stance along with his serrated hunting knife, using the two weapons in unison. "Are you familiar with this technique?" he asked, as he held its primary position.

"Actually, no," Flynn curiously admitted.

"Try it," Walther suggested. "Take one of those throwing knives and hold it upside down in your off-hand," he said, as the old Sergeant stood up and joined him out of genuine interest. "The idea is to grip them together if you can, but as you can see, I can not fully join these two," he explained, indicating the size of his own weapons as a drawback. "The technique is good for close quarters and for going around corners. The blade can sometimes be there before you even have a chance to fire," he went on, continuing to demonstrate exactly what he meant by turning into Flynn's side, making direct contact with the edge of his hunting knife before the barrel of his gun was even in alignment. "You see? Before my aim was even on, and even then, I still had to pull the trigger," he added, before the old Sergeant attempted the technique in a convincing manner. *"Good,"* Walther said, and stepped aside to glance in Kimberly's direction, prompting her to begin drawing on a new page in her sketchbook. "If you bend at the knees and lower your center of gravity, you can shift your weight forward and still ensure a strong footing," he advised, while demonstrating exactly what he meant. "That way you can force the blade forward and still maintain a solid defense. A bend at the elbow is key," he went on, "so that you can still *thrust forward* without stepping forward," he skillfully explained and demonstrated, before holstering and sheathing his two weapons at the same time without even looking. "Now it is perfect," he said, when the soldier mirrored the technique. "Well done," he added, without being patronizing.

"It is a practical concept," Flynn admitted. "I'll use it well," he added in thanks, before he began to hide away the rare and unique service revolver that he'd been illegally concealed-carrying, and under the nose of the county sheriff, no less.

"Go back to that, Gramps, I'm not done yet," Kimberly complained, from a few feet away, as she continued to draw in the sketchbook on her lap. "A solid minute is all I need. I can finish it up later."

"I'd gladly oblige, Ms. Hunter," he responded, "but there's the challenge of keeping the gun raised for that long," he said, in admission of the fact that he was getting to be out of shape, but still managed to provide the persistent Englishwoman a good thirty seconds more before an old shoulder injury put a stop to it.

"Stand there anyway, will you?" Kimberly immediately pleaded. "You too, Walther, you're going to love this when it's finished."

"I imagine I will," he responded, and tipped his hat ever so slightly.

"Hmm, yeah, that's good," she judged from his subtle action, and began using an eraser to alter part of the drawing, not having considered at the time that her growing collection of sketches would become illustrations for the story she would eventually complete.

A short time later, the Dark Hunter wandered off to the northwest, separating himself from the others in order to center his thoughts and focus on his own exercise. Ending his routine with a set of push-ups during which he reminisced about finally winning out against his father in a competition, he looked up from staring down at the greenery of the meadow he'd spent much time training in only to find the pretty face of a young woman in front of him, smiling brightly as she held herself in an identical position before resuming the exercise she had been quietly mirroring. He smiled wide before asking her, "How many can you do?"

"I dunno," Trinity replied, as she balanced herself in proper form. "Maybe thirty?" she guessed. "Before, I could barely do ten."

"Well, that was fifty," her mentor truthfully admitted, as he stood to his feet in front of the struggling young woman and the sword that lay on the tamped-down grass next to her.

Believing that she didn't have a prayer in getting that far, the young apprentice gave up at a count of twenty-seven and collapsed into lush green upon hearing what she considered to be an unattainable number for a single set of push-ups.

"Let us head back," Walther told her, turning to face southwest. "We should not over-exert ourselves. Save your strength, and I will continue your training if all goes well tonight."

"Tonight?!" Trinity repeated from ground level, picking her head up from a bed of clovers in the meadow, stopping the hunter in his tracks as she stared up at him from behind.

"We do not have the luxury of time," he responded assertively, before continuing toward the house in the distance.

Silently and suddenly arriving at her mentor's side in an effort to test his nerves, "Are you sure about that?" she wondered, seeing right away that he was grinning and wasn't unnerved in the slightest. "Within Scarlet's Blessing, we're not in any danger, ya know."

"It would be more accurate to say we are not in any *immediate* danger," he corrected. "It is true that she cannot exit the Mere during the hours of daylight, but, each night she remains unchallenged is one we may live to regret. At least, until she kills us, of course."

Wide-eyed, the sword-bearer drew in a deep breath and nodded her understanding. "Scarlet...is in agreement," she said, with an exhale. "The sooner the better."

Amid the sound of birdsong coming from the northern woods, the mentor and apprentice headed southwest to the beginning of a freshly-trampled path of tall grass at the edge of a spacious, but overgrown property. Walking along in silence, they took in the sunlit beauty of a variety of butterflies that fluttered by as they made their way, in single file, toward the atypical dark wood design of the Looms' house. Although the Looms family no longer lived there. the darkly-dressed man leading the way could only think of it falling under one other family name – that name having nothing to do with the actual owner.

Still seated in the wooden deck chairs that faced north in the back yard, the ex-soldier – old Sergeant Flynn – glanced up from the Englishwoman's sketchbook and did a double-take when he spotted a dark figure in a black cowboy hat emerging from the tall grass. "They're back," he quietly announced, setting the sketchbook in the lap of the woman sitting next to him without looking or considering what she was doing, interrupting her focused process of writing.

"Hey," she lightly complained, though she would receive no apology or acknowledgment of fault.

"Hay is for horses, my dear," he instead responded, before raising his raspy voice a few decibels louder. "We must soon take action?!" he called out, when he stood up from his chair to await the return of the sole-surviving member of the Walther family.

"Aye," the Dark Hunter answered, coming to a stop at the edge of the patio, causing the old man to grin upon hearing what was clearly an anticipated word of reply. "For now, we take respite in readiness for the battle of the century. If there *is* a God, He or She, likely neither, could very well be tuning-in to watch the action. So, if any of you happen to feel even the slightest amount of apprehension or fear, just remember that your actions during these difficult times may not go unnoticed. If the unexpected happens, we will deal with it. There can be no more past or future if there ceases to be the present moment. That is what we are fighting to preserve in this world: The right to life. For all those who cannot fight with us, may they continue to live on, unaware that we fight for the ongoing freedom of their eternal souls."

With that being said, the Dark Hunter stepped onto the square stones of the patio and proceeded forward, opening up the back door, disappearing into the house as the others watched in silence, left to ponder his words.

Realizing that she, in the very least, should have been taking notes, "I can't keep up with all this," Kimberly lamented, tossing her pencil into her open satchel, at the time having no awareness of the method whereby she would be able to recall each and every detail of a journey that was, for the most part, yet to unfold.

Appearing to be empathetic toward that feeling, the old Sergeant raised his eyebrows and nodded a few times before relaxing his wrinkled brow. "It does seem strange that even if we succeed, no one will even know they've been saved," he thought to mention.

"We will," Trinity said, while inspecting the starsword's blade, afterwards performing a minor flourish with the weapon before bringing it to rest alongside her right leg. "But, isn't that why *you're* here?" she asked the writer, who was by then seen to be resuming work on the shading of one of her most recent sketches.

"Oh, *me,"* she realized, after a moment of unanswered silence. "No. I'm pretty much here out of personal interest at this point. Nobody would publish any of this, anyways, save for those God-awful tabloid newspapers. My editor would have me thrown in the loony bin."

"Then write it as a fictional story," Flynn immediately proposed.

Her demeanor and tone of voice indicating disbelief apart from some level of amusement, *"Pardon?"* Kimberly replied.

"I said you should write it as a fictional story," he repeated, though the writer had clearly heard him. "Change our names, the dates, places, details, and you weave them into a fictional story," it was idealized.

Giving her head a quick shake and allowing her response to sustain for a time, *"No..."* she said, rejecting the idea, still managing to maintain her English charm throughout the forthcoming explanation. "I'm more interested in the journalistic style of writing. I've never written anything fictional before, what with characters who say things and a narrative that says what they don't. It's...odd," she decided, being succinct, letting her personal taste for non-fiction stand firm.

"It wouldn't actually *be* fiction, though," Trinity chimed-in with her two cents. "It'd be non-fiction masquerading as fiction. If you can't sell it as fact then you might as well sell it as myth," the mythical sword-bearer reasoned. "I knew this boy in high school," she vividly recalled. "He published a collection of short stories for kids and made twenty thousand dollars. God, I hated him," she suddenly remembered.

Taking notice of the writer rifling through the contents of her satchel, "*Now* what are you up to?" Flynn asked her.

"Writing the story," she casually responded, having found her only fountain pen, getting a laugh out of both Flynn and Trinity as a result.

Chapter 6

Greased Lightning

10:00 hours.

Within the safety of the Looms' house, the party of four – five, in a way – sat in the comfort of the living room, about to enjoy a cup of tea being served in colorful vessels that two of them knew from previous experience rather than from mere obvious assumption were the former resident's beloved chinaware teacups.

“Can you believe it?” Trinity said to Walther, taking a seat in the oversize, dark red chair along with her counterpart and her chosen cup and saucer; all four being of a relatively similar shade. “The Earl Grey was still stashed in the bread box,” she told him, as she adjusted the position of the sword at her left side, being careful enough not to make direct contact with it.

“Hmm,” he replied, with his thoughts lying elsewhere.

“I am absolutely in love with this house,” Kimberly commented, from her seat on the dark blue sofa. “I especially like the mini grand piano. Can anyone play?”

“I was never very musical,” Flynn confessed, in his thick, raspy voice, in between sips from a green cup, “but, my brother used to play the spoons,” he joked, getting a laugh, a chuckle, and a grin out of the other three in his company.

“Even without words, or perhaps, especially without words, music expresses the inexpressible,” the only musician in the room said.

“Walther can,” Trinity told the group. “He's amazing,” she said, as she stared at the darkly-dressed man and sipped from her cup along with the others. “What was it I pried out of Leona last year? It was the night you were busy outside,” she began to recall, though not entirely on her own, with her jovial expression suddenly becoming serious. “He's the embodiment of everything I've always desired in a man.

Adventurous, strong, independent, intelligent, funny and passionate. But, all of that isn't what did it for me. It was the sound of a Moonlight Sonata that truly stole my heart."

Burying his emotional response deep down, the Dark Hunter swallowed hard as he set his gray teacup down on the coffee table. "She...really told you that?"

"Perfect recall," Trinity answered, while tapping her left temple. "She's anything but inaccurate," she added, in a sort of mocking compliment of the enchanted sword leaning against the front of the chair alongside her left leg. "So, come on, play something."

"I doubt it is in tune," Walther said, excusing himself from the request, having recalled that it was last tuned over a year ago and likely wouldn't be tolerable by his advanced ear for tone. "Too many notes would be off-pitch. It would sound terrible," he reasoned, wanting any performance to be on a well-tuned instrument. "When this is all over, perhaps I will tune it up and play something."

"You know how to do that?" Kimberly asked, as she stirred another lump of sugar into her tea.

"Sure do," he replied. "Beethoven had gone deaf and still he insisted on tuning his legless piano on his own by placing his ear to the floor, sensing the direct vibration of each note."

"Wait a second...Beethoven, the famous composer, was *deaf?"* Trinity asked in disbelief.

The Dark Hunter nodded. "He gradually lost his hearing and continued his craft, regardless."

"Talk about dedication," Kimberly said, feeling inspired, drinking from a blue and white teacup featuring a bluebird motif.

"The man's music played a role in the restructuring of Europe, inspiring revolution and uprising. Of course, he later regretted supporting Napoleon, who defiantly declared himself an Emperor...but my point is that the power of music can have a profound and lasting effect on people. For better or for worse, in fact," he was sure to add.

Though old Sergeant Flynn was very much enjoying listening to a conversation revolving around music and history, he felt a strong need to interject with an unrelated question regarding something he couldn't quite put his finger on. "Trinity?" he said to the sword-bearer.

"Hmm?"

"Just what is it you're making in the kitchen, now?"

"Nothing," she replied, before sipping more tea.

"Something's definitely burning," the alerted ex-soldier announced. "Can't you smell it?" he asked the group, looking to each one of them.

"Yeah," Walther agreed, after deeply inhaling a breath of air through his nose. "Yeah, I think something is," he followed up, becoming suspicious of a possible cause. "Everyone outside, right now," he calmly, yet alarmingly stated, prompting the group to get up from their seats right after he did.

"But what about the tea?" Kimberly complained.

"No time, Ms. Hunter," Flynn told her. "Come along," he said, and ushered her to hurry.

Not a minute later, the party of five unlikely companions, including Trinity's counterpart who had already told her exactly what was happening, exited the house via the front door. An orange glow emanating from above was all they needed to see to know for certain that the roof was indeed on fire. As the group backed away from the house while looking up at the flames, they came to realize that the fire was isolated to the lower roof, directly above the kitchen, and hadn't yet spread very far.

"What could have started it?!" Kimberly wondered aloud. "Perhaps a grease fire in the kitchen?!" she speculated.

"I don't think so," Flynn mumbled to himself, as he turned his attention away from the house in favor of watching their backs.

"The ground is a bit wet," Walther said, upon taking notice of the simple fact. "Look. There are dark clouds overhead. It actually could have been lightning," he reasoned, before turning his attention to his apprentice. "Tell me that you can do something about this," he practically begged of her, after grabbing a hold of her shoulder to pull her in close, knowing there was nothing that he, himself, could do.

A flame of this intensity is nothing. I have quelled forest fires. Simply throw me into it and retrieve me in haste.

"What?" Trinity said, as she looked down at the sword by her side.

Do it!

"The fire's starting to spread," Kimberly warned, amid the

increased crackling sound of scorched hardwood.

"Alright, here goes!" the sword-bearer announced as she stepped forward, raising up the Starsword and positioning it over her head like an ax, preparing to send her counterpart flying.

"What could you possibly..."

The writer received part of her answer when the scarlet sword was thrown as hard as possible, up above the roof, spinning around and around until it suddenly came to a halt in midair and plummeted blade-first into the flames. "Did you see that, Gramps?" she asked Flynn, who repeatedly nodded a confirmation after the amazed Englishwoman tugged at his jacket with one hand while looking up at the fire.

"What are you planning to do?!" Walther asked, the moment he detected his apprentice heading toward the wide-open front door.

"Move away from the house," she calmly commanded, before she quickly ran back inside, leaving her perplexed, bewildered, confused companions standing among the weeds and overgrown grass of the front yard, wondering whether or not to go back in after her.

"No!" Walther told Flynn and Kimberly, who both seemed intent on reentering to stop the brave young woman from getting herself killed.

"Are we just going to stand here and let her risk her life?!" the writer inquired, over the crackling of the flames.

"If she is seriously wounded, our mission becomes much more difficult," said the veteran soldier, offering a warning that especially caught the ear of the Dark Hunter.

"I know," Walther responded with regret, "but, do either of you believe you can stop her?" he rhetorically asked, knowing that they could not. "We will have to trust her, *and* the other one, as well. If they can stop this inferno, I will be convinced they can handle anything."

The three remaining comrades then stood in helpless amazement, watching the flames that would soon be devoured by the Starsword, beginning from the moment its human counterpart emerged from a window on the second floor and began walking atop the roof through the flickering tongues of orange that seemed to flee from her very presence. By the time she stepped forward to reacquire her fine-edged friend, the disaster seemed averted to all others, and in its place stood a darkly-dressed woman with scarlet red eyes, holding high a sword that contained a fiery-orange glow – a containment that would breach with the shock of a sonic boom, violently discharging and dissipating the gathered energy evenly across the evening sky.

Near the edge of the property where the hunter, ex-soldier, and writer had retreated to a safe distance, Walther was suddenly forced to hold onto his hat as he ducked down in reaction to the delayed sound reaching him. Kimberly, too, was compelled to hit the ground due to the sheer intensity of the blast that was immediately accompanied by her own startled, effeminate scream. Having been a miner and then a soldier and heavy weapons expert for much of his life, Flynn was the only one on the ground who was unaffected by the sound that he equated with exploding dynamite and simply tipped his duster hat forward, holding onto its brim as dust and leaves swept by in a torrent of hot air.

From the rooftop, Scarlet performed a victorious flourish of edged self and released control back to Trinity by simply shifting herself into her host's gloved left hand. She then headed back along the blackened but intact roof while reequipping her alternate black glove, eventually reentering the second-story window that had previously been used as a direct exit onto the roof.

“I don't believe it,” Kimberly said, as Flynn helped her to her feet. “She really did it.”

“She did it, all right,” Walther confirmed, as he brushed his jacket clear of debris. “Come on,” he said to the others, after visually confirming that they were fine.

Not a minute later, the group of three reentered the house in haste out of great concern for their other party member only to discover her sitting quite peacefully in the living room, almost exactly as she had been prior. With her sword resting flat in front of her across the arms of her and her counterpart's favorite chair, she appeared to be sitting quite comfortably, sipping on a cup of Earl Grey.

“Still hot,” she said to the others, who either laughed, smiled, or shook their heads in the presence of her nonchalant attitude.

With great relief over the safety of the house and, of course, for their vitally important companion, the returning group sat down as they were prior to the fire and resumed their enjoyment of the aromatic tea.

"That was quite the sight," Walther said. "I am impressed," he told his apprentice. "I *have* been since you became better acquainted with your friend there," he added, mentioning the sword that guarded her.

Saying nothing, Trinity continued to take small sips from her teacup as she occasionally eyed Kimberly, completely aware of the fact that the sketch artist was in the process of drawing her yet again.

"What did you think of *that,* Ms. Hunter*?"* Flynn asked the busy, blonde Englishwoman.

"All I can do is remain focused on my work," she replied, as she continued to develop her newest work of art. "I'll lose my mind if I keep telling myself none of this is possible, even though I've seen the impossible with my own eyes several times today."

"The impossible is only impossible until it is possible," Walther philosophized, and struck a match with his thumbnail to light the cigar that he puffed on while rotating it around and around, knowing that it could very well be his last one ever.

Four of the five companions sat drinking tea in the living room of the assumed-to-be-abandoned Looms' house, completely unaware that a masked figure on the outside was watching them through the front window between the narrow divide in the curtains.

~

21:30 hours.

With the setting of the sun underway, the Dark Hunter rightfully decided it was time and so those who were participating, already equipped from their ordeals with the house, headed west across the front yard and south down the forest path leading toward the vacant Camp Scarletmere. Along the way, a straightforward plan of action was reiterated: The sword-bearer was to remain at the edge of the forest in stealth until an opportunity for attack presented itself. Leaving the young woman to wait and observe from a distance, the Dark Hunter and the old Sergeant continued south to the docks to initiate the confrontation that, according to the hunter, was not between good and evil but rather life and anti-life.

"Come on out, demon!" Walther spoke aloud, when the last light of day had nearly faded from the horizon. "We know that you dwell here! Come on out and meet your maker!"

Moments later, despite a warm summer breeze, the rolling waves of the water suddenly reduced to a state of unnatural calm. In the center of the Mere, from below a surface as smooth as glass, a black figure rose up, emerging as a silhouette shadow standing atop a mirror that slowly began to lose its reflective quality. Not a wave nor a ripple broke through its sleek, blackened appearance, even as the darkness flowed down along the figure of the young girl that remained standing in the moonlight, adorned in a tattered, once white dress, by then a faded gray, that covered a body of seemingly perfect health.

As the Dark Hunter and the old Sergeant wisely kept their distance from the shore, firearms already drawn, the Dark Demon lightly began skipping across the water's surface in the way that a little girl would on a summer's day, until the Mere began locally rising beneath her delicate feet, allowing her to effortlessly skip forward and onto the end of the dock, effectively concealing the aura of darkness she released with a hellish scream from within herself from the moment she touched down. With waves of purplish, dark energy emanating from a youthful female frame, the embodiment of anti-life began casually strolling down the dock toward the shore, looking not at the two who openly sought to challenge her, but elsewhere, slowly turning her pretty little head from side to side and back again, observing her surroundings.

Just as the two decoys were about to engage, something entirely unexpected occurred. A masked figure appeared from out of nowhere and ominously stood in their line of fire, standing still, staring at them through the narrow eye slits of a black and blue mask that bore an expression of great sadness. Uncertain of the masked woman's intentions, Walther and Flynn held their fire and watched with dismay as she suddenly turned away and began approaching one who used to be her daughter. Wanting to stop the woman whom he knew to be the Caretaker, the hunter stood firm by verbal order of the old Sergeant, accepting that the risk was too great, and thus he was saved from an almost certain death. Seeing her stop at a distance of but a few feet from the advancing demon-girl, hearing the screams of the enslaved souls from a distance, they helplessly watched the Caretaker bow her head and place a hand over her heart in what seemed to be a pledge of obedience to a creature that clearly did not have any further need for her – a fact that was evidenced by Lydia's inability to spare even her own mother from death. In the blink of an eye, an open, down-turned hand was violently thrust through the chest of the masked woman who remained loyal to her child even in death, until her instantly-rendered-lifeless body was launched fifty yards from the dock and into an area of the water that prematurely rose up to snatch her out of the air, swallowing her whole.

"Shoot her!" Walther ordered, after snapping out of the paralyzing horror he had just witnessed, and so the duo began their attack with ammo conservation in mind while retreating and reloading when appropriate, all the while being walked down by a casually strolling foe that horrendously moved forward into each hail of bullets as if they were a meaningless curiosity. At best, each impact from the Dark Hunter's powerful M29 magnum revolver would momentarily stun the demon or knock her off step, but with her enchanted blood healing each gaping wound one by one in sequence over a matter of but a few seconds, it was accepted through a subtle exchange of a shaking head and a nod of agreement that purely physical attacks were quite useless.

That was when they each took notice of someone and something else, silently but swiftly approaching from the rear with her inactive sword held at-the-ready, and when she came within range of her seemingly oblivious target, she gripped the ancient weapon with her bare right hand, evoking the Spirit of Fire as she leapt through the air and sliced the Dark Demon's head clean off her youthful shoulders, leaving a cauterized wound where her pretty head once was.

Victory seemed well enough at hand. However, while speaking a Recitation, much to everyone's astonishment, Lydia's headless body suddenly rose up to her feet in a flash and grabbed hold of the Starsword's ancient blade, sealing its blazing inferno within the darkness of an ebony void. In that moment, the mental and spiritual connection with Trinity's symbiotic counterpart was lost.

Retreat---

"Scarlet!" Trinity yelled. *"No!!"*

"Run!!" Walther and Flynn commanded, at the exact same time.

Feeling the full terror of where she was and the imminent onslaught of what was looming toward her, Trinity fell backward and began frantically scampering away on her hands and feet in a reverse fashion as Walther and Flynn resumed firing at the creature masquerading in young Lydia's shell, who was then in possession of an ebony sword with a burning black and purple fire that illuminated her surroundings. Tolerating heavy fire, the decapitated demon soon took repossession of her own head, securing it back atop her shoulders within an instant of bloody regeneration.

With the Starsword having been stolen and its captor beginning to legitimately give chase, the Dark Hunter, the old Sergeant and an emotionally distraught young woman ran as fast as they could, having no choice but to head west up the camp's dirt road in order to put as much distance between themselves and the Mere as possible. When they finally turned north into a grove that was about a quarter-mile away, the hunter stopped the group to rest under a big oak tree, fairly certain that they were no longer in immediate danger.

"I lost her. She's gone," Trinity sobbed, and fought against her tears as she sat down on the grass and rested her back up against the trunk of a moonlit tree. "There was nothing I could do."

"Whoever that masked woman was, she has placed the success of the mission in serious jeopardy," Flynn said, as he recovered his breath, not having run such a long distance in quite a number of years.

"The Caretaker," Walther informed him, as he comforted his visibly distraught apprentice. "She got both of them."

"That's it, then," Trinity spoke, amid her falling tears.

To that assumption, *"No,"* Flynn strongly responded. "She may have won this battle, but we aren't dead yet. I was hoping it wouldn't come to this, but we must now head east, straight into the deepest part of the forest."

"Surviving the descent will be impossible for the two of you," Walther immediately responded, knowing exactly what the old Sergeant was thinking. "One wrong step and it would be your very last. I will have to go it alone. We will return to the house for Ms. Hunter, but, after that, all of you must get as far away from this area as possible."

"I need to help you!" Trinity exclaimed, as she quickly got to her feet. "I *have* to do *something!"* she practically begged of him.

"Surely, one of us should go along with you, if only to watch your back," Flynn proposed, seeing that it was at least being mulled over. "I'd only slow you down if we got into a pinch, so, why not take the girl?" he suggested. "She's light and fast. Certainly faster than these old legs. She looks like she can handle herself."

"Hey, that's right!" Trinity suddenly realized. *"Look* at me!"

"What?" the hunter wondered.

"Don't you see?" she said, presenting herself with open arms, as if the answer was obvious. "I'm still the same."

"...A remote possibility, but a possibility nonetheless," Walther agreed, in understanding what little hope she was clinging to. "But, even Ol' Loudmouth here was ineffective," he reminded them, while tapping his holstered, but unclasped weapon. "If we have to engage her in close range she will undoubtedly use it against us," he said, referring to the even more deadly combination of Lydia and the stolen Starsword. "I am not opposed to the idea of you coming along, but, without a solid plan, we are as good as dead."

Upon hearing a rustling sound coming from the edge of the forest to the south, the Dark Hunter and the old Sergeant simultaneously drew their weapons and took aim, directly alongside the other since they were left and right handed, respectively, in anticipation of Lydia storming out of the woods after them, but, instead, a deer ran into the grove and stopped to look and listen at a distance of about twenty yards. Standing in the moonlight, its ears twitched as it observed them before it began grazing, apparently deciding that it was in no danger.

"Let's get the hell outta here," Trinity said, as she watched the deer nibble at the grass from a protected view behind the men who holstered their sidearms with no small amount of relief.

"We should take the long way 'round," Flynn advised, as he took point, leading the company forward in the direction he knew to be safest. "As I understand it, her range is limited, so if we maintain a mile radius from the Mere we'll remain out of danger and get back to the house in one piece."

"I wonder how Ms. Hunter is doing," Walther thought out loud. "The whole world could be crumbling down all around her and still she would not put down her pen. I cannot help but worry about her."

"I'm not worried," Trinity said, choosing to believe in Scarlet's continuing existence and in the Divine Blessing that had been cast upon the Looms' house the previous night.

When the three companions left the grove, heading west along the winding dirt road and then going north from the crossroads, a lone, young girl emerged from the forest, entering the grove afloat a small black cloud that spared her from having to touch the ground, taking immediate notice of a deer feeding on grass in the moonlight. When the animal took one look at her and attempted to run, she trapped the beast at a distance using her newly acquired weapon's inherent ability. Her white skin and even her tattered white dress became a jet black as her screaming aura flared up like a swirling tornado, was concentrated into the Starsword's ebony blade and was then released as a four-pointed, star-shaped projectile of death, resulting in a violently contained explosion of fire-like darkness that was reabsorbed back into the sword and on through to its captor and supposed dark master.

Not a trace of the poor animal remained to be seen.

Chapter 7

Blind Ambition

23:00 hours.

In the Looms' house sat a relaxed, yet focused writer, steadily working on her illustrated narrative, having fully realized that her two loves, writing and art, could actually be combined into the singular goal of telling the Scarletmere story – even if it would only ever remain fictional. After completing her most recent sketch, coloring and all, she continued to add to her point form notes until she arrived at the present time in the details of the story before allowing herself to drift off to sleep in the sword-bearer's favorite living room chair.

Several minutes went by in the quiet house until the sudden sound of the front door being quickly opened caused the blonde Englishwoman to instantly awaken with the fear that something unnatural had come back to get her while the others were away. Flipping herself around to her knees, she peered over the top of the big, comfortable chair, waiting to see who or what was there. The door was soon heard closing and locking and, luckily, the sound of many advancing footsteps on the hardwood floor indicated the welcome return of her companions.

"You're back!" she happily exclaimed, before she sprang up from her seat to offer Trinity a congratulatory hug that was not only accepted, but eagerly welcomed out of need. It wasn't until the first teardrop was seen falling down the face of the young woman did she begin to doubt the success of the mission that was thought to be a guarantee if the three of them returned alive. "What's wrong?" she softly asked, as she glanced between Walther and Flynn while Trinity held onto her tight, reminiscent of herself as teenage girl, still needing a hug from mum in order to feel alright. "You're shaking... What on Earth happened out there?"

"She killed Leona, and she took Scarlet from me," it was confessed, in a clear withholding of bottled-up emotions. "They're...gone."

"The girl's *mother?* Where did *she* come from?"

"Pack up," Walther sternly interrupted, quite disinterested in wasting time with idle conversation. "We must leave immediately."

Doing what was requested of her, the writer began gathering up her books, pencils and pens from the table, becoming even more concerned after seeing the usually stoic hunter's altered temperament. "What exactly is going on?" she asked, while placing her possessions back into her leather satchel. "Where are we going?" she curiously asked, as she lifted the satchel by its long strap that was pulled over her head and adjusted diagonally, across her body and between her breasts, allowing her to comfortably carry the bag that hung from her right shoulder and alongside her left hip with little to no effort.

"This is the end of the line for you, Ms. Hunter," Walther told her, flicking a switch on the wall that turned out the lights of the chandelier above their heads, leaving just enough light spilling into the living room from the corridor to allow them to see. "You will drive Mr. Flynn back into town and then head far away from this area. *Very* far," he said, as he peered through the window, looking directly south rather than to the walking path at the western edge of the property.

"Alright," Kimberly partially agreed, "but, where are *you* going?"

"They have a mission to carry out," the old Sergeant said, as he stood between the double doors to the living room, diverting the writer's attention from the hunter who was seen to be pacing back and forth in the corridor. *"You* are driving me home."

"I want to go, too," she quickly declared.

"No," Flynn responded, with a stern shake of his head. "Believe me, my dear, you don't. I once asked his grandfather where he was going, and I was told that I was better off not knowing the road to death's door."

"Where I am going, you cannot follow," Walther summed up, as a statement that was intended to dissuade the persistent writer. "A single error. You fall to a certain death. No second chances," he said, remembering and reciting for her his father's haiku. "The descent alone is intimidating enough to stop anyone."

Smirking, the writer raised and lowered her eyebrows as she looked the hunter up and down. "Except, of course, for you."

"Nearly anyone," he corrected.

"I suppose I have no choice," Kimberly begrudgingly accepted, in a tone of voice that the old Sergeant found to be somewhat suspicious.

"I require a good length of rope," Walther informed his apprentice, who by that time had laid down to rest on the sofa. "Have you ever seen any around the house or the yard? Trinity..?"

"I...I don't know," she responded. "I don't know anymore..." the lost young woman admitted, in a sort of sad realization of the fact. "God, I never realized how much I was relying on her."

"Rely on what you have learned," her mentor strongly suggested, as a confidence-building reminder for her to draw upon, knowing something of the emotional difficulties brought on through losing someone near and dear to the heart.

"There's some rope in the back of the Volkswagen," Kimberly remembered. "It might be enough."

"Let us go," Walther announced to the group, before leading the way out of the living room and down the hallway toward the front door. *"Trinity!"* he hollered, when he detected only two sets of footsteps following behind him, knowing that his apprentice was still lying on the sofa in a mix of anger and sorrow, strangely reminding the both of them of the mask of red rage that her biological father, Bennett Looms, and the mask of blue sorrow that Lydia's mother, Leona Looms, were seen to be wearing before they died at the hands of their daughter – the Resurrected – the Dark Demon.

~

When the old Sergeant obtained a length of rope from the VW's messy trunk and tossed it into the back of the Chevy, the four broke off as pairs and drove in separate directions for nearly half an hour, with the time ticking closer and closer to midnight, soon ticking over into the earliest hour of the morning on July 21st, 1967. Kimberly and Flynn were to take the Volkswagen southwest to the town of Scarletmere, while Trinity and Walther planned to drive further north and then east before finally parking and hiding the Ruby Red in the woods. The mentor and apprentice would then head out on foot, traveling south by southeast into Scarlet Forest from a safe direction, though they'd be moving further and further toward the northern edge of Lydia's growing domain of influence. But, the Dark Hunter would not dare speak so far in advance of the many dangers they were venturing toward, not with his apprentice more or less having returned to normal and, amazingly, still wished to accompany him. Going forward, he would tell her only what she needed to know with the hope that she would progress in experience and gain confidence on her own, without the benefit of her counterpart.

"Are you sure you know where you're going?" Trinity asked, as she followed behind her mentor, catching only split-second images of his dark figure in the frayed moonlight that made it through the lush treetops overhead. "I can hardly see a thing," she complained, right before she stopped herself from falling after stumbling on a large tree root that the hunter somehow managed to avoid.

"Your eyes will adjust," Walther assured her. "Now, listen, we should not make too much noise out here," he quietly told her, as they walked single file down a woodland trail. "And, yes, I know exactly where we are going. We will soon arrive at the river that flows into the Mere a few miles away. Once we find it, we follow it to the falls."

"The *falls?"* she questioned. "As in waterfall?"

"Yes," it was confirmed. "It is not wide, but quite high. You will have to take it slow and follow my every instruction. If you do not..."

"The haiku?" she remembered. "About falling to certain death?"

"I have traversed it a few times," he replied, reassuringly. "Just do exactly what I say. Or, perhaps..."

"Why couldn't we just go at first light?"

"You know why," he responded, forgiving her interruptions as he led the way through the overgrowth and into a murky part of the forest before suddenly stopping in place to look around.

"What's the matter?" she wondered, having almost bumped into the man before she peered around his right side in order to see what the problem was. "Hey, everything's dead here."

"Not dead. Dying," he corrected, detecting no immediate reason for them to retreat. "This is all unnatural. See there?" he said, nodding in the direction of a tree that was literally withering away in front of them. “I thought this might happen. We cannot travel this way. Come,” he said to the captivated young woman as he changed direction, heading east by northeast down a narrow animal trail with the intention of arriving further upriver, having only to go a little way south from there to get to their actual destination.

After a few minutes of traveling what appeared to be a safer path, the pair took notice of a terrifying singing voice that seemed to be echoing to their left, just north of their position. Fearing the absolute worst, the Dark Hunter opted to boost his young apprentice into a tree before climbing up, himself, where they remained in silence to observe and hopefully elude whoever or whatever was onto them. When the sound of footsteps on leaves and branches grew nearer, Walther quietly drew his revolver, fully prepared to fire down on whatever crossed the magnum's sights. Thankfully, the one that had been following them had been no one more dangerous than a curious and persistent writer who, at the sound of a clicking gun hammer returning to its neutral position, looked up into the nearest tree and discovered the two people she had been hoping to catch up to.

“There you are,” Kimberly said, just as she activated a flashlight and shone it up into the nearest tree above her head.

With a sigh of relief, the Dark Hunter holstered the high caliber weapon in his left hand and dropped several meters down from the big tree, the tails of his long coat flapping behind him as he landed with a heavy thud. “What are you doing here?” he asked, upon returning to the ground. “I thought I told you to go home? And put out that light before you get us all killed.”

“How did you find us?” Trinity wondered, while slowly but surely climbing down from the tree on her own, with the writer's flashlight shone on her to help her see what she was doing.

“I managed to cleverly pry some information about where you were headed, you know, for my story, from Gramps before I dropped him off,” she explained, and turned off the heavy flashlight before sliding it into a pocket on the side of her satchel. “Then, I drove back as quick as I could, found the trail further north...and now, here I am.”

Trinity rolled her eyes and shook her head in disbelief of such tenacity and stubbornness. “What should we do with her?”

"...So be it," Walther soon decided, after looking down on the troublesome Englishwoman for a time. "However, just so you know, we cannot stick our necks out for you. Not at this stage of the game. The success of the mission must take priority over a single life. If you wind up in a dangerous situation, assume you are on your own," he warned. "You know, I have been wondering something about you, Ms. Hunter."

"Yeah, and what's that?" she responded, as she began to follow behind Trinity, though she would be instantly turned back around by the grip of the hunter's strong hand, to be given a piece of his mostly self-educated mind.

"How one can be so dedicated to their own cause that they become dangerously naive as a result," he said, to the woman whose blonde hair could barely be seen in the dark. "The Chinese symbolize the concept with an image of a serpent or dragon swallowing its own tail, slowly killing itself in irony, unaware of its impending doom until it is too late for awareness to make any difference whatsoever."

"So, what are you saying? That I'm unaware of the risk to myself?"

"In this case," Walther strongly replied, "the dragon represents not only *your* life, but *all* of life. I am saying you unwittingly placed humanity in the path of greater danger for your own selfish reasons, and if there exists a fine line between noble ambition and blind stupidity, you were quite literally treading on it by walking this very path. Traveling alone in this forest, with no way of defending yourself, was most...unwise!" he quite sternly said, and stepped around her, placing himself between the two women. "Keep close," he soon followed up, at the very least recognizing the scholar within her naivete, "and if anything happens, stay right behind me and do exactly as I say. *Exactly.* Do you understand?" he asked, with his back to her.

"Perfectly," Kimberly acknowledged, after swallowing the hard-hitting truth and adjusting her rectangular eyeglasses.

Continuing on through the dark forest, down a narrow animal trail, time passed uneventfully until the Dark Hunter and his two female followers emerged from the forest, entering into a wide-open grove with tall grass, thistle and wildflowers in a variety of moonlit colors.

"It is quite safe here," Walther remarked, sensing the ladies' shared desire to proceed beyond the protection of his close proximity.

Loving the sights before their eyes, as well as the sweet fragrance of the night air – feelings and senses that Walther not only expected, but shared in, given the natural beauty of the mostly untouched environment – Trinity and Kimberly went on ahead, leaving the darkly-dressed man alone to sit cross-legged on a large, flat rock where he was seen to be breathing-in deeply and exhaling slowly, his eyes closed in meditation, apparently conceding to them a few minutes of literally stopping to smell the roses.

"If the two of you are about finished," he eventually said to the lovely women, who were both quite busy smelling and admiring the flora and fauna of the moonlit grove, "we must be getting on with it. The falls are close."

"If we're near the falls, then where's the river?" Trinity asked, as she began threading a lock of Kimberly's long, blonde hair around the short stem of a blue flower – a pretty poinsettia that she positioned above the charming Englishwoman's left ear.

"Listen," Walther replied. "Put your ear to the ground," he added, minding where he stepped as he continued on through the length of the grove, having lifted up the tail end of his coat by wrapping it around his left arm so that he wouldn't harm the flowers.

Doing what was suggested, Kimberly was the first to realize that the river was directly below them, running underground. "I can hear it!" she told Trinity, who lay right next to her with an ear to the ground as well. "We better go," she realized, in the interest of remaining close to Walther – a feeling that was suddenly brought on through remembering that the gentle, lovely young woman lying next to her no longer carried with her a divine passenger who could protect her. The ancient, sentient sword of fire had been lost – stolen by the very hand of darkness, herself. The blade that ignited in a liquid-like fire and blazed with the power that its aptly given name suggested had been extinguished, only to be replaced by a black blade and an ever-growing, lifeless shroud that was spreading across the land from its origin point.

"Now that we're almost there, are you finally going to explain what we're doing out here in the middle of the forest, in the middle of the night, in the middle of nowhere?" Kimberly asked, after catching up with Walther and matching the unusually casual pace he set.

“Yeah, tell us,” Trinity chimed in, appearing from behind her mentor to walk alongside him as well.

“The first thing we will have to do is take a reading of the moon and the stars,” he said in response, and awaited a reaction from both of the ladies walking on either side.

“You're kidding,” Kimberly replied. “Whatever for?”

“What do the stars have to do with our mission?” Trinity mumbled.

“We are not going to any place resembling anywhere either of you have ever been,” he informed them. “Where we are going, there are deadly traps, secret passageways and different laws that are only in effect at certain times during a Great Year.”

“A great year..?” the writer repeated, questioningly, missing the fact that it was a proper noun until she remembered her freshman astronomy class during the hunter's explanation.

“It takes three-hundred-sixty-five and a quarter days to complete the yearly cycle, but a *Great Year* takes approximately twenty-six-thousand Earth years to complete one full cycle through all twelve of the major constellations.”

“I'm sorry I asked,” Trinity commented.

“You need to know this stuff,” her mentor insisted, correcting the young woman's renewed sense of an easygoing attitude. “You will learn to appreciate what knowledge offers. It can easily mean the difference between life and death. In the case of where we are going, I can assure you that knowledge will be the one thing keeping us alive.”

“And what about wisdom?” she thought to ask.

“Aha! Very good,” he replied, acknowledging participation in the same manner that his father was known for. “It is much more evasive than we would think. Wisdom is knowing what to do *with* the knowledge you have acquired. Pops always said that a man who possesses both knowledge and courage can accomplish a great many things, if only he had the wisdom to know when it was unwise to do so.”

“What about *women?”* Kimberly said, in a tone of accusation.

“Obviously, it is no different,” Walther responded. “In the case of my Pops, the masculine reference was for himself and his son, who, as far as I can tell, is also a man. A mother or father could educate their daughter in the same way, using the feminine, which brings me to my next point," he said, flashing the writer a stern glance, "accurately interpreting both context and intent – a skill that fades away when we are unwilling to give people the benefit of the doubt."

Feeling a bit silly for even insinuating sexism on the part of the hunter, Kimberly scratched her head, wondering if an apology was due.

"Perish the thought, Ms. Hunter," Walther said, knowing just what was on the writer's mind. "Our thoughts are sometimes not our own."

Puzzled by his words until she took the time to ponder their meaning, the writer wished she could stop to record her interpretation. "How am I supposed to remember all this?" she soon complained, in reference to the ongoing story she was writing and the fact that she was unable to continue adding to her notes at that very moment.

"We remember the tragic, the important, and the interesting," Walther responded, causing Trinity to then wonder aloud if he was speaking as himself or as his father, only without the southern accent, and to that inquiry he replied: "It is both."

"What's that over there?" Kimberly had to ask, as they walked on through the moonlit grove of blossoming flowers, motioning with a simple nod of her head in the direction she meant.

"Never mind that," Walther sharply answered, discouraging any further question regarding what seemed to the curious writer to be a clear indication of a grave marker – one that the Dark Hunter apparently did not wish to speak of.

That was around the time and place that the falls became clearly audible to them. The steady, ceaseless crashing of falling water only grew louder as they inched their way toward the edge of a two by three meter crevice that formed the elliptical shape of a large eye in ground. Instinctively, without so much as thinking about it, Kimberly placed her left hand on Walther's right shoulder as both she and Trinity joined him in lying on their stomachs to peek into the moonlit crevice and down to a rocky river passing through an underground cavern, over a hundred yards below. The sound being generated by the impact of crashing water on what could only be described as unnaturally shaped stone was nearly as memorable as the view of the rather unique area that was, unfortunately, only accessible by descending into the crevice and along the somewhat concave wall of the underground. As a constant vibrato, the high-pitched, yet soft and gentle resonant tone emanating from the stone pillar jutting up from the riverbed was not unlike the sound between radio frequencies, pulsing amid the kind of television white noise heard when there was no signal being received.

The hunter's description had been accurate, but fell quite short in regard to how unique the hidden, natural phenomenon actually was. It was certainly true that the falls weren't very large, but what seemed to imply in plural was in fact only a singular wave of smooth, flowing water no more than three meters wide, continually extruding from the face of the stone to the left of the group's clifftop position. Beginning perhaps twenty feet below them, the underground river plummeted the remaining eighty feet down and into a circular pool whereby the excess created a continuation of itself, spilling over and flowing onward for miles to eventually connect with the Mere. Combined with the protection of the rounded stone interior that would seem to prevent any kind of grip or leverage, except along a single, hard to spot route, the exterior of the isolated location in the middle of the forest was a well-kept secret, camouflaged almost entirely by the biology of nature's lush plant life.

"We may have to do this the same way my Pops first did with me," Walther said, as he continued to take in the moonlit view through the clifftop crevice. "It will be the safest way, so long as you do not fidget."

"How's that?" Trinity wondered.

"With me on his back," he answered, after re-positioning himself on one knee. "Climb aboard, Ms. Hunter. You first."

"Are you serious?" Kimberly sincerely asked.

"I appreciate the setup, but we do not have time for joking around," Walther replied, and quickly winked at his apprentice as the writer stepped around to his back amid a young woman's background laughter.

"Hey, aren't you going to use the rope?" Trinity suddenly asked, the moment she realized it was still coiled up, tied securely around the strap of Kimberly's satchel for safekeeping.

"The descent is not the reason I need it," he responded. "Now, hold on tight," he said to the Englishwoman behind him, "but do not strangle me. You will have to wrap your legs around my waist so that you do not dangle and throw off my balance. Trinity, better take Ol' Loudmouth and stay hidden until I come back for you," he instructed, as he unhooked the belt and holster at his waist and tossed her the heavy magnum.

"You never taught me about guns," she mentioned, just as she caught the belt in both hands. "I'm not sure I can handle this," she added, after withdrawing the weapon from its holster and taking aim at the brightest star in the sky before choosing the crescent moon as an appropriate target and pretending to fire.

"It is simple to operate, but difficult to utilize," the weapon's owner explained, while trying to accommodate his suddenly bashful first passenger. "When you pull the hammer back as far it goes, she is set for six. She kicks like a mule, so squeeze her tight or she will go flying right out of your hand. As your first firearms lesson, always keep both eyes open when aiming," the experienced hunter advised, noticing the novice tendency to shut one of them.

"And lesson two?" Kimberly asked, speaking almost directly into the hunter's right ear, causing him to slightly flinch in reaction.

"Not one single death has ever been caused by an inanimate object. The cause exists always in the action of the human being, whether on accident, or for better or worse. And by the way, Lydia, herself, cannot travel any further than her current power will permit."

"Then what do I need *this* clunky thing for?" Trinity asked, noting the weight of the weapon as a serious drawback for her in comfort.

"For bears and the like," Walther answered.

"Bears?" Kimberly said, reacting fearfully.

"This *is* a forest in America, after all. The Dark Demon, as Scarlet called her, can take control of the mind of any beast she comes into contact with, hijacking its body and using it to travel a ways beyond her sphere of influence. You had better hide like we did before, out of any distant line of sight."

Hearing all that, the Dark Hunter's apprentice quickly moved to take cover in the nearest tree on the outskirts of the nearby forest, fearful of being left alone and out in the open to be preyed upon by God knows what. "Hurry back, will you?" she called out, as she fast-walked while strapping and adjusting the belt and holster around her slim waist.

With a slight turning of his head, and with his left eye, Walther glanced at the saddled-up writer on his back. "Ready?"

"Giddy up," she told him, after twice clicking her tongue on the roof of her mouth.

Amused by her accent and sense of humor both, the Dark Hunter tilted back his cowboy hat and carefully shuffled closer to the edge of the elliptical crevice. Stepping down from one knee into the underground, he began slowly lowering himself and his first passenger along a highly dangerous descent, feeling with his feet for every accurately recalled groove in which it was safe to step.

"Oh, good Lord," Kimberly mumbled, and held onto her ride tighter, having made the mistake of looking down. "I must be going mad," she admitted, as she hung on for dear life, not even realizing with all the noise from the falling water that the flashlight stored in the open pocket of her satchel had slipped out and had fallen over a hundred feet down, straight into the rocky pool at the very bottom of the cavern.

Before long, the hunter and the writer were adjacent to where the waterfall began. Feeling with his feet to find the grooves in the face of the rock, the darkly-dressed man then began muttering to himself as he progressed, causing his passenger to inquire of what he was doing.

"Making certain that I am remembering the pattern correctly," he answered. "My Grampy must have known the pattern, probably from that Old Book of his. He taught it to my Pops, who taught it to me. If you fail to step in only the correct slots, the paired stones will give way under enough of your weight, and down you go," he said, in answer to her next question before she could even ask it. "I wonder what they would think of me bringing not one, but two people down here, with neither one of them being of my own blood..? Under the circumstances, I think they would understand."

"Are you still feeling concerned that word will spread 'round if I write about all of this?" Kimberly wondered, even as her life hung in the balance. "Assuming it gets published, of course. As I recall, you and Scarlet had differing opinions in that regard."

"Well," Walther replied, as he shifted over by one position to the right, “the Sergeant has apparently been getting the word out for decades, but everyone just thinks that he is crazy. Now, if you would remain silent, Ms. Hunter, I really must focus.”

“Oh, right,” she said, before silencing herself, seeing that their lives were quite literally dependent on his concentration.

Focusing on the daunting task and succeeding without incident, the Dark Hunter eventually slid his hands and feet into horizontally cut grooves that ran directly toward the waterfall, and in shuffling toward it, it became clear to the writer on his back where they were actually headed. They wouldn't be descending anywhere near to the bottom.

“My back is *soaked*,” Kimberly soon complained of the misting water behind her, though she was thankful that her satchel was protecting her invaluable possessions.

“You will be dry in no time,” Walther responded, as he held himself firmly in position and allowed his passenger to disembark to safety. “Give me a hand, would you?” he requested of her, and waited to be pulled up behind the arc of the falling water.

“Aren't you going back for your protege?” she wondered, as she assisted the man in climbing to his feet on a hidden ledge of stone.

“Of course I am,” he replied. “I just need to rest for a few seconds.”

Behind the shimmer of moonlit water, the writer adjusted her glasses and tugged at her wet clothing. “Oh, that's wonderful,” she said with sarcasm, as she wrung-out her wet blonde hair and slowly turned around when she began to take notice of the pathway that led away from the waterfall, heading straight into a series of jagged rock formations that constituted a divide in the face of the wall. “Is that where..?”

“Do not get any foolish ideas,” Walther interrupted, knowing, without even looking, what the writer's attention had been set upon. “Under no circumstances are you to go in without me. You will wait here until I return with the girl,” he demanded, before he carefully began stepping down from the ledge and back into the grooves in which he could again shuffle along the face of the underground, disappearing out of the writer's sight with a spray of water that repelled from his jacket.

As she stared down the dark path that penetrated through the rock,

Kimberly shivered upon feeling a chilling coldness well up inside of her – a chilling coldness that had nothing to do with her cold, wet clothing. In that moment, curiosity was repelled by fear.

*What **is** this place?*

She instinctively reached for the flashlight at the end of her satchel and soon realized that it wasn't where it should have been. "Huh!? It's gone! Oh, no, I must have dropped it..." she commented, feeling scared, cold and alone, with nowhere to go and nothing to do but wait.

With his ascent only halfway complete, the sound of a loud, booming gunshot echoed into the night, telling the Dark Hunter that Ol' Loudmouth had been called into action. Increasing his rate of climb, he was nearing closer and closer to the moonlit eye above when a female figure suddenly flipped over the edge of the crevice, momentarily eclipsing the moon as it hurriedly began the dangerous descent, dislodging a pair of stones in the process and miraculously managing not to fall to her death.

"What *is* it?!!" Walther yelled out, between easily avoiding each of the falling stones that whizzed on by, that had they struck him, would certainly have sent him falling to *his* death.

"A mountain lion is chasing me!!" Trinity frantically hollered in reply, as she dangled from a single stone with both hands, praying that it wouldn't come loose.

After restraining his primary instinct to laugh at her unexpected response, he yelled out, "Hold on!! Do not attempt to move!!"

When the hunter climbed up beneath her, he allowed her feet to go past his shoulders and down his back as he continued to carefully ascend, putting himself in position between the young woman and the face of the subterranean cliff so that she could simply let go and take hold at his back. With his next passenger safely aboard, he began the descent once more as he focused his attention on choosing the correct stones to bear their weight rather than even once looking up at the fierce, purple eyes of the mountain lion that was smelling the air and growling as it looked down on the prey it could not pursue.

After carefully making his way back down and across with the added weight of his apprentice, who, during the trip, commented that she'd managed to prove the haiku wrong, the hunter awaited the help of the cold, lonely writer in getting his passenger safely onto the hidden ledge behind the waterfall, where, after a short breather, the group of three turned their attention to navigating the next route that loomed in their midst.

"Do exactly as I do," Walther said, as he began to lead the way along the narrow, dark and dangerous path that had the function of immediately discouraging travel. "This rocky tunnel is called Deadly Ebony," he explained, as he slowly walked between the spiky walls of a barely visible path leading away from the waterfall. "The rock is sharp and difficult to see. Because it is so dark, a jagged shard of ebony could be right in front of you and you would not even notice. Keep one arm in front of your head at all times and, whatever you do, try not to stumble or lose your equilibrium. Beginning a few yards in, the path narrows, and neither sunlight nor moonlight will be of any aid to us. Even if your eyes have adjusted to the dark and you can still see, at that point you will be effectively rendered sightless as if you were blind."

"I lost my flashlight, but what about a match?" Kimberly suggested.

"No good," he replied, knowing that she was misinterpreting his words. "There are ancient forces at play in the forgotten depths of the Earth...forces that even I cannot comprehend. From this point forward, you can both consider the laws of physics as being entirely mutable."

"Could you explain what that means to us normal folk?" Trinity asked, in a request for clarification, but also to poke fun at her mentor's typically complex explanations.

"Get ready," Kimberly offered as a rather blunt translation, taking the middle position behind Walther and copying his slightly-bent-over-forward posture.

After a few more seconds of carefully evading the jagged rocks that stuck out every which way on the narrowing walls, the Dark Hunter stopped in place. *"There,"* he said. "I cannot see a thing. Make certain that you do not react to the loss of vision. Follow my voice in single file at all times."

"All of a sudden I can't see you," Kimberly announced, upon taking but a few more steps. "This is really freaky."

"Me too," Trinity said. "I can't even see back the way we came.

There's just nothing but black in all directions."

"Remain calm. Grab onto the tails of my coat," Walther offered, feeling that it was the best way to keep them feeling safe and secure. "Trinity, you can hold onto Kimberly's satchel. We will make a chain, but you should also feel your way as we go along, just to confirm what I say. For instance, the side of a huge spike can be felt just over your head, right *here,"* he announced, and smacked it a few times with his palm so that they could hear.

In following all of his directional and cautionary instructions while slowly feeling their way blind along the dangerous path, the women suddenly found their vision restored by a struck match.

"Stop," Walther commanded, from a position facing them.

The two ladies both looked down to discover that they stood amid several potentially crippling rows of stone spikes, two to three feet high, aimed up at their thighs and midriffs.

"This way," he immediately said, before he led the way around the sharp spikes with the aid of a torch he lit, obtained from seemingly out of nowhere. "There is one more trap to cross before we arrive."

The ladies carefully walked around the spear-like shards of ebony, avoiding the potentially devastating leg injuries they would have suffered had they been moving at any faster a pace.

"So, you consider these traps?" Kimberly asked.

The hunter was seen to be nodding based on the movement of his hat – a hat that happened to be in the pinch-front Cassidy crown style. *"Oh,* yes," he confirmed. "These are definitely traps meant to not only discourage travel, but to prevent anyone without the proper knowledge from ever getting through, whether they be bold enough or foolish enough to try without said knowledge. You might call it an ancient security system. Without a proper guide, the odds are insurmountable."

"So, the Ancients built this place," Trinity surmised.

"I know of no other civilization that could have," Walther responded. "There is an invisible rift that will show itself in a few yards. The trick," he said, as they entered and walked through a perfectly rounded, cylindrical tunnel, "is simply to keep moving through it. Lower yourself over the edge and then drop down. You will feel it pushing on you from all directions, almost like a steady gust of wind. It is a force you have never felt before, but the more you resist, the less of an effect it has," it was explained, before the hunter lit a second torch already in place in a stone fixture on the wall just outside of the end of the short tunnel, leaving it there to illuminate part of the wide-open chamber before them. Without delay, he then hopped down from a six-foot-high ledge to stroll headlong into the barrier of what he termed *the Fray* – disappearing into an energy field existing as a result of distorted spacetime.

"This is intense!" Kimberly called out, after she entered its area of effect, feeling her voice fail to reach even as far as the hunter's ears a mere five yards away due to the peculiar quality of the starry, inverted black and white environment that surrounded them.

Knowing the Fray permitted almost no sound at all except for the constant wispy tone it generated, and in the interest of making sure that the other two in his company were progressing fine without him, the Dark Hunter, appearing to be dressed in an ensemble that was rendered a silvery-white, did a quick one-eighty that produced a slight afterimage of his motion. Seeing that they were making slow and steady progress, he grinned and spun back around to continue leading the way across the brilliance of the expanse, carrying with him a torch bearing a flame that burned black.

Noticing that their leader had turned around to check on them and had a rather pleased look on his face before he turned back around, Kimberly, out of concern for the young woman behind her, turned around and stopped in place to do the same. In the blur of the Fray, she suddenly felt herself becoming dizzy and weak. The feeling of her very consciousness being pressed-upon was causing her to begin to black out. That was when a scarlet red aura, exposed by and resistant to the Fray, caught up to her, turned her around and began physically encouraging her to continue moving. With her thumb and index finger, the writer signed an okay and continued striving forward on her own.

After only a minute had passed in normal time, the group emerged one by one from the highly strenuous environment a good ten minutes later, returning each of them to normal spacetime.

"That was...not so bad, was it?" Walther asked, breathing heavily to recover his drained stamina.

"It actually kinda felt like being underwater," Trinity suggested. "Everything was slowed down."

"Yes," Kimberly agreed, "and much like a shark...I could breathe only if I continued moving," she pointed out. "I couldn't even begin to offer a scientific explanation for what we've just gone through."

"At first, the danger was over-action," Walther explained, as he again began to lead the way in standard darkness with a torchlight that was back to looking as it should. "This time, it was under-action that could have killed you. I have been through it a few times, but it never gets any easier, and the bigger you are the more difficult it is to resist. Come, now. The rest area is just ahead."

"No more traps?" Trinity pleaded and wondered at the same time.

"No more for the three of us," he responded, as he led the way through a gradually widening tunnel wherein the surrounding rock eventually gave way to a ceiling of star-filled sky above a danger-free path, made of and surrounded entirely by the smooth, polished stone of a courtyard.

"Where *are* we?" Kimberly wondered with amazement, being that she was second in line to take in the sights of their moonlit surroundings.

"What is *that?"* Trinity asked, when she became aware of the haunting structure that stood in isolation at the back of the courtyard.

"Our ticket to the underworld," Walther replied, feeling that it was proper to respond to the latter question first. "Do not go near the arch. Just know that it is safe, so long as you remain on this side," he informed them. "This is the Courtyard of the Moon. There are torches and a sealed vat of oil to the left. Set a fresh torch into each one of these holders and we can light this place."

"This place..." Kimberly said, repeating the hunter's last two spoken words while taking in the sights, "it's like a natural solarium."

"Lunarium," he corrected, "and though it may appear to be natural, you are not actually seeing the sky. Well, not directly, anyway. What you *are* seeing is light passing through an enchanted ebony ceiling," he informed them, taking the time to observe their reactions as they came to realize it was somehow true. "If there is one thing I know about these ruins, it is that the people who built them were far more concerned with studying the moon and other celestial

bodies than with studying the sun."

"Unbelievable," Kimberly said, under a breath of amazement, accepting that they were not at all above ground.

As the Dark Hunter began examining the layout of a clock-like mechanism he called an *ancient moon dial,* four torches were dipped in a thick oil and set into four stone fixtures, between five and six feet off the ground, evenly spaced around the semi-circular courtyard.

"I need the matches," Trinity said, as she stood behind her mentor, watching him continue to stare back and forth between the moon dial and the moon itself using a pair of micro binoculars sold to him by a nameless supplier of military equipment – his quite roundabout way of saying *black market.*

"Here," Walther replied, just as he tossed a very small box over his shoulder without turning around. "Actually, on second thought, better save them," the experienced hunter said in realization, before he proceeded to slash with his serrated knife, over and over, at the stone wall, causing the young woman behind him to back away from his suddenly violent behavior, confused. When sparks were produced by his repeated effort, the torch underneath his multitude of slashes ignited a welcome flame. "Here," he then told her, picking it up and handing it to her before returning to his calculations. "This will take more time. The alignment is not yet true," he muttered, while taking notice that the Englishwoman was already in the process of sketching the crescent arch with only the moon's cold light aiding her vision.

Soon, three additional torches that in turn crackled to life under a sky of stone were lit, further illuminating their enclosed surroundings. The area beyond the arch, however, was strangely and noticeably unaffected by the increase in illumination, remaining pitch black, admitting the passing of no light whatsoever beyond its crescent arch. Becoming aware of the strange phenomenon in their midst, the writer was drawn a few feet closer out of curiosity, taking notice of her own reflection amid a wall of darkness.

"Walther?" she somewhat nervously called out.

"Step away," he calmly but immediately instructed, not even having to look up from his work in adjusting the moon dial to know what the curious Englishwoman had taken notice of.

"What happened?" Trinity wondered, as Kimberly backed off

without looking away from her fading reflection. "What did you see?"

"...Myself," she somewhat fearfully replied.

"It is the Lunar Mirror," Walther stated, between double checking his mathematical calculations in a small notepad using the remaining quarter of a very old pencil in his left hand.

"I thought it was an archway," Kimberly replied, upon hearing the apt description of it, having become somewhat annoyed by the ambiguity of the information she was receiving.

"It *is,*" the Dark Hunter asserted, as he stepped away from the adjusted dial and joined the two ladies in the upper middle of the courtyard, just a few yards away from the wonder they spoke of.

"Then, it's both," Kimberly gathered, and quickly made the correction in her journal. "What now?"

"Hmm," Walther thought, or rather, pretended to think, since he knew full well what he was planning to do next. "Coin toss," he suddenly proposed, while reaching into an inner pocket of his jacket, eventually presenting a heads-up gold coin in the palm of his hand.

"A coin toss?" Trinity repeated, in a funny combination of amusement and curiosity.

"Why?" Kimberly asked, as the hunter showed them the item that he flipped over, just to demonstrate that it was not a trick coin.

"Call it," he said, as he flipped the coin up into the air between the two women, and stepped away.

"Heads."

"Tails."

They spoke their choice at nearly the same time, and when the coin clattered on the stone floor, it bounced around and rolled in the younger woman's direction before coming to rest beside her foot.

"Tails it is," Walther announced, as he retrieved the valuable coin, placing it back into his pocket along with another that went unnoticed.

"So, what does that mean?" Kimberly asked.

The hunter sighed. "I dare not venture past this point with three," he informed them. "I can in good conscience protect one of you, but, not two. We either go as a pair or I go it alone."

"I'm going," Trinity affirmed, and began pacing around while doing stretches and twists at the waist to prepare herself for what lie ahead.

"You want me to stay *here?"* Kimberly complained.

The hunter nodded. "Three people have not been inside at the same time before, at least, no one in my family," he said, correcting himself. "There were likely many people inside at once, a very long time ago, but, I have learned from firsthand experience that it is better not to meddle with what one does not understand. Trust me, it is far safer out here than inside. There is enough oil and wood to last many hours and, besides, it is a chance to get caught up on all of your work," he rightly pointed out.

"Yes, but..."

"I expect to return in approximately two hours...maybe three. Trinity can tell you all about it when she gets back."

The saddened writer groaned with disappointment as she crossed her arms and turned away, obviously wishing to experience everything for herself instead of hearing about things secondhand. A moment later, she turned back and approached the hunter, not yet ready to give up. "But, I only want to learn from *you*," she softly confessed, and glanced up at him, doing her best to avoid blushing in his close proximity.

"You should try to remain on her good side," he quietly suggested. "When she gets the sword back---" he began to point out.

"If she gets it back," Kimberly corrected, while glancing back at the confident, jovial young woman who was exercising and apparently not paying the slightest bit of attention to their conversation.

"---she might decide to kill you if you upset her."

"You think she'd really do that?" Kimberly seriously began to wonder, as the hunter turned to face the crescent arch. "Walther..?"

"Go on, now," he replied, ignoring the question for his own amusement, playfully shooing the woman into stepping back a few paces. *"Trinity,"* he called out to his energetic apprentice. "Let us go."

"Me first?" she wondered, and out of playful spite along the way, kissed the left temple of the cross-armed writer who was staring down at the ground, resentfully kicking pebbles around.

"Yeah..." Kimberly said with a sigh, ineffectually acknowledging a kiss of consolation. "I want *details*," she told them, before rooting

around in her satchel for a piece of candy.

"Within this particular lunar cycle, we must go through at the same time," Walther explained to his apprentice, so that the writer could easily hear him. "If we were to go through separately we would both end up in entirely different places. And, by the way, this is going to feel quite strange."

Trinity and Walther stepped forward together, side by side toward the crescent arch of the Lunar Mirror, heading directly into their own static reflections that appeared as if frozen in time. When physical contact was made, the dark mirror began to ripple and flow outwardly, enveloping them in soft shades of pink and blue, representing what Kimberly incorrectly assumed to be distinguishing signs for the feminine and masculine, respectively. The mentor and apprentice were then pulled up off of the ground and into the center of the mostly unaffected darkness of the mirror, akin to entering a vertically contained pool of blackened quicksand that sucked them in as if consuming them whole, leaving in their wake only fading silhouette's of color. The amazing sequence that lasted all of twenty seconds left the writer standing in the Lunarium courtyard in a stunned, lonely silence.

Chapter 8

Ancient Underground

Absence. Endless chilling darkness, stretching through infinity. Enter a single point of light: The violent birth of a star. Matter colliding, merging, expanding. Boundless destructive force, radiant and divine, sustaining molten and vaporous nature. Lashing tongues, swirling nexus, erupting pressures. A rendering of heat and light; defying, rivaling, vanquishing the dark with that of finite life.

A young woman found herself awakening from a dream, emerging from nothingness, bathed in a softly glowing pink light that gently lowered her down to a smooth, stone floor on the other side of darkness. "I feel...incredible!" she exclaimed, as the shape, brightness and color of the mirror slowly returned to normal behind her, providing a view of the courtyard on the other side with a two-way effect in that one could only see through from the inside. "Can I do it again?" she called out into the gradually darkened, clearly man-made underground corridor.

In the courtyard on the other side of the two-way mirror, sat Kimberly, cross-legged and writing beneath the glowing light of a torch near the clock-like moon dial. From her view on the outside, the mysterious Lunar Mirror – a portal to God knows where – had returned to a solid black, allowing no light or sound to pass through, even as Trinity looked back at her from within the darkness of the other side.

"Walther?"

"We will have to, upon our return," his deep voice responded, from further within, before striking a match that revealed his location a few yards down the stone corridor. "This way," he said to his apprentice, just as he lit a torch taken from a small pile of wood that had been set against the wall. "Carry a few for backup and stay right behind me."

"Right," she acknowledged, and hurried to gather up a few of the torches in her arms. "Hey, um, why did the mirror turn pink and blue?" she asked, when she caught up to her mentor following close behind him. "Is it a male and female thing?"

"Your active link shone through, pink," he answered in rhyme. "That was the first time I saw it do that."

"Active link?"

"A metaphysical connection with a non-biological entity."

"Oh," Trinity responded. "Wait, what does that mean, exactly?"

The hunter grinned a grin that couldn't be seen as he continued to lead the way down the rectangular corridor. "Well, in the very least, it is additional proof that your counterpart is still having an effect on this world. If your connection was truly broken, your spiritual aura would have been blue – the same as anyone. Well, almost anyone," he said, correcting himself. "Though I figured Lydia would retreat in order to hide your sword where it could never be found, it seems that she has chosen to enslave it and use it as a tool for destruction. Either that or she is actually being deceived and, when the time comes, even this Dark Starsword may remain as our ally."

"May?" Trinity repeated, zeroing-in on her mentor's uncertainty. "Well, it's comforting to know that if you're wrong, we'll all be incinerated under the blade of a sword containing the power of a compressed star."

To the Dark Hunter, her words sounded rather like those of another. "I see that you retain a portion of her knowledge," he commented. "You could do without the sarcasm, but there is still something there. You should draw upon it for strength."

"Actually, when I went through the mirror, I felt the sensation of what it must be like to be one of them. So much raw power trying to force its way out. She does everything she can to restrain herself in the interest of protecting life, all the while knowing that, I mean, if she really wanted to, she could flare-up and destroy everything."

That was when the hunter began replaying in his mind the events he had since perceived as only failure. "Perhaps she allowed herself to be caught..?" he soon theorized out loud, as they walked the featureless corridor that seemed to stretch on and on, unchanged.

"What exactly are you saying?"

"It is what *you* are saying," he countered. "We were too close to you. Her very nature could have prevented her from taking the necessary action. I should have made it clear to her to let loose, no matter what. Then, perhaps, we would not be in this mess."

"Yeah, because we'd all be dead," Trinity sarcastically pointed out.

"Mind where you step and what you touch from here on," Walther warned her. "Do only what I do. We must be cautious and quiet."

"Alright, but who's cautious and who's quiet?" she continued to joke. "I thought you said you've been here before."

"I *have,"* he told her, when he stopped in place, "but that was five years ago. In fact, Ms. Ryder, it would be better if you did nothing at all, or you might end up like this guy," he said, right before he held the lit torch he carried up to a lone human skull resting in a small alcove.

Instinctively, Trinity drew-in a breath that her mentor correctly interpreted would come out as a scream, and so in the blink of an eye he securely covered her mouth with his hand, allowing only a brief, shrill sound to echo throughout the corridor ahead, causing it to physically twist and groan before its walls violently collided in what would have been a crushing agony had they been standing there.

With her fear increased even further as a result of witnessing the deadly phenomena, Trinity froze in place, paralyzed by the thought of uttering another sound with such life-threatening consequences abound. While staring into a fiery reflection in her eyes for his own assurance that she would remain silent, Walther slowly removed his hand from over her mouth. "I think I forgot to carry the one," he whispered, causing the eyes of his apprentice to nearly pop out of her head in disbelief of what she was hearing. "Speaking as a whisper has no effect," he assured her. "I have seen this once before, though I could swear it was further down."

"I-it wasn't," she nervously replied, as quietly as possible.

"I must have miscalculated on the dial," he surmised. "You know how every action is supposed to have an equal and opposite reaction?"

Unwilling to take her eyes off of the deathly corridor, Trinity nodded, having heard the scientific principle in school.

"Well, that was a tenfold reaction," he informed her.

"What do we do?" she softly whispered, quite afraid to proceed any further – a fact evidenced by a tug on the tail of her mentor's long coat.

Pausing his advance, the hunter considered for a moment how best to alleviate her fear. "Refrain from sneezing," he told her, successfully employing the use of humor before insisting that they move on.

For at least a minute, Trinity was forced to restrain herself by only smiling wide at the absurdity of his joke, containing her urge to laugh out of the fear of what might happen to them if she actually laughed out loud, and so she continued along the corridor, proceeding as quietly as possible, with her Dark Hunter for a mentor slowly and silently leading the way down the lengthy stone hall that arched almost imperceptibly downward into the Earth. With no small amount of tension and growing suspense over whether she would survive to reach the next stretch of corridor, and then the next, and then the next, Trinity cautiously followed close behind, trying to step silently in an environment that echoed even the slightest sound.

Further and further the duo went, having only to turn left down the occasional forty-five degree change in direction, with each passing corridor appearing to be no different from those prior, rendering the unwary traveler with an anxiety-ridden spell of uncertainty. Further and further they proceeded unspoken, with Trinity becoming more and more certain that they were traveling in a never-ending sequence from which they would never emerge, when at last they arrived at the end. The end that was only the beginning of what lie hidden in the underground.

"As you were," Walther said, signifying that it was safe for them to speak as he continued leading the way, though at a quicker pace, unafraid of the wide-open darkness he was venturing into.

"Where *are* we? *Where* ***are*** *we..? Where* ***are*** *we..?"* Trinity's voice echoed throughout the massive chamber, causing her to feel entirely humbled by the constructed greatness of what little she was able to see. *"Whoa,"* she said, suddenly speaking a lot softer.

"Come along," Walther immediately instructed, feeling that his apprentice was lagging behind in a vain effort to see how high the ceiling went, knowing, himself, that it remained out of sight within darkness high above their heads. "Pops once told me that his father was convinced there was even more to this place."

"You mean..?"

"Yes," he said, as he passed through an open, oval shaped doorway leading into an adjacent room, carrying with him a single lit torch that suddenly proved to be more effective in an area with a lower ceiling. "More than what we have gone through thus far."

"Great..."

After lighting a second torch, boosting it off of the only one in use, the pair separated and moved to opposite ends of the circular room where they began visually scanning the walls for any sign of a possible way forward.

"I'm not really sure what I'm looking for," Trinity admitted.

"Anything different," Walther replied. "I have not spent enough time investigating this area. Be sure to examine every inch."

"What if there's nothing but this empty room?" she wondered, as she carefully scanned up and down the face of the smooth stone wall in front of her, before sidestepping a few paces to repeat the procedure. "You really think there's something down here that can help us?"

"There better be, or we are in deep trouble."

"Seriously," she said, attempting to draw a direct answer out of the man possessing quite the flair for the mysterious, receiving only his silence as a reply. "I can't imagine what it would be."

"I thought your counterpart would have tipped you off."

"Yeah, well, she didn't," Trinity confessed. "She was very secretive. I asked her a lot of questions; how it was even possible for her to exist, where she came from, even the meaning of life, but she just wouldn't give me any answers. I knew what she allowed me to know, but, that was it."

"I know what it is you are wondering," Walther said, as he continued to scan the stone wall by torchlight, "but it is beyond my understanding. There are unseen forces that we, as humans, are unable to take measure of. Perhaps, through establishing a link with one of these beings, these Element Spirits, as it was translated, we can gain a vague insight into what they represent. However, to truly know what makes it all possible is probably impossible from our low-lying, human perspective. There may not be any scientific or rational explanation at all. One has to see the signs and experience phenomena before it truly sinks in as being real, despite all you have been taught, otherwise. There exists a moment when one comes to the inevitable conclusion that there is much that lies *beyond* the narrow limit of our senses. As an example, people sometimes have what are called out-of-body experiences, disconnected from the restraints of the physical self. Upon returning to a conscious state, they find that they cannot explain the experience in specific terms. A vague insight into a different state of consciousness is all that ever remains."

"And here I was thinking your family knew everything about that sort of thing, and about this old place."

"No," he replied, through a slight laughter in his voice. "We have only been picking up the pieces, doing what we can and passing on the knowledge. I am only the third generation to exist since its rediscovery. My knowledge is limited, but, as I understand it, these ruins are a relic of a once great civilization from which even the dullest individual could teach us a thing or two about energy manipulation and harnessing the power of light. They most certainly understood more than anyone in my family ever did, including myself. The Ancients must have been an enlightened people."

"Enlightened," Trinity repeated. "Isn't that Buddhism?"

The hunter instinctively nodded. "The first step on the path to enlightenment is admitting you know nothing. Or, was it the path to wisdom? The path *of* wisdom? No...perhaps it was truth..." he went on, gaining the amused attention of his apprentice while trying to remember the exact phrasing of the Buddhist principle, still visually scanning the walls for any sign of a possible clue.

"Is *this* anything?" Trinity suddenly asked, as she stared down at one of the square-shaped, stone panels on the floor.

"Is *what* anything?" Walther questioned, upon crossing over to her side, unable to take notice of what it was she was seeing.

"That," she stated, while pointing down at an area of the dusty, stone floor, seeing that it was carved into four square-shaped panels. "It's a slightly different color than the others...and just in this one spot," she realized. "All the rest are exactly the same."

The Dark Hunter squinted and brought his torch closer to examine the stone slab at his feet. Part of it was indeed a different shade of gray. "Hmm. I did not notice this before. Very interesting. If you recall, Pops taught me not to meddle with things I did not understand," he said, while taking position above the panel in question.

"What are you doing?"

"Meddling," he confessed, right before he shifted all of his weight down onto his left foot, activating a hidden pressure mechanism that closed off the exit behind them, while at the same time presenting a new path forward. Stone rumbled under immense mass, shaking the room by effect, until only the sound of crackling torches remained amid their stunned silence – silence that was preceded by a loud *thunk* at the end of the ancient fulcrum's cycle.

"Well, lead the way," Trinity suggested with apprehension, as she observed her mentor apparently hesitating to simply take charge with his usual demeanor and determination.

"No," he decided, after taking but a few steps toward the newly revealed path.

"Me?" the inexperienced young woman asked in disbelief, upon being summoned to walk in front.

"I mean to say that I wish to keep a closer eye on you from this point forward," Walther explained. "I do not know what awaits us, or of the trials that may yet lie ahead. If we have to react in haste, I want us moving together as a single unit, and I can only do that if I can see you and grab onto you. Trust me, I will remain quite close behind," he said, as he began nudging her along.

"So, *I'm* the guinea pig?"

"Come on, just walk," he insisted. "This is the best way I can protect you. Just take it slow. The sooner we find what we need, the sooner we can get out of here."

"Yeah," Trinity agreed. *"Yeah,"* she strongly repeated, and with confidence, stepped into the next short corridor that she could already see led straight into another dark, open environment but a few yards away. "Looks like it goes into another room," she announced, with her torch-bearing hand extended out as far as it would go.

What the two discovered upon exiting the short tunnel was far and away from anything they might have predicted. To the immediate front was a balcony of sorts, one that was made of a reactive material that began to glow a soft shade of orange from the moment the first foot was set upon it. In nearing the balcony's smooth, rounded guard rail to see what was beyond their view, they began to realize that the structure on which they stood was reacting to Trinity's very presence, and hers alone. From contact with her hand, a build-up of bright, fiery orange light began to appear and intensify within the metal rail. Reaching maximum charge and illumination, it suddenly bolted off to the right, drawing dual gazes and counterclockwise rotations of two pairs of eyes as golden light raced around and around a grand interior structure that had begun from its origin point high atop the lone balcony where it traveled a half-mile, spiraling descent, warming candle-like spheres situated along its path, producing soft, multicolored light as it rapidly progressed narrower and narrower on its journey to the bottom. An impressive and mysterious sight that would surely capture the attention of anyone, the mentor and apprentice hadn't immediately noticed that straight across from where they stood, two hundred yards away, on the other side of the broad expanse before them, several other lights had illuminated here and there, offering a dimly lit view of a once flourishing underground city.

"T-The Lost City..." Walther said under his breath, barely able to get even the first word out of his mouth after his apprentice tugged on the sleeve of his long coat, trying to get his attention as she continued to stare straight across the void. "So, this is what was hidden here, all along," he said in realization, before he leaned on the glowing rail, apparently overwhelmed, lowering his head, soon laughing quite maniacally into the vast emptiness of the underground.

"The hell is going on?" Trinity nervously asked, amid the echo of her mentor's jarring, sustained laughter. "Walther, you're scaring me."

"People have been speculating about the existence of lost cities for centuries," he soon explained, when he managed to restrain his excitement a little. "Atlantis, Lemuria, what have you. What you are looking at, Ms. Ryder, is the oldest remaining city in human history and, if my assumption happens to be correct, you are the second person to lay eyes on it in thousands of years," he said, counting himself as the third, not yet knowing that someone else had gained entry just one year prior to their arrival.

"It's...beautiful," Trinity decided, while gazing at the lights above and beyond the stone wall on the other side from where they stood. "What do you suppose is down *there?"* she couldn't help but wonder, as her gaze shifted to the narrow bottom of the funnel-shaped interior, accidentally dropping her fading torch into a dark abyss. "Oops..." she said, cringing when it finally clattered on something below.

"That is what we are going to have to find out," Walther replied, discarding his own nearly useless torch before taking his apprentice gently by the arm and encouraging her to once again take the lead as they headed off to the right, away from the balcony, beginning a time-consuming descent into the depths of the unknown.

Chapter 9

Seeking Justice

Minutes passed like hours in such unfamiliar territory as the deep underground of ancient Earth. The hospitality of *Theravylia,* the flourishing, earth-dwelling city built under a mountain was at one time known throughout the land. Following a great cataclysm, it had endured the passage of time and thousands of years of uninterrupted silence before it was finally rediscovered by chance and the persistence of an old man on a quest for knowledge – knowledge that he one day hoped to pass on to his son and soon to be born grandson – a possibility that seemingly came to an end in July of 1947.

Some of that history Marcus Walther was aware of. Some of it, he was not. At least, not at the time, but in the summer of 1967, at a young and uncommonly experienced age of only twenty, he became determined to follow in his grandfather's legendary footsteps.

The air that was dry and stale-smelling upon the arrival of a Dark Hunter and his accompanying apprentice was, for reasons unknown, becoming humid and more easily breathed once again. Around and around a softly lit, circular pathway they went, with a young woman leading the way and her mentor remaining in close proximity behind her, studying the details of the intricate, old-world architecture in a conserved but active readiness to react to unforeseen danger.

"What do we need these for?" Trinity asked, in complaint of the four unlit torches she still carried. "We can see just fine, now."

"You never know," Walther reasoned.

"But, *sometimes* we know," she countered.

"Sure," he quite easily agreed, "but in this place, neither of us actually does."

"Well, I don't think we have to worry about this path," she told him, after running her hand over one of the multicolored globes on her way past it, enjoying the fact that it reacted to her touch, and hers alone. "Even so, I wish *you know who* was still with me. With *us*. Whatever... She might have known something about this place. But, of course, she has a problem with volunteering information."

The hunter was already nodding. "Rain falls. Wind blows. Earth crumbles," he said, "but fire would have been extremely rare and difficult to comprehend."

"What do you mean?" Trinity responded. "They *had fire.*"

The mentor shook his head, though the young woman walking in front of him was in no position to see it. "I speak of naturally occurring fire, *before* ancient peoples learned to create it at will," he explained. "To encounter it naturally would have been exceedingly rare. Forest fires...beyond comprehension. To a mind of that era it would have seemed that the world had gotten too hot, or some other basic, yet rational thought. Perhaps they believed that God had intended to destroy the forest. Who knows. We as a species had to learn to manipulate and control materials in order to create fire at will, and to sustain it, indefinitely. We still do that, actually, though *now* it is more a form of technology when compared to what our ancestors had to do, which was to interact with the raw materials. We originally began to understand the nature of frictional heat by rubbing two sticks together. Or perhaps it was more like the Flintstones, smacking a pair of *flint stones* together, creating sparks with the potential to birth flame."

"Flintstones?"

"That *is* how they got the name, is it not?" Walther said, in defense of his animated assumption. "My point is that if you wish to understand more of the nature of your lost friend, perhaps you should treat her more like a *real* fire, and there is no point in asking a *fire* a bunch of indirect questions. Instead, why not try more of a direct approach?"

"I'm listening..." Trinity let him know, as she continued leading a steady pace along the spiraling stone pathway.

"Well, you mentioned before that you felt she was secretive. Fire is just that. It requires effort to create it and to comprehend its volatile nature. Effective use practically demands human intelligence. Birds fly on the air, fish swim in the sea, and insects burrow into the ground, but even the smartest animals have not the intelligence to make proper use of fire, nor can they truly be taught to understand it, which is what you must do."

"You're saying it's *my* fault?"

"Unintentionally," he smoothly pointed out, "but, just like a real fire, you will have to figure her out. She will not, or perhaps, *cannot* give you answers to that which she does not know, herself. She exists. She is here, but, like all of us, she does not know for how long. For example: Say you manage to create some sparks while attempting to start a fire. You will undoubtedly wish for the sparks to ignite a flame and for it to grow in size and strength."

"That's exactly what I tried to ask her about," it was confirmed. "That and a whole lot more."

"Then, apparently, asking even the Spirit of Fire, herself, how you would go about doing that is not going to yield anything but a silent reply. You must determine what her needs are without her telling you outright, and you do that by paying attention in the moment in order to understand what works and what does not. It's a *yes or no* game. Positive or negative. The answers lie within *you* as much as they do within *her."*

"Within *me,"* Trinity repeated. "If that's true, my approach was all wrong. How do you know so much about Scarlet?"

"I don't," Walther confessed, allowing a verbal contraction to slip into his speech. "That is just what I know of women."

After a brief conversation and an uneventful period of silent travel, the mentor and apprentice at last came to a divide in the path, forcing them to work out what to do. The route that veered off to the right entered into a tunnel and passed under a message carved into the ebony stone above the entrance – a message that they both surmised had been written in the Ancient language – the language spoken on Earth during the First Age and in the yet to be known Golden Era until it faded from memory in the wake of great tragedy. The route that continued to the left seemed a continuance of the safe path they were traveling, and that fact, alone, became the intuitive reason for knowing where he had to go.

"Looks like we have a need for those torches after all," Walther said, as he stared up at the faded red symbols carved into the stone above the entrance to the dark tunnel, where, unfortunately, the rail of golden light and the multicolored, illuminated globes did not follow. "Pass them here. The last of the matches, too."

"I can lead the way," Trinity volunteered, as she reached into her pocket to pull out a small box that she shook to indicate to her mentor of its last remaining item.

The Dark Hunter shook his head and proceeded to try to light one of the four remaining torches by slashing with his knife at the nearest stone wall. Having been previously dipped in oil, a few sparks were all that were required to get it to ignite in a fiery instant. "You have done well to accompany me thus far," he declared, and quickly snatched the box of matches away from her in order to avoid her imminent refusal, "but, I have definitely seen those symbols before. The fact that I cannot recall their meaning is troubling enough, but, I have a bad feeling about this. I will go it alone."

She already had her hands on her hips, somewhat shocked by his boldness and deftness, alike, though her grin indicated she was actually impressed by his ability to predict her actions in advance. "Well, then, let's just continue in *this* direction," she suggested, looking toward the lit route they had been following as the ideal best and safest option.

Again, he shook his head. "Under normal circumstances I would not dare venture past this point without first discovering the meaning of those markings. However, we are in dire straits and this is most likely where he went, never to return."

"What makes you think that?"

While staring at the unknown symbols, he sighed before turning his attention back to her. "Call it a feeling. Wait here for me, and stay within the light," he instructed, nodding toward one of the small, evenly spaced, multicolored globes situated atop the light rail behind her as a clever misdirection.

"But, I---" she began to complain, but her mentor had already receded into the darkness by the time she glanced back to look at him. "Why does he have to do that?" she mumbled to herself, crossing her arms, then having nothing to do but sit and pass the time in solitude, awaiting the hopeful return of one whom she was beginning to admire and respect.

~

After a planned separation from his apprentice, who was to him a young woman in an exceptionally unique position to both learn and effect real change in the world, the Dark Hunter, traveling alone, discovered yet another wonder of the ancient underground: *the Spire.*

Earlier travels had led them around the interior of an expanse on a magically lit pathway, and though he despised the term *magic,* knowing, instead, that it was a form of technology, it was nonetheless an apt description of what it was like to behold. The path he intended to travel by himself, however, was perceived to be a dark and dangerous one that began when he emerged from a tunnel atop a tower of black stone that stood high and alone in an underground void, with dimly glowing, dark red energies highlighting sharp features and demonic faces so grim and foreboding of peril that only those with an iron will would dare tread upon it. Taken aback by yet another unexpected discovery, the Dark Hunter quickly discarded a very old torch that was found in a nearby recess and replaced it with the lit one he carried, using its flame to light the first of his spares before reluctantly continuing his journey with only two torches remaining pinned under the same right arm as the hand carrying the light, encumbering only one in order to keep his dominant hand completely free. Stumbling and having to navigate his way around and over upturned stone that seemed as if a great force had demolished the pathway proved initially difficult until he passed into an area that was more or less normal – normal for the environment he was venturing through, of course, since what began within the ebony of the sealed tower on his right were voices that barked, growled, shrieked, snarled and otherwise antagonized him quite suddenly. Startled enough to grip the stock of his Smith and Wesson M29, aptly named *Ol' Loudmouth,* by reason of its booming calibre, the Dark Hunter at first stood silent and frozen, wary of making any sudden movement as he stared at yet another phenomenon of the ancient world. Eyeing the shifting, horrifically demonic faces within the sealed stone right next to him, time quickly passed with no harm befalling him, causing him to begin to suspect that they were simply reacting to his presence. Though they wailed and cursed and screamed, he appeared to be perfectly safe so long as he stayed on the outer edge of the winding pathway, keeping himself at an outstretched arm's length from the treacherous walls of the accursed tower full of vengeful, dark spirits that even in death held onto a corrupted and agonized existence. So very long had they been sealed and locked away that they'd become a part of their enchanted ebony prison; the passing of time causing the stone to reflect the twisted, evil souls contained therein.

With a lobbed stone confirming his theory that the angry spirits held no power over him, he slowly and carefully advanced on his way before choosing to ignore them outright, first believing and then knowing that the only thing holding him back from advancing was his own fear – fear that was quite rational, but through observance and consideration had quickly become illogical, allowing him to continue onward, somewhat emotionally unfettered, toward a goal that was both known and unknown at the same time.

After several minutes of proceeding at a decent pace amid a nonstop verbal assault that he considered to be an auditory nightmare, he began to grow increasingly fed up with having to endure it all while not having any clue where he was going or where he would end up. No matter how many times he looked over the edge to his left, the hunter found himself staring down into total darkness, eventually helping him conclude that he probably couldn't see the bottom even if he were on the last and largest loop away from it. With that thought in his mind, he looked back up at what he had journeyed through so far, realizing in that moment that the path he and his apprentice had traveled and the path he currently traveled gradually came together in the center to form the overall shape of a giant hourglass. It was a moment of revelation that was ruined by persistent cruelty.

"Come closer!"

"Closer!!"

"Die!!!"

"You will die like the other one!"

Having heard quite enough upon receiving an unsavory comment he immediately associated with the death of his grandfather, the third generation Dark Hunter's frustration suddenly got the better of him.

"Will you *shut the hell up!!?"* he commanded those within the tower, in effect only seeming to encourage its prisoner's more, until an otherworldly voice called up from somewhere in the darkness with its last ounce of power.

"Young Master..."

Instantly, the threatening voices silenced in unison and would not dare utter even the slightest sound thereafter, due to the presence of a much more powerful voice – one that the hunter deduced was recognized and feared. Swallowing hard, he continued on his way, once more having to battle his own fear and apprehension toward actually obtaining that which he sought. Until that point, with his thoughts having been solely attuned to the moment, he had ceased thinking about it. There was no choice in the matter but to carry on, however, for the lives of a blissfully unaware humanity rested on his finding what had just called out to him.

Walking alone in the dark with only the sound of footsteps on stone amid the crackling of a fading torch, how he wished that he could turn back. Back to a simple outdoor life of hunting for his food and occasionally accepting bounty contracts to find and capture the murderers and criminal psychopaths that the authorities could not. But it was not a fear of the dark interfering with his concentration, nor was it even the fear of death, rather it was a fear of who or what he would become should he actually discover the lost artifact he was in search of. A fear of loss over his own mind. What would become of his own intentions? His own judgment? His own morality? What *is* morality to a non-biological entity? Did it even care? *Could* it care? Furthermore, what of *life* to such a being?

The last spiral around the wide base of the tower took the longest by design. Just as he previously suspected, he did not even realize that he was one level away from reaching the bottom, but when the decline steepened and met with a totally flat stone floor, he realized that he had at last come to the end of the path. That was when a new thought came to the forefront of his mind.

Now where?

It was pitch black no matter which direction he faced. That much was unchanged and would remain. The one thing that was different was that he was now free to wander in any dark direction of his choosing. So, which direction? Standing there with the glowing ember of a nearly expended torch in his right hand and two to spare still pinned under the same arm, he began to accept that he in fact had no solid plan or intelligent method of traveling any further. Any straightforward direction was very much a shot in the dark, and so rather than risk becoming lost in venturing too far from the only known point of return, that being the spiral pathway leading back up the silent ebony tower behind him, he opted to enact the only remaining approach that he could think of. What else could he really do, he figured, but to begin with searching around the wide base of the tower before systematically proceeding with mapping the place in his mind by moving in concentric circles and slowly expanding outward. Luckily for him it would not come to that, as his trained, methodical approach to every situation would soon render him justice.

After passing around the smooth, featureless base of the tower where the first section of the winding path began just above his head, he suddenly stopped in his tracks, hesitant to take even one more step toward the still-clothed skeletal remains of a man he strongly suspected to be of kin. The third generation Dark Hunter stood there staring down for a time, conflicted, as a part of him wished to respectfully leave the remains of the legendary man undisturbed, though the teachings and knowledge within his family suggested that the dead were nothing more than an empty shell.

A spirit bound in flesh, set free upon our death.

In the case of his grandfather, that had occurred quite some time ago, therefore he decided that no reason existed to justify his apprehension. That decision, however, would not stop an array of questions from forming in his mind.

What the hell happened to him? Why did he not leave the ruins and return to the surface? Was he that intent on discovering its secrets that he was willing to stay until he died? Doubtful. Perhaps he died of natural causes. Or perhaps something else is to blame...

Quickly searching the man and examining his final position yielded no clues or additional information until the hunter's eyes naturally followed in the direction of the outstretched left arm and to the pointed bones of joined middle and index fingers that he surmised could very well have been intentional.

Perhaps he hid it.

It was then that he decided that following the twenty-year-old, one and only possible clue left by his grandfather was his best hope and chance, having no viable option other than the random success of a concentric search that could take anywhere from minutes to a multitude of days – the latter not being an amount of time that anyone could live with.

After igniting one of the spare torches he carried, done by pressing together, twisting and blowing on the last moments of hot ember in the one that lit his way down, he placed a newly vibrant torch into the recesses of a column that braced the spiral pathway, set at a forty-five degree angle, leaving it there to serve as a far-off visual marker that would aid a hopeful return. Then, after igniting the last remaining torch in his possession, he began heading away from the tower in the direction that a long-dead man did actually intend for a descendant to follow.

Even with the largest of the spare torches lit and in his grasp, firelight would serve as no aid other than that of mere comfort from that point forward, as the dark expanse of the ancient underground seemed to stretch on endlessly. Other than his own body and the stone floor at his feet, absolutely nothing was visible in the environment ahead of him. There were no walls, no markers, no signs and no clues as to what he was heading into. All there was, was darkness. Darkness and the sound of his own footsteps amid the crackling of a torch. Into the void, a voice from the past echoed to the forefront of his mind.

~

My father, your Grampy, would not show me the ancient weapon that came to him so many years ago, but, he spoke of his connection to it and what he learned over the years. He would always begin by telling me of its rival: The Shadow. Do not be afraid to venture into the dark part of your soul, he would say. The darkest part of yourself. To know, fully, what you are capable of is to claim power over it. To avoid delving deep into the depths of your psyche is to live in ignorance of the complete self. Until you do, you can never know who you really are, but when you do, you will discover the truth – that you are the master of choice. One cannot fully control, nor are they truly the author of, their own thoughts, however, it is true that you have all the power when it comes to exercising choice. When you realize this, from that point on, the Shadow of the soul can be bent. It can be broken. It can be silenced and it can be humbled. It must be, for it is secondary to the Light – Light that is not intimidated by its eternal nemesis, for when the two are matched in strength, its benevolence and brilliance always finds a way to reign supreme.

Though opposite in their natures, the Shadow can be turned to explicitly service the interests of the Light and vice-versa, he said to me. Be especially warned in that regard, my son. The Shadow's greatest desire is to subvert and control its greatest foe. The two are powerful counter-forces that, depending on the motives of the individual, can be utilized from a perspective of good or evil. Through knowing the nature of both aspects, one attains a true sense of balance and enlightenment. Indeed, it is the only way, for you are most unenlightened if you cannot accept the truth around and within yourself. The singular, universal truth that is only subjective in the eyes of the unprepared, whose facts are skewed or misinterpreted or nonexistent. Truth is readily identifiable until a level of deception or misinformation enters the fray. Without accurate facts, my son, opinions become varied and contradictory, creating chaos...and a spirit of darkness thrives on the chaotic to achieve the advantage in strength. That is about all I can remember, for now, though there was certainly more.

Hey, Pops..? Have you ever been afraid? Like, really afraid?

Yes, my boy. Now, climb into bed.

Really? Even you?

Living in fear is a common path in life, however, there is an answer to fear: Bravery. To be afraid and to live in constant fear is certainly difficult, but the more difficult path is accepting that although you are afraid, you are still in control if you choose to be, and that if and when you choose to be, nothing can stop you from changing your life. Except, of course, for yourself. Fear can be pushed aside. Beyond it, courage and bravery are found. Ultimately, you are the only thing holding you back from that which you desire or hope to achieve. What stigmas do you cling to that, if examined, would prove to not even exist? You are not a victim if you decide otherwise. There is no one and nothing standing in your way that cannot be circumvented. Through meditation and focused thought, one can achieve an even greater sense of control over one's life. Even for the blind who cannot see anything but darkness, the light is always there. You have only but to close your eyes to see it and feel it. It exists within the self as energy. It is the real you. You can fall back on it for support when you need it, but it also serves as a tool for learning and for remembering. It is a tool for orienting, reorienting, and even disorienting oneself and one's beliefs. In your study of Buddhism, confusion is a prerequisite of enlightenment, remember.

***I** know.*

I know that you know, Marcus. None are born with all the answers. One must learn, and quite often, learning involves unlearning. Now, go to sleep, my son. Seek out the truth with courage in your heart and you will not need to find it. ***It** will find **you**.*

~

With glossy eyes that reflected the flickering flame of a torch, straight on the hunter went in search of the one thing in existence that held a genuine fear over him. The one thing he had to find, but was afraid to find, was very much weighing on his mind. When the fate of the world rests heavily on your shoulders, what is one to do? Turn away in spite of it all? Run off to some untouched part of the world to live out the remaining days of what little time would exist until death, herself, at last came calling? To Marcus Walther, these were neither options nor desires. Courage had been trained and instilled in him as a value beginning from the time he was a young boy.

Doing the right thing, even in the presence of your greatest fear, is the greatest challenge one can face.

His father's greatest fear had been public speaking, at least, it had been until the man became what *his* father had termed, *Specialist Bounty Hunter,* while traveling under the guise of a wandering preacher. What better way to cover himself than with a Christian white collar as he traveled around the world with his son, doing God's work, in the truest sense of the phrase, in order to protect those who had not the knowledge nor the skill to protect themselves. A man who was afraid of public speaking found himself compelled by others to speculate on God or to help them with advice concerning personal problems. When word spread around the towns and cities he visited, people very much began to seek him out to confide in him and, as a result, the man opened up a veritable treasure house of knowledge in the service of others. Problems that started out as personal would be spun into a larger tale that practically anyone within earshot could identify with and learn from. Once he knew what the problem was and what you were asking of him, the sometimes embarrassing nature of personal issues would be cleverly removed in such a way that anyone could listen in and not even feel the slightest threat of offense or embarrassment. The man was that good with metaphor. A man, who was at one point afraid of public speaking, found himself speaking publicly on an almost daily basis. Small crowds would sometimes gather as they passed by on the streets, always stemming from a single individual or couple in need of advice. Great knowledge and wisdom he would impart unto them, never in the form of direct sermon, but rather in the form of rational biblical interpretation that could be applied to the knowledge of the present day. The people seemed to take comfort in learning that he was very much one of them, since he purposely shied away from, and even spoke out against, religious fundamentalism and extremism, blaming such ill-sought values and out-of-date information as the root cause for historic and ongoing problems that faced the world over.

Even as a boy, Marcus found it funny that although his father was not ordained by any church, and therefore was not an official preacher, minister, or pastor, he possessed a more detailed knowledge of the history of Christianity and the Bible, New *and* Old, among other religions, than any actual preacher they would ever meet. His father would even laugh about how they were *Soldiers of God.* In retrospect, what started as a joke in good-natured humor seemed to be more fact than fiction as time went on.

In quieting his overactive, yet inspired mind as an adult, the Dark Hunter soon found himself literally looking back to see how far he had gone. In the distance, a few hundred yards back, the lower half of the hourglass spire was thankfully still marked by a single point of light at its base. If the torch went out on him, he realized, might he suffer the same fate as his grandfather, lest his apprentice defy his orders and foolishly come looking for him?

Continuing forward at a mindful pace in the direction he had been traveling, quick enough to make timely progress in the midst of a finite flame, yet cautionary enough to avoid overextending himself into an unseen trap or pitfall, he began to wonder how much time the world had left if Lydia was left to her own devices. If her growth went on unchecked and unchallenged, perhaps it would only be a matter of weeks or months as opposed to any number of years remaining. If she were to reach the town – the town being full of souls to capture and enslave – she would likely become more and more powerful by the minute. He would do whatever he could to prevent that from happening, but the uncertainty of even being able to challenge the Dark Demon was troubling, to say the least. With the apparent loss of Scarlet, a singular hope now remained. A hope that would instantly be found when the light of a fading torch suddenly revealed a dusty blanket of darkness on the gray stone floor at his feet. Having quite nearly stepped on it, he restrained his foot out of reflex and a desire not to disturb what surely lay beneath, realizing as a result of the butterflies in his stomach that his own apprehension in actually finding the Relic from the bedtime stories of his childhood was very much real and not just a product of his imagination.

Without so much as peeking under the black cloth to visually confirm the find, the Dark Hunter attempted to lift up the long object that was unpredictably heavier than he ever imagined it would be, so much so that he had no choice but to carefully lay down his torch in order to use both of his hands, requiring nearly all of his strength just to get it moving. When he managed to lift it from just one end to an upward angle of forty-five degrees, he set it to lean up against himself and in keeping its weight balanced and divided between his chest and the stone floor, he wrapped the partially exposed underside with the long black fabric of its makeshift cover in order to completely avoid making direct contact with it. Then, requiring a great deal of leg strength, he squatted and arced the hidden, long and heavy object behind his neck and across both shoulders, bearing all of its weight as he returned to a standing position with a grunt and an exhaled breath between his teeth.

Having at last retrieved what he set out to find, the sole-surviving member of the Walther family reversed his direction with a careful one-eighty and began making his way back the way he had come. Fortunately for him, though ultimately for all, he had a solid fix on his point of return, barely visible from several hundred yards away as the torch on the ground behind him extinguished, leaving him in near total darkness but for the single point of guiding light fading away beneath the ebony tower in the distance.

Chapter 10

Renewed Hope

Trinity sat on the stone pathway near the divide, waiting with a patience she didn't know she had, facing to the right and down the dark tunnel that her mentor had insisted he investigate alone. Above and behind her, the golden glow of the illuminated light rail that activated upon her arrival spiraled upward on a widening route to the top. Below it all, where the path was most narrow, the young apprentice shuffled close to the comforting light with her back to the stone half-wall on which the rail was supported, awaiting the return of the Dark Hunter.

When the loneliness and isolation finally began to get the better of her, she stood up from the stone floor of the pathway and turned around to look high up at what she and her mentor had discovered to be a balcony of sorts, where the unusual light rail had first been activated. Inhaling and exhaling a deep breath and gripping the rail with both hands caused it to react with a small flare-up of warm energy that in effect seemed to calm and mitigate her anxiety. According to the petite silver watch that adorned her left wrist, over an hour had passed since the separation that left her by herself, and it had been over two hours since they had come through the mysterious mirror under the Lunar Gate in the Lunarium's courtyard, where, hopefully, the writer was still chronicling their journey thus far.

Upon hearing the initial sound and corresponding echo of heavy footfalls drawing closer and closer, she instinctively whipped around and was soon relieved to discover a familiar face walking up the incline, from out of the darkness and into the light, with a large, covered object seen being carried across his strained shoulders. *"Whoa!* You found it! It's *huge!"*

"You alright?" he asked, ignoring her comments.

"Fine," she responded, opening up her arms as if to demonstrate that she was uninjured. "Why is it wrapped in that blanket?"

"...This is no blanket. It was my grandfather's cloak," Walther plainly stated. "We must leave immediately," he added, as he stepped past his intrigued apprentice and began heading back up the lit pathway.

The hidden object, however, was far too much a curiosity for her to just ignore. "I can't get over the size of it! Is it heavy?"

"Quite," he admitted. "Perhaps I should rest a moment."

"Then, you haven't---?"

"No."

Curiously enduring a long silence during which her mentor exerted himself in order to very carefully set the cloaked weapon down to the stone floor, Trinity watched him lean the heavy, hidden object up against the stone guard wall overlooking the dark interior, leaving it pointed upward in the direction of the balcony situated half a mile above their heads. "I don't understand," she soon stated, as she stared at the cloak-covered relic. "The more time you have with it, the stronger the link will become. I mean, I know that for a fact."

"So do I," Walther said, as he hung his head while leaning over the golden, glowing rail, crossing his arms atop it.

"Then, what is it?" she pressed.

The Dark Hunter drew in a shallow breath and sighed as he raised his head ever so slightly. Gazing across the narrow expanse of the very center where the primary pathway and the spiraling light rail came to an end on the other side of the next level down, his eyes focused in on what he assumed to be a door that led into the remains of one of the lost cities of the ancient world, though, unfortunately, they hadn't the time for further archaeological or architectural endeavors.

"What?" Trinity repeated.

"I am...afraid of it," her mentor confessed.

She couldn't help but laugh in reaction, at first assuming it was some sort of joke. *"You? Afraid?* Linking with it will probably remove fear, for the most part, like *she* did for *me."*

"That is partly what I am afraid of."

"So, you're afraid of not being afraid? I'm confused."

"What is courage without fear?" he wondered aloud. "Who will I be? Who will I become..?"

"Find out," it was casually suggested to him.

"There is no reversing it..." he seemed to be saying to himself.

"Yeah, you're right," Trinity seemed to agree, as she pulled the cloak away from the tall object without her mentor noticing what she was up to. She then proceeded to pick up the sleek, faded gray, still-inert relic, requiring all of her improved physical strength to do so, having to exert herself vocally in the process.

"Girl, what in holy hell do you think you're *doing?!"* Walther yelled out, suddenly taking notice of what she was up to.

"There *is*... no going...*back!* We have to go...*forward!"* she stated, just as she heaved the heavy weapon straight at her unsuspecting mentor.

"No---!" he abruptly said, before he instinctively caught the Relic in midair, using both hands out of a desire to protect it from sustaining damage, though the hefty weapon that was suddenly rendered as light as a feather in his bare hands could not so easily be broken.

A burst of silvery-white light exploded all around, knocking Trinity to the ground by surprise and completely illuminating the vast interior of the underground, including the remains of the seemingly unreachable ancient city located beyond the high stone wall on the far side. The light that had expanded in an instant was then recalled inward at an initially slow but ever-increasing rate of speed and was reabsorbed along with all other available light, rendering the balcony along with the spiraling light rail and its several hundred globes of multicolored light completely dark. For a few moments that seemed like an eternity in the silent underground, nothing at all could be seen – not until two silver eyes at last blinked open, having just awakened in bright and stunning fashion after a twenty-one-year slumber.

"My eternal gratitude to you, young one," a deep, masculine timbre of dual voices spoke to a visibly frightened young woman as the guiding lights along the pathway reactivated in sequence. *"Fear not, for I have awakened once more to restore hope to a forsaken world."*

So much history, knowledge and power was flowing through the

Dark Hunter, it felt as if his body and soul would together explode in a violent burst of the light energy that was coursing through his entire being. He could both hear and feel the distant echoes of time – everything that had happened to his bloodline for millennia, beginning thousands of years in the past leading all the way up to the present moment. Images of the many forbears who wielded the same Relic then in his possession, and their many battles that most recently included his grandfather's epic triumph against the darkness that was once again overtaking the land, were shared and openly made available to him. In an instant, with the benefit of true hindsight, he was made into a veritable man of the Ages. When in direct contact with the reawakened Element Relic of Light, his strength and resilience was dramatically increased, so much so that placing the brilliant weapon back across his shoulders was child's play in comparison to any previous difficulty.

Feeling and knowing that she was in the presence of an immensely powerful being – what Scarlet would have called a Light Spirit – Trinity could barely bring herself to look up from the ground at the man whom she already respected and whom she was now in complete awe of. Entirely humbled and quite nearly afraid to stand with what she understood to be a divine presence, she remained on her knees until she was suddenly instructed to do otherwise.

"Rise, young one," she was told, as softly as the powerful voice could speak. *"You need not humble yourself before me. Take my hand."*

With hesitation and mixed emotions, she reached up to touch the hand being offered in her aid. At the moment of contact, she felt as though she was touching a hand of pure, loving energy, as if *God* was personally reaching out to uplift her body and spirit. The strong, smiling face looking down at her through radiant, silvery-white eyes was enough to let her know that she was in the company of a kind, grandfatherly being who would not only protect *her,* but all of life. There was nothing at all to fear from a being of such virtue.

"I can feel your connection to my kin, the Lünaflara. The one you call Scarlet. Yes. It is faint, but it is still there. She calls out to you."

With those words uttered from the lips of the divine, tears began streaming down Trinity's lovely cheeks, causing her to instinctively relax her grip on his hand in the interest of wiping them away, but he, however, would not let go.

"She calls to you from the void. From the hand of death. I will restore for you a portion of what has been lost."

A silvery-white light began emanating from the hand that engulfed her own. Feeling pure energy flow into her body, her sudden reaction was to vocalize her astonishment while squeezing the hand of her mentor. When he let go, the light surrounding his hand stayed with hers and shifted in color from a sparkling silver to a familiar, flaming red. Closing her hand in a tight fist, the flame absorbed into her and was gone, yielding a momentary flash of scarlet in her eyes.

"How do you feel?" it was inquired of her.

"Oh, yeah!" she quite positively responded. "I can feel the fire in my heart and soul!"

"Very well. Go, now. Make haste for the gate."

"Huh?"

"The enchantment on the spire below has quite nearly dissolved. An unfortunate side effect of the reawakening. They are coming."

"Who's coming?!" the partially rejuvenated young woman exclaimed. "I want to help you!"

"They can no longer be thought of as ***who,*** *but* ***what****. They can no longer harm this body, but that will not stop them from attempting to kill you, or worse."*

From the dark path that the hunter had returned from, horrible, nightmarish, violent voices could be heard echoing up from below, originating as nonstop howling, raging and screaming that only grew louder and louder.

"Kill her!!"

"Devour her!!"

"Tear her apart!!"

"Destroy her soul!!"

Across the Dark Hunter's shoulders, the ancient weapon began to hum and glow brighter as its interior components lit up Silver in a compression of light energy. *"Run."*

In a figurative blaze, having no idea of what was coming for her, Trinity took off along the spiraling pathway toward the top. From a level below, a searing projectile of pure energy tore through the air at the speed of light, vanquishing with ease the first Ghast; a fast-moving, undead creature from a bygone era, free at last from its ancient prison in the underground city of old. One after another came through the tunnel with a motivated vengeance and hatred for the living, so many in number that they spread out as wide as the passage allowed and together seemed to represent an unconquerable threat, at least until dual voices spoke aloud a recitation in an ancient tongue.

"Lyth..."

Midway through the unusual dialect of an all-but-forgotten language, the spiraling light rail again went black, completely blanketing the expanse in darkness as a humming sound of compression that began rather high-pitched and ended quite low reverberated all around, absorbing the available light energy in the underground environment directly through the source field of reality.

"...nüvah!!"

A wide, radiant bolt of silvery-white light violently blasted down the corridor, penetrating every nook and cranny, vaporizing the ghoulishly evil spirits and leaving behind nothing but a vaporous cloud that quickly faded away. All but one of the fast-moving Ghasts that desperately pursued a tasty young mortal were vanquished in the blink of an eye, and the young woman who had stopped in place in the dark went on running for her life while being unaware that her final pursuer did not even have legs with which to give chase. Instead, the remaining winged creature flew directly up the middle of the massive expanse between the spiraling pathway, cackling and hissing in spite of the one it could not harm, though it would certainly try in vain while on its way toward reaching the level its prey had made it up to.

Having realized what was coming straight at her in an attempt to cut off her escape, Trinity again stopped in place and then began to back away out of fear until a fiery anger flashed in her eyes. Having no other course of action, she picked up the nearest melon-sized globe of multicolored light from atop the golden rail and threw it at the ghoulish specter. Striking it directly, the globe shattered upon impact, igniting in a bright burst of golden light that rendered it sightless and shrieking in pain as it burned down to nothing more than a pile of ash.

Chapter 11

Perilous Return

Staring at the stone moon dial in the Lunarium courtyard stood Kimberly Hunter, sketching her viewpoint on paper. Having apparently forgotten to wind-up the silver and white gold watch on her wrist, she tapped on its glass face and again observed with dismay that its hands had in fact stopped moving, forcing an exasperated sigh out of her upon realizing that she'd gone and lost track of the time in such a place as she was. Getting back to the unusual clock-like device in front of her, the ebony hands and dials serving unknown functions remained a complete mystery from those of her charming watch, though Walther, the Dark Hunter, most certainly understood their purpose, as she'd seen him spend a significant amount of time adjusting them before going through what was quite possibly even less understood – the Lunar Mirror at her back.

Having already sketched a front and back view of the Courtyard of the Moon in order to capture the full scope of the Lunarium – one that included two darkly-dressed individuals passing through an ancient, color-changing mirror, and a second that displayed its undisturbed isolation from the rest of the known world – the English, Cambridge-educated writer and artist flipped through the pages of her most recent works. While staring down at a drawing of her twin selves on paper, she turned around, flipped the page over, paced forward, raised up and then slowly lowered out of her own field of vision the self portrait in her sketchbook, behind it revealing the reflected reality of what her eyes previously beheld on paper. The eyes being the window to the soul, the person in the mirror's strangely static reflection, as well as the one drawn on paper, seemed to be of a colder demeanor than she imagined herself to be.

Could that really be me?

Standing there in the light of four burning torches and the presence of her own side-to-side-moving reflection that eerily followed her when she changed position and always faced to the front, even with her back turned to it, knowing that it would fade away whether she stepped forward or backward by seven paces, she began to wonder if her two companions would ever return from the enigma of the other side. With a small amount of food and water in her satchel and with plenty of torches and oil to spare, she knew that she could likely remain alive and well for at least a couple of days, but the inescapable feeling of a growing loneliness was beginning to overtake her, making her wish that she had never come to know of the Lunarium's foreboding and mysterious existence. Oh, what she wouldn't do for a cup of tea and a nice, hot bath.

Turning away from the unsettling mirror and its crescent arch in favor of sitting down to contemplate the moon dial with a newly lit torch set into the wall nearest her for added warmth and security, Kimberly soon began to yawn out of boredom and decidedly rested herself up against the smooth, ebony wall of the courtyard. There, the dedicated writer and artist slept in peace for a time, beneath a view of the sky beyond a mostly transparent ceiling that, according to Walther, would have required a high level of knowledge to construct. Though it appeared to be magical, the ebony had been altered at the molecular level, allowing light to pass in, but not out. From the outside, the upper face of the steep, dark and dangerous cliff appeared to be entirely opaque and more or less normal in both form and function. Inside, the Ancients had been using their creation to observe astral and lunar phenomena from within a protected environment.

You can forever shield an environment from light, the Dark Hunter had previously philosophized, *but forever not from darkness.*

While she was dreaming of him disappearing from her sight into darkness as more or less a normal man, the mirror before her began to bubble and change color in an isolated area of the center. Before long, the silhouette of a man in a cowboy hat with a large object arched across his shoulders took shape within an aura of pink and lightly sparkling silver. Suddenly, the man's complete form emerged from the liquid in midair, and slowly down, the Lunar Mirror lowered the changed man safely to the ground. His footsteps, much heavier than usual, echoed throughout the courtyard, awakening the sleepy-eyed Englishwoman who had drifted off with her sketchbook open in her lap as she lay in the flickering light of a burning torch.

"Oh, thank God," she said, being alarmed for a split second after opening her eyes. "You're back," she noted, as the Dark Hunter came to stand over her in observance of her condition in a manner she had not seen prior. "Something's different about you," she correctly interpreted from his grinning expression alone, afterward taking notice of the concealed object carried diagonally across his shoulders, balanced and held in place with minimal continuous effort. When the large, covered item was set down on the stone ground and leaned upright against the wall of the courtyard with a force that told of its unsuspected and unbelievable weight, the Lunarium environment echoed the deep sound of the violent impact tremor out into the darkness of night beyond the cliff. *"Crikey!"* she exclaimed, feeling the stone shake beneath her feet.

"My mistake," Walther instantly admitted, faulting himself for being careless. "It seems that I no longer know my own strength."

"What *is* that thing?"

"I will have to be much more careful," he continued commenting. "If *Nüvah* falls on you, you will be no more."

"So..." the curious writer said, "that's it, huh? The old man said it was a Winchester. I figured it would be *a lot* smaller."

"Nearly seven decades ago, it was."

Rubbing the sleep from her eyes, it was only then that she gained enough cognitive awareness after waking to realize that a member of the party was missing. "Where's Trinity?"

Before the hunter could offer an explanation, the bubbling sound of the Lunar Mirror drew their attention as it began to swell a deep red in the center of its vertically contained pool. Soon, the pink silhouette of a finely shaped feminine form appeared in the mass of red and, only a few seconds later, a rejuvenated young woman let out a sigh of satisfaction just as her tightly-laced boots touched down, prompting the artist to begin fast-drawing a sketch of her rather elegant appearance.

"Miss me?" Trinity asked, amid the crackling of torches and fast-moving strokes of graphite pencil.

The focused artist wouldn't offer an immediate response other than looking up from her sketchbook to first take in the features of a spirited young woman's eyes reflecting the torchlight, followed by her dry hair and clean clothes that were, on last sight, wet and a bit soiled in appearance.

"Oh, come on," the symbiont to the Spirit of Fire said of her new friend's silence, with her hands placed on her hips in a teasing attitude as she shifted her weight to one side.

"Perhaps a little," Kimberly acknowledged, though she was actually quite pleased to see the both of them return to her alive, mitigating a great deal of her withheld anxiety that in the absence of the others could only be controlled by focusing on her work.

Apparently curious, the Dark Hunter positioned himself in close proximity to the writer and artist with a newfound interest in her work, nearly cheek to cheek, causing her to stare at him out of the corner of her eye while she kept the strokes of pencil moving at a speed that slowed and slowed as she admired the features of his rough-bearded face and strong jaw. Hoping to keep her attraction a secret, she quickly returned her eyes to her work and resumed sketching at a fast rate of speed from the very moment her staring drew his gaze.

The Spirit of Fire, perhaps due to being a heated and passionate secret in and of itself, allowed Trinity the gift of noticing and being aware of minute changes in the body chemistry of those around her. Changes that, when coupled with the innate ability to detect subtle physical signs that likely only a woman would ever notice, resulted in a rolling of eyes and a light scoff of amusement when the eyes of the others diverted back to the image that was forming on paper.

Having greater knowledge and power within him, granted in no small part by the Light Spirit bonded to the ancient weapon at last in his possession, the mindful hunter understood that a victory over the Darkness of Lydia was yet uncertain and would remain as such until it was attained with absolute certainty. Feeling that they shouldn't waste any time other than what was necessary for adequate rest and preparation, the trio made their way to the foot of the snakelike, winding pathway leading out of the wide-open, underground courtyard and back into the narrow passageway of the mountain, taking their leave of the Lunarium with a final look back from the group's record keeper at the mysterious and wondrous Lunar Mirror.

Advancing through the white air, streaking black stars and amplified gravity of the Fray without directly channeling the Spirit of Light was the most difficult challenge of the way out. Even the Dark Hunter's slightly increased strength and endurance proved to be no match in besting it, with the effect of its power being directly proportional to that of one's own strength and mass, forcing a struggle with every movement made. And so, with *Nüvah* carried across his back and with the help of two female followers holding it up as they advanced in equal stride, they eventually reached the other side of the Fray's expanse and burst into darkness, free from its inverted black and white, kinetically draining area of effect. After a rumbling crash that reverberated for several seconds in the pitch black dark, and though they were quite out of breath, the mentor and apprentice both agreed that the Fray at least offered a good full-body workout. The poor writer, however, being so unaided and unaccustomed to extreme physical challenges, fell to the ground along with the others, the difference being that she remained laying face down with a cheek pressed to the cold, stone floor in an effort to recover her totally drained stamina.

"It always feels worse on the way back," Walther commented to an exhausted Kimberly, who, from the ground, barely managed a nod.

"I won't be able...to roll out of bed...in the morning," she speculated, absolutely dreading the experience of her next-day condition while continuing to lay flat on the stone ground of a suddenly match lit environment that was soon to be torch lit.

"Should we fail, there will soon come a morning where none will rise again," he responded, warning of a possible future that had Trinity nodding her understanding with much regret. "On your feet, Ms. Hunter," he added, and together with the other symbiont with an Element Spirit, they hoisted the exhausted Englishwoman back to her feet, satchel and all, with little combined effort.

"What are our chances?" Kimberly wondered.

The Dark Hunter responded to that inquiry by explaining that the chance of success after the loss of the Starsword was bleak and likely somewhere in the vicinity of one in one million. With circumstances changed, odds had improved to a margin greater than one in two. Though the sentient sword was in the hands of the enemy – the enemy being the ancient darkness within young Lydia's shell – he was not at all concerned about the stolen relic being used against them.

As a burning torch was passed along to her from the hand of her mentor, Trinity had to ask. "How is that not a concern? I'm terrified of the thought of her being used against us."

"Fear not," Walther said, and motioned for his apprentice to lead the way back. "If you recall, I suspect that she spared Flynn and I by allowing herself to be captured. If *Nüvah* knows her intentions, and I think that he does, she is currently playing the part of victim and hostage, to a degree."

"How is it *you* know that, and she didn't?" a confused Kimberly asked, with a forward motioning of her head in Trinity's direction, having no idea how the hunter possessed information about Scarlet that eluded even her symbiont counterpart.

Beginning with a grin, the Dark Hunter explained that the conditions that brought the two artifacts back into active existence in the world were actually quite different. The Starsword, *Lünaflara,* the word that meant *Moonfire* in the Ancient language, was transmigrated through the source field of the universe, directly to Trinity's unwelcoming hand. A re-genesis; de-materialized from its last location and then re-materialized with a new blood and silver catalyst in another. The Divine Justice, *Lythnüvah,* the ancient Lythian word translated to mean *Light Nova*, on the other hand, was awoken from a twenty-one-year slumber, providing its Young Master with instant access to all memories, benefits and abilities attained by former symbionts, going all the way back to the last time of its re-genesis.

"Nüvah, for short – made of *Lythnüvian* silver – is highly experienced, having accompanied one man for nearly five decades. *Scarlet,* on the other hand, has been reborn. Created anew. She is but a growing child whose master is that kid right there, though she no longer looks like one."

Having a lighthearted attitude and an accompanying sense of humor, Trinity acknowledged her mentor's teasing comment by glancing back at the writer with a smile and a wave of her free hand – the one that wasn't occupied by a lit torch that with but a few more steps was suddenly of no aid to their sight. *"Whoa.* There it is. I can't see," she announced for the group.

"Here we go, again," said Kimberly.

"Discard the torch," Walther instructed. "We will not need it."

Back along the Deadly Ebony route they traveled, making a chain as they did before, with the Dark Hunter guiding their slow and safe progress. He wouldn't disclose to his female friends that even the sightless spell that had been permanently and irreversibly cast upon the area, thousands of years prior, no longer posed any danger – to him, specifically. He could see everything with the spiritual aid of his reawakened counterpart. Every sharp and deadly spiked rock, every trap and every pitfall, some of which he never knew were there and from which one could never hope to climb out of, were revealed to him in white air and of silver and black stone. The only real challenge was to transport the terribly heavy, five-foot-long object that the hunter insisted on keeping inactive with the ongoing use of the cloak of his long-departed grandfather, requiring him to expend a great deal of energy re-positioning it to fit the passageway as they maneuvered through dangerously confined space – but at least it wasn't nearly as burdensome as carrying it through the Fray.

Near the entrance and exit to Deadly Ebony, it being the narrow path of spiked rock walls that began from the ledge behind the moonlit waterfall, Trinity and Kimberly suddenly found their vision restored, though the man walking in front of them as their guide required no light other than the silver light in his eyes to see what lie ahead. From behind the thin sheet of falling water, the distorted view of a half moon shone down through an elliptical crevice up above, giving them an impression of a great eye with a lunar iris in the sky. For Walther, only one question remained at the time: Who to transport first; the women, or the weapon?

After a brief respite during which the writer withdrew rations from her satchel and distributed them to her new friends, the Dark Hunter lifted the ancient weapon up and arced it across both shoulders, positioning it behind his neck. The length of rope that hours ago was taken from the trunk of Kimberly's Volkswagen was at last needed to fulfill its intended and hopeful purpose. Holding steady the cloaked Relic, he instructed the women to tie the heavy object in place by wrapping the rope around his chest and shoulders, bound as tight as possible in preparation for the climb back to the surface. Since the women were lighter than the first load he was to bear, even in combination, Walther began the ascent with a splash, leaving them safely behind the waterfall out of a desire to finish the final climb with the lightest passenger.

The way up took twice as long to traverse than it would if he were unencumbered, but he would eventually return to accommodate his next passenger after hiding the invaluable artifact in an area where he felt it would be watched over and kept safe. Then, with his apprentice on his back, he began the ascent again, teaching her the secret math-based pattern of selecting the safe stones that could bear their weight in case she had good reason in his absence to climb down on her own.

"Wait right here," Walther soon instructed, as he waited in place for Trinity to disembark onto the clifftop.

"Out in the open?" she questioned. "I could climb up into a tree, like before," she instead suggested, as she turned to look back down into the crevice and into the moonlit eyes of her mentor.

"You could," he replied, not even bothering to climb all the way out, "however, that particular tactic was to be used to avoid anything she may have corrupted and sent beyond her limited range. It is entirely possible that enough time has passed for that distance to have dramatically increased. I would not dare venture into the forest until well after sunrise."

"...Understood," Trinity conceded, and sat down cross-legged, facing north toward the closest part of the forest in nervous waiting, very near to the crevice that led back into the cavern where the eyes of the hunter had already disappeared below ground.

At the edge of the forest to the east, a pair of low-lying, fierce violet eyes among the bushes came alive and quickly vanished before they were detected, compelled by a force stronger and more prevalent than the hunger that typically ruled over animal instincts.

Fifteen minutes later, the Dark Hunter returned to the top with the featherweight, hundred-pound blonde writer on his back, and the moment she disembarked with Trinity's help and set foot on solid ground, she took notice and stared, frozen with fear, at a menacing presence hovering near the outskirts of Scarlet Forest.

"That was fun, huh, Kimberly?" Trinity asked her, and received no response whatsoever. "Kimberly..?" she repeated, before realizing that something had drawn the writer's silent attention, and not in a good way. *"Ah...Walther!?"*

"What?" he replied, as he struggled to pull himself out of the crevice, having spent a great deal of his energy on those who came before himself. "What is it?"

Following their gaze, he took notice of a raven-haired girl whose skin and summer dress that were at one time a milky white and a sign of her purity and innocence, had become a thinly veiled, flat black armor of darkness protecting a youthful body that stood afloat a wisp of black cloud bearing a hint of violet to its swirling interior. With a sudden pulse of energy in her suddenly-revealed dark purple eyes, she began to move in on her prey, beginning her advance with an otherworldly, demonic, deathly scream unlike anything the trio had ever before heard.

"Stand your ground!" Walther commanded, after glancing beyond the edge of the cliff behind them, toward the far-off horizon, knowing there was nowhere to run.

"What do we *do?!"* Trinity shouted, as Kimberly frantically grabbed at the hunter's arm in an attempt to get him to flee.

"Stand your ground!" he strongly repeated, and held the two women firmly around the waist in place with him, so as not to become divided targets.

With steadily increasing velocity Lydia soared at the trapped trio with intent to kill. At just the right moment, the Dark Hunter forced the women to hit the deck just as the light of the morning sun arrived on the distant horizon, sending a blinding light into the Dark Demon's ferocious and murderous eyes, as if God's sun – the light of the world – had returned as their savior. Shrieking in pain and agony as the sun pierced her with its penetrating rays, the cloud of darkness on which she rode was quickly vaporized into nothingness, halting her advance and exposing her underlying human form that, on two legs, much to the shock and relief of her would be victims, spun her around and sent her racing back into the forest in desperate retreat from her eternal nemesis.

Hearts pounded amid rapid breaths as the women glanced back and forth between one another and the darkly-dressed man standing between them, who appeared, at least on the surface, to be quite calm.

"That is why I insisted we make the journey during the night," Walther explained, once their nerves had more or less settled. "For cover of light on the return," he said, and turned to face the horizon, pressing his hands together in what could easily be mistaken for prayer, the same way his father would when showing gratitude or paying his respects.

"Crikey," Kimberly said, as she sat down on the ground, shaking her jitters away and beginning yet another sketch to capture the horrific encounter. "That was really her. This is insane," she added, having just seen the resurrected girl's actual body for the first time, rather than the mere form of her arachnid doppelganger.

"Gather some wood and get a fire going," Walther instructed his apprentice. "Use whatever kindling you can find, but do not enter the forest. We must await the rising sun," he said, before he began to take leave of them.

Immediately, the blonde Englishwoman ceased her fast-paced sketching and quickly sprang back to her feet. "Hey, wait! Where are you going?!" she asked, seeing Trinity in her peripheral getting right to work in gathering stray branches for firewood, having learned to trust the wisdom of her mentor implicitly. "You're *leaving* us here? With *her* out there?"

"God was our savior, this time, ma'am, not me," she was told. "There is nothing to worry about for the time being. Consider yourself under divine protection. Feel free to finish your work as you await my return. I will not be gone for long."

"We're out of matches!" Trinity called out, already holding a pile of branches in her arms.

The Dark Hunter, symbiont with the Spirit of Light, turned and smiled. "Ah, yes, well, for that, you no longer require anything other than concentration and strength of will," he revealed, before taking his leave of the two women who exchanged puzzled expressions with one another as they stood there on the clifftop overlooking a valley.

Northeast around the perimeter of the forest the hunter traveled, intent on retrieving his counterpart from its hiding place in the array of naturally growing flowers that the group had earlier passed through while en route to the falls. Remaining within the sunlit safety of the colorful grove running north and south, dividing the woods in the east and west until they merged a few hundred yards ahead, Walther, at the silent request of the interested spirit within, took time to enjoy the sights and smells of the flowered environment while ignoring the sensation that he was being watched.

Removing his cowboy hat in the center of the grove, the hunter came to a stop at a four-sided, six-foot-tall standing stone that on the south side had a face carved into it. Having picked a white lily, the variety of flower that grew in multitude in a circle around the stone, he touched its soft, delicate petals to a feminine cheek in fondness and remembrance and, finally, down the flowing hair of the carved image of a woman with whom he had an implicit connection. He then tucked the lily into the breast pocket of the dark gray collared shirt beneath his matching vest, flattening it as he pressed it to his heart, and knelt down to one knee as a sign of respect before rising with the weapon that had been placed in the care of his dearly departed mother.

With the excuse that she was going for a pee, though Trinity rightly suspected otherwise, a crouched down, persistent writer evaded the returning hunter's line of sight by keeping low to the ground below the top of the flowery overgrowth, only returning to a standing walk when she was far enough down the hill leading back to the cliff overlooking the valley below.

Meanwhile, Trinity had gathered enough firewood and had taken a seat on her heels, with her feet pointed toward the edge of the cliff several meters behind her. Having understood to some extent of what her mentor had revealed, interpreting it as a challenge or test from him, she closed her eyes and thought only of her blazing counterpart. Picturing in her mind's eye a spark within an endless darkness, suddenly igniting the blade of a four-pointed, star-shaped sword, she concentrated intensely as the aura surrounding its indestructible nature grew stronger in a rolling, liquid-like fire. Reaching out with a desire to touch and claim her once again, and upon making imagined contact with an outstretched hand, a small, incendiary burst of explosive fire shot down from the reality of her palm, managing to ignite the layered pile of wood directly in front of her.

"Whoa! Whoa!"

Startled by the dramatic result of her efforts, the fiery young woman was forced to quickly scamper away from the flame she herself generated, for fear of it catching her clothes on fire. Kneeling on the ground while staring at the surprising accomplishment, she then turned up the palm of her hand and stared at *it,* instead.

"Neat."

It was then that she remembered what Walther had told her about having no fear of her own Element. In thinking about it, she approached the flames, closed her eyes and decidedly thrust a hand into the flickering orange tongues, awaiting a nearly instantaneous desire to withdraw due to the onset of pain. But, lo and behold, that desire did not present itself. Wiggling her fingers in the warmth of the fire, Trinity opened her eyes and was amazed to see that her mentor was yet again correct, for there was no damage done.

Elsewhere, in the overgrowth of the grove near the edge of the forest, a partridge perched upon a tree branch and began pecking at a meal consisting of ladybugs that were themselves busy feasting on green leaves, when the bird suddenly and unsuspectingly found itself met by an accurately and violently thrown serrated hunting knife, losing the life that would serve to sustain the lives of three others.

Before long, the hunter was making his way down the grassy, flowery hill leading back to the clifftop where his female companions were seated on the ground around a strong-burning fire. Motionless, Trinity was staring deeply into the dancing flames, while Kimberly seemed hard at work on catching up with the details of a written story using the drawings in her sketchbook for recollection and inspiration. "I see that you have realized your renewed capability," Walther pointed out, appearing to the women from seemingly out of nowhere, startling only the busy writer before he dropped three plucked partridges on the ground near the fire.

"You mean to say I could have done this before?" Trinity gathered from his chosen words. "Why didn't you tell me?"

"I did not possess that knowledge until recently," he answered, as he swung the cloak-covered weapon down from his shoulders, setting its butt end down first before carefully laying it flat, not because he was worried about damaging an ancient artifact, but rather the ground and the clifftop itself. He then sat cross-legged around the fire with the others. "This was an appropriate time for you to attempt it, so, congratulations."

Sitting in silence, the hunter unsheathed his trusty knife and began carving the end of a stick into a sharp, spear-like point, and after producing three of them in a very short time, they would be used to impale the fowl that would then be set to roast over the fire. As they slowly cooked, he would periodically rotate the three sticks that were purposely stuck into the ground and leaned up against a well-placed rock, supporting the weight of the game birds above the fire – the fire that his apprentice couldn't seem to take her eyes off of. Watching her with multiple, undetected glances, he grinned at her newfound inter-reflection and fascination with her Element, knowing what would develop with time.

The Divine Light had so easily become a part of him that he hadn't taken the time to reflect on its gifts and bestowed abilities, most of which he would not yet demonstrate nor speak of. Staring into the fire, himself, recollecting historic events that his ancestors took part in, and the accompanying vivid flash of memories, including the ones far more distant in the past than those of the time of his grandfather, he quickly became reluctant to delve into for the time being, wishing to remain emotionally unaffected in present company. Declining the offer from the Great Voice in his mind for emotional isolation, he refocused his attention on the present task of evenly cooking a rather impromptu breakfast.

When they were finished cooking, "How do you expect me to eat this thing?" Kimberly asked, after setting her notebook down to accept the stick being offered to her.

"The Sheriff managed to overlook this," Walther responded, as he withdrew a slender object from a hidden pocket inside of his jacket, and in pressing the button on the side, a blade was quickly released from hiding. Flipping it around in the air and catching it by the tip, he offered the jet black hilt to the surprised Englishwoman.

Using the accepted switchblade, the writer began to slice off a piece of partridge breast. Freezing in place before putting it in her mouth, "How is it?" she first asked the young woman on her right, who had already begun to eat the bird directly off the stick that was held horizontally in her hands.

“Pretty good,” Trinity quite happily mumbled, with a mouthful of succulent meat.

With a small slice pinned between her thumb and the side of the switchblade, Kimberly took a somewhat hesitant bite and, with her eyes to the sky, she chewed in consideration of whether or not she could agree with the opinion of another. “Better than expected,” she admitted, “but it sure isn't my idea of a lovely Sunday dinner.”

Surprisingly, the hunter took no offense to the comment and nodded in complete agreement. “When this is all said and done we will enjoy a special southern dinner to celebrate our success,” he idealized, in confidence of their chances. “Fried chicken, black-eyed peas, mashed potatoes, and my mother's special cornbread recipe,” he added, in reminiscence of his early childhood.

Unable to silence her inquiring mind, the writer opted to use the relaxed opportunity to ask a tough question that had been in the back of her mind for some time. “In the center of the grove...”

“Yes,” Walther answered, anticipating the rest of her question, knowing that she was not likely to resist asking it for much longer.

At that moment, Trinity was compelled to cease her constant chewing as she stared at her mentor from behind her food in anticipation of learning more about the man who rarely spoke of his mysterious past.

“She was Native American. Some people call them Indian, but that inaccuracy of history was very likely due to the fact that when America was discovered by Europeans, they were actually looking for India. In other words, they were lost. In *my* view, the only *Indians* are from *India.* In the truest sense, my mother was an American, and her ancestors were Americans long before this land was given its name. My Pops met her while traveling alongside my Grampy in the winter of 1944. Less than three years later, I was born. Pops fell under her spell from the moment he first laid eyes on her. He chose to stop traveling around that time. He gave up the life of a bounty hunter in order to remain close to her. Grampy, of course, objected and said that his training was not yet over...that their mission in this area was incomplete. There was a difference of opinion and an argument ensued, resulting in them parting ways in frustration. They never spoke again after that, though I now understand that Grampy stopped in to check on them a few times...without them knowing it. He was pleased to see that she was carrying the next generation within her, but, as you both know by now, he never made it back from the ruins."

"And you know all this because..." Kimberly surmised, with her pen pointed at the cloak-covered weapon on the ground, having already set her food down to make a record of the new information she was hearing.

With the sharp edge of his serrated hunting knife cutting off a tender slice of meat, the hunter nodded a confirmation as he chewed away, tapping twice on his right temple before he continued slicing the fowl that he hunted many a time.

"I see," said Kimberly, understanding a little of what was implied by the gesture to the symbiotic Spirit of Light.

By the time they finished eating and had allowed time for the writer and artist to catch up on her work, the sun had risen high enough in the sky to penetrate through to the forest path, leading the Dark Hunter to assume that their enemy must have been compelled to take refuge within the dark and treacherous waters of her rebirth.

"Let us go," Walther soon said. "Trinity, put out the fire, would you?"

With a controlled and concentrated placement of her hand, the apprentice began to do as she was asked with apparent ease and, much to the wide-eyed interest of a blonde-haired Englishwoman, the flames slowly quelled and were soon no more.

And so, at just after six o'clock in the morning, the trio made their way north through the flower-filled grove and into the forest to the west, heading back along the safest and most sun-lit route around the densest and darkest part of the forest, hoping to avoid trouble. Much sooner than expected, they arrived at the edge of the Lifeless Zone within Scarlet Forest that, in its radius, spanned an estimated six to seven miles from its center point: The Mere.

"It's gotten worse," Trinity acknowledged for the writer, who, having bypassed its earlier progression entirely, was seeing the unsettling, unnatural phenomenon for the very first time.

"What happened here?" Kimberly asked, as the group moved southwest and into the misty shroud of gray, having no other choice but to do so if they wished to avoid the steep valley directly to the southeast.

"This is her sphere of influence," Walther immediately replied. "The Lifeless Zone. She loses power beyond the edge and the further out she travels."

Immediately understanding what that meant as it related to their previous close encounter, still, Trinity felt the need to clarify for herself and for Kimberly, the implications of their leader's chosen words. "So, if I have this right, what we saw...what was about kill us...was actually in a weakened state."

Kimberly's body practically froze in a physical paralysis as she awaited a response to the shocking statement.

"Correct," Walther confirmed, just as he and Trinity instinctively stopped in place, knowing that the fearful writer had already done so.

"H-how much weaker would you say she was?" Kimberly asked, which was a question she very much had to force from her lips, for once not looking forward to actually knowing the answer.

For a moment, the hunter appeared to be considering his reply, but his response indicated that he had instead been listening to the silent voice of another – a voice that spoke, but could not be heard by any ear. "Based on the perimeter of the Dark Demon's anti-life in relation to where the incident took place on the clifftop, we calculate a seventy percent reduction of her current level of power."

"Great!" Trinity enthusiastically exclaimed. "She's not going to stand much of a chance against you," she figured.

"You misunderstand," her mentor had to say. "The power loss was temporary and was restored as she retreated closer to this point of decay. The Lydia we are dealing with is upwards of seventy percent more powerful than the one we encountered."

"Great..." she said, for the second time, only with much less enthusiasm than that of the first iteration, maintaining a smile for comedic effect, alone.

It was only then that they heard a heavy, earth-pounding gallop among the dead trees and fallen branches of the gloomy, misty interior of the woods that served to lessen the sun's penetration. Coming straight at them, in full sprint, was a roaring, monstrous grizzly bear with intense violet eyes and a thirst for blood to match. Trinity, being the first to react, drew Ol' Loudmouth from its holster at her mentor's left hip, took aim with it and was prepared to fire when six gunshots of a lower caliber sounded off in rapid succession, ringing out into the mist of the dying forest and slowing the big animal down to a nearly defeated, off-balance pace. To spare the beast a slow and agonized death, a killing shot from the high caliber magnum became necessary to stop the creature's near-death, endlessly compelled advance. Following the discharge of the powerful round, the black-furred grizzly fell to the ground a few yards away, dead. No longer able to rise under the Dark Demon's infectious and subversive control, its unnatural black fur faded away, revealing the natural color of brown that one would expect a grizzly to bear.

Out from behind the largest of the dead cedar trees in sight stepped a man with a grim expression and whose eyes were hidden behind a tipped down green and black duster hat. Resting at shoulder level, his smoking hot pistol was blown clear and cool with a full breath before it was holstered beneath a camouflaged trench coat, exposing a set of worn army fatigues that altogether with the rest of his features gave away the old man's identity.

"Gramps!" Kimberly said, finally exhaling a held breath.

"Nice shooting," Trinity quietly acknowledged, before attempting to return the magnum revolver to its owner.

Casually declining the return of the firearm for the time being, the Dark Hunter carefully leaned the larger, heavier, still concealed weapon up against the trunk of a dead tree that creaked and cracked under the weight of the weapon. He then moved both hands to his midsection and proceeded to remove the brown leather belt and holster from around his waist. "Keep it," he told her.

"You sure?"

"Sergeant," Walther acknowledged, with his attention set on the welcome return of the fourth member of the party. "Change of heart?"

"Something like that," Flynn admitted, in his typical, raspy voice that the others learned to miss in his absence. "I see that you've succeeded," he commented, after glancing at the covered shape of the weapon he had not seen in over twenty years.

"Not yet," Walther replied, preferring not to count his chickens before they hatched, though had he not been successful in obtaining the lost Relic, the chances of their survival would have remained slim to nil, and not just for those closest to him.

The old Sergeant nodded his understanding. "You've no need for your M29?" he wondered, referring to the Model 29 Smith and Wesson magnum revolver holstered and hanging from a belt requiring readjustment to fit the small waist of a fit, young woman.

"She can carry it until we get to the store," Walther explained, while in the middle of handing over a supply of bullets. "Carrying this," he said, as he picked up the heavy, concealed weapon once again, "I feel a little too encumbered to be of much use to anyone."

The hunter then eyed each of them for a brief moment before asking the youngest among them to take point and guide the way along the deadwood, shrouded path.

"You don't want to take the lead and protect us with *that?"* she questioned, confused as to why the task was being assigned to her when a much more fearsome weapon was in the hands of her mentor.

The Dark Hunter shook his head in confidence. "Have you ever played poker?" he asked her, with a guiding hand on her shoulder to start her off in the right direction. "Texas Hold 'em?"

"Yeah," Trinity replied.

"It would be most unwise to tip our hand before the showdown."

In the single file line, those in first, third, and fourth position nodded their understanding of the hunter's disclosed strategy, revealed to them in the form of a poker analogy.

"So, I take it we're going shopping if we make it out of here alive?" Kimberly wondered, as she walked along in third position, right behind the hunter, preferring to travel as close to him as possible while also dying to catch even a glimpse of the weapon he insisted on keeping covered.

With the old army Sergeant willingly bringing up the rear to keep an eye on their six, the group moved on and was forced to slay many a creature along the way, putting a strain on a dwindling supply of ammunition that had them understanding why a trip to the store was necessary. Before they made it back to the nearest vehicle, that being Kimberly's VW Beetle, still a mile away, a night owl with a large wingspan, corrupted and desiring to attack no matter the time of day, swooped out of the sky and was instantly blasted out of the air by a young woman gaining more and more control over the powerful revolver on loan to her. Next, a pair of wily black foxes, with cunning, violet eyes attacked the traveler's from behind, but were quickly dispatched by the even more wily old Sergeant Flynn and his Colt Single-Action Army. Then, from out of nowhere, a deep purple-eyed, black-furred jackrabbit began viciously biting and clawing with its hind legs while hanging from Kimberly's satchel, and as a quick reaction, the writer screamed and dropped her leather bag before booting the mad creature like a soccer ball, sending it right into a tree, breaking its neck on impact with the petrified deadwood. The others couldn't help but stop and stare at her as she picked up her belongings, amazed at the result of her powerful kick. *"What?"* she said in her own defense, tossing back the ponytail of her long, blonde hair, all set to continue the perilous journey.

"Nothing," Trinity said, looking away, secretly impressed by her sudden and effective action.

"I'm just glad she's on our side," Flynn said, directing his comment to Walther, seeing him nod his approval.

Not long after that, the Dark Hunter suddenly placed a hand on the shoulder of his apprentice, halting her in place and preventing her from taking another step. *"Wait,"* he whispered, managing to signal to those behind him using the fingers of his other hand – the same one being used to balance the ancient weapon pinned under his wrist and held over his left shoulder.

"Yeah, I see them," Trinity confirmed, from the head of the line.

With his right hand still on her shoulder, the Dark Hunter pointed his index finger at an upward angle for the benefit of the two behind him. Looking up into the lifeless, unnaturally petrified trees, the group stared at numerous small, dark figures that swayed randomly from side to side and back and forth from the bottoms of hundreds of branches in their midst. Saying nothing, the mentor removed his hand from the shoulder of his apprentice and slowly guided the readied gun in her hand back to its holster, knowing that revolvers would serve no purpose whatsoever against the sheer numbers they were facing. Aware of his cautionary action, the Sergeant did the same.

"What do we do?" Trinity whispered back over her shoulder.

"The answer is within you."

She didn't have to think for very long about what he meant by that.

"You sure?"

"The valley would be far more dangerous. There is no other way. Like you said before, there is no going back, and so we must go forward," Walther advised, and nudged the young woman to take care of the situation on her own.

Much to the puzzled and worried expressions of the writer and the Sergeant, they obeyed the hunter's signal and copied him in getting low to the ground behind the remains of low-lying thorny bushes for at least a small bit of cover, and when the lone Dark Huntress stepped but a few paces further, the bats took flight by the hundreds as a living whirlwind, shrieking loudly in a deafening high pitch being generated by their combined numbers.

Closing her eyes and standing still in concentration, even in the horrific presence of the indigo-eyed bats that began swarming together as a collective, the young woman, symbiont to the Divine Fire, looked deep within her consciousness knowing that she was metaphysically linked with a powerful force – one that came to exist on Earth in the form of a weapon containing the power of a compressed star, and all at once the solution became as clear as daybreak. Corrupted or not, she could sense the life forces of them all.

As the horde of bats descended from above, a single word grew in intensity as a voice that was thought to be lost echoed up from the depths of her soul.

Ignite.

Opening her eyes and snapping the thumb and middle fingers of both outstretched hands in unison, the indigo-eyed bats – every single one of them – altogether ignited from the spark of a consuming scarlet flame that began from the inside out, and alas, the shrieking, winged creatures fell from the sky like a rain of fire and disintegrated before their burning bodies could even hit the ground.

Trinity drew in a slow, deep breath as she stood motionless beneath the masses of petrified trees, looking at an upward angle, enraptured by the perpetual twilight of weakened sun rays that barely made it through from beyond the misty shroud of darkness pervading the forest. She soon felt a gentle, yet firm, familiar grip of a hand on her shoulder.

"Well done," Walther softly spoke, thoroughly impressed by her performance. *"All clear!"* he announced for the other two members of the party, who were still looking on through the remains of thorn bushes from a side by side crouched position in shock and awe, and who managed to turn their heads toward each other to exchange stunned glances after witnessing the unexpected display of fire power.

Having entered the Dark Demon's sphere of influence from the north and subsequently traveling southwest a few miles, the group soon spotted the western perimeter of the Lifeless Zone through a weakened, temporarily halted misty shroud that only partially blocked out the light of the warm sun. Beyond the cutoff point, the forest was bright and green, lush and vibrant, and quite free from the Dark Demon's dominion, though the writer couldn't help but wonder how long the outside world would remain as such, knowing that the arrival of nightfall meant the expansion would resume.

"There it is," Walther said, being the first to see the end of the path as a result of his superior vision. "Lead on," he told his apprentice, standing off to the side so they could go by him. "Go. Go," he said to Kimberly and Flynn as they passed by him in turn, giving them each an encouraging pat on the back as he kept his eyes on their flank, reminding the old Sergeant of his days in the army going all the way back to boot camp before the start of the second world war.

Though his eyes led him to believe that they were free from danger, a finely-tuned sense of hearing indicated otherwise and was quickly confirmed by a God-like voice within that calmly spoke a single word.

Run.

Trailing each of the Dark Hunter's long-stride steps, the ground rumbled and caved in as he moved as fast as he could while sweating profusely and bearing the weight of a dreadfully heavy Relic on his shoulders, leaving the path behind him totally destroyed. Struggling to catch up to the others who were but casually jogging, he burst clear of the misty shroud of the dead woods by launching himself into a barrier of healthy, green bushes and into direct sunlight knowing that momentum would carry him on through. "Run *faster!"* he hollered, trusting the intuition that they were not at all safe in the sun from what was coming after them this time.

A steadily increasing hissing accompanied by the sound of

millions of crawling legs belonging to a collective hoard of furious fire ants, millipedes, centipedes, spiders, cockroaches and God only knows what else, emerged as a swarming mass intent on devouring alive the fleeing four who were unfortunate enough to have crossed their guarded path.

"Oh, my God..." Kimberly said under her breath, when she momentarily looked back and saw what was coming for them, prompting her to frantically remove the car keys from her pocket in readiness to gain entry to the VW Bug parked at the edge of the forest.

"I can destroy them," Trinity declared, when she suddenly stopped near the back of the car and turned to face the advancing hoard in preparation to repeat her previous feat of fire.

"No!" Flynn yelled, before he forcibly picked up the brave, but foolish young woman around her waist using only one arm. He then opened up the passenger side door that had been unlocked for him and shoved her to the middle of the front seat as he got in and shut the door behind him, all while Trinity put up a fight to free herself out of a desire to save everyone from the impending onslaught of corrupted, falsely carnivorous creepy-crawly's.

With the driver's side passenger door open for his imminent arrival, the Dark Hunter sprinted as fast as possible with the weight of the heavy weapon he carried, knowing full well that he could use it to destroy the hoard in the blink of an eye. Refusing to do so for tactical reasons, he quickly, though as gently as time allowed, set the edge of the covered object down on the floor of the VW's interior and slid it under the seats at an angle, causing the vehicle's rear shocks to fully and suddenly compress as a result of the added weight before he dove onto the back seat, somehow managing to shut the door as he did so, barely evading the legions upon legions of maddened insects that blanketed the car in a disturbing darkness that was followed up by the driver's high-pitched screams.

The engine having already been started, Kimberly stepped on the gas pedal, violently ejecting the bugs that were attempting to crawl up the vehicle's tailpipe. The constant crunching and mushing of crushed exoskeletons under the tires, and the guts being smeared all over the windshield from the activated wipers was sickening, especially to the driver, whose effeminate screams and properly disturbed English sensibilities were mitigated only by the application of the washer fluid that allowed her to at least see where she was going. Sharply turning left onto the road to head southwest, her three passengers were suddenly thrown hard to the right in a verbal declaration of the pain they each received, and she drove on while breathing heavily and trembling with a somewhat fading fear.

"I told you that you would get more than you bargained for," Walther said, as he relaxed in the back seat and adjusted his clothing, directing his voice to the other three members of the group who were trying to get comfortable being squished together, side by side in the front. For a good thirty seconds, no one said a word while watching an unlikely mix of insects attempt to cling to the car's exterior as it gradually accelerated down the paved road, getting up to the posted speed limit of fifty-five miles per hour.

"You're gonna have to get this car washed," Trinity eventually said – a comment that managed to yield a good laugh, that although was delayed on the part of the shaken driver, was nevertheless accompanied by a sense of relief that they had made it out of Scarlet Forest alive.

Chapter 12

Darkstar's Python

July 21st, 1967. 10:00 hours.

Clean as a whistle, at least, on the outside it was, a sky blue VW Beetle beeped its horn twice as it exited the line of a full-service car wash and was then driven around a corner and along the town of Scarletmere's Main Street where it soon turned left into a parking lot, eventually coming to a stop behind a car with a vanity plate that read: RUBYRED.

"Anything you want from this store is on me," Walther announced to his companions, who naturally gathered in the vicinity of the two vehicles. "My family has a longstanding relationship with the owner, so, do not allow the price of any item to deter you from selecting it. Suffice it to say, there will be a considerable discount."

With that said, the four headed for the store, but not before making sure that the doors of the VW were locked out of respect for the invaluable and priceless Relic that barely managed to fit at an angle across the floor. Staring up at the sign above the store and entering second to last, the writer made a mental note of the shop's unique and unusual name while the hunter held the door open and flipped the *OPEN* sign around to read *CLOSED* to anyone on the outside.

Darkstar Guns & Hunting had everything an outdoor enthusiast would likely need or want, but, even if they didn't, they could special order what you wanted or even custom make it for you. Reinforced glass case counter tops lined much of the perimeter, securing and protecting the expensive handguns on display within them. On the walls at the back, a wide selection of locked-down rifles and shotguns were held on vertical gun racks between tall book shelves on which individual boxes of ammunition were stacked. The rest of the store was divided into aisles featuring everything else such a place would be expected to carry. Bows, binoculars, scopes, tents, sleeping bags, blankets, decoys, targets, camouflaged clothing and clothing that edged toward a southern appeal. It was easy to see that it was a shop where Walther's southern eye for fashion and need of special items could be fulfilled and maintained while on mission in the region.

"Welcome to Darkstar," a sweet-sounding female voice called out.

With the others having separated to look around the impressive store on their own, the hunter made his way directly to the lone female shopkeeper who was putting away inventory behind the waist-high line of display cabinets. She had only glanced up from her work to notice the first three of the four customers who entered the store.

"Hello, Wendy."

Hearing what was apparently a familiar voice to her, the shopkeeper stopped what she was doing and turned to face the man who knew her name, while the admittedly curious writer, who was of course watching them as she pretending to shop around, took notice of the young, redheaded shopkeeper's smile from her vantage point at the end of an aisle, surprised and intrigued to see the young woman respectfully bow to the Dark Hunter, who immediately returned the dignified sign of respect before they happily hugged over the top of the counter before disappearing out of sight from the storefront.

Uninterested in shopping for herself, not even considering her wants or that she was in need of anything, the writer made her way over to the east side of the store where the old Sergeant was seen to be examining various revolvers through one of the glass counter tops, apparently interested in obtaining something a little more modern than the old Colt she knew he was concealed-carrying.

"Find anything to your liking, Mr. Flynn?" the attractive redhead asked, as she returned to the counter from the back room, alone.

"This," he replied in his raspy voice, while tapping an index finger directly down onto the glass to indicate which one had caught his eye.

"Ah, the Python," Wendy said, as she unlocked the display cabinet from the rear. "An excellent choice, I must say," she added in compliment. "We bought it from a young man who came in looking to sell it last week. As I recall, he said it was gifted to him. It's second-hand, but this particular model is only two years old, and still in prime condition," she explained, as she handed it to the prospective customer, who, being no stranger to firearms, began to look it over, nodding in agreement with the shopkeeper's assessment. "Based on the significant impact wear of the hammer when it came in, which was replaced by yours truly, it definitely saw at least semi-frequent use. The original owner took very good care of it. Came in clean as a whistle considering the number of times it must have been fired."

"I'll take it," Flynn said, in possibly his raspiest voice. "How much if I trade *this* in?" he then asked, setting his old Colt down on the counter for the young shopkeeper's consideration.

"Whoa," she said, after an initial gasp escaped her lips in immediate recognition of an iconic American revolver. "This is a first-gen Peacemaker," she declared, as she glanced between the two customers in front of her. "What's the year?"

"Well, it was awarded to me in 1933," the retired Sergeant informed her, "but, according to the high-ranking Army Officer who issued it to me, the year of manufacture was 1890. It's been chambered for the .41 caliber Colt."

"May I?" she respectfully asked, quickly receiving a nod of approval from its owner. "This is quite the rarity, especially in this condition," the informed shopkeeper noted. "A prewar SAA, Cavalry Standard seven-point-five inch barrel," she said, taking a couple of seconds to look along it while aiming at a pristine target that was taped to the wall, apparently for just that purpose. "Chambered for .41 Colt, just as you said," she confirmed, being extra careful when rotating the cylinder. "Hammer and trigger action are...smooth and unobstructed. No sign of any fractures or stress-related damage that I can see. Intricate silver and ivory stock. Lovely pattern. This has been very well cared for," she declared, after many other declarations, to which the old Sergeant nodded. "Yup, she's a real beauty, for certain. Hmm... Are you absolutely sure you want to sell this?"

After observing the blonde Englishwoman who was hastily penning everything mentioned about the much older Colt in the notebook she'd opted to set down on the counter, if only to ease the effort being put into it, he nodded to the shopkeeper.

"We're going to owe *you* money on this trade," Wendy speculated. "I'll need my father to appraise it to determine the value and make you a fair offer. I know he'll be interested, so, there's really no worry in that regard, but, feel free to shop around and pick out a few more items so that we can get this trade down to something *we* can afford," she suggested, knowing that a custom-made historical weapon was going to have a high dollar value assigned to it. *"Daddy!"* she called out, as she walked toward the back room with the seventy-eight year old Colt lying flat in her hands. "Got somethin' you're gonna wanna take a look at!" she added, as she passed by a certain other someone who was on his way back to the storefront.

"I thought *I* was buying," Walther commented, seeing that Flynn intended to sell the old Colt to help finance the rest of the mission.

"Just doing my part," he replied, as he looked down the Python's sights, and with a squeeze of the trigger, test-fired the empty cylinder of the like-new weapon to his satisfaction. "Besides, from what I've seen, I think it's high time I upgraded to a weapon with a little more stopping power," he reasoned, in reference to the ineffectiveness of the older Colt in penetrating all the way through the Dark Demon's youthful body.

"You would certainly be more likely to acquire her attention," Walther admitted. "And, hey, that model is chambered for .357 Magnum *and* for .38 Special. An excellent choice, if I do say so, myself," he added, giving an informed opinion, afterward clearing his throat twice in what was surely the most commonly heard way. "There should be something engraved on the stock."

Hearing that, the old Sergeant flipped the weapon upside down and closely examined the bottom. "W.M.," he read out loud, barely able to make out the small letters that had been carved into the heel of the revolver's wood stock. "Just how is it you knew that?" he inquired, looking to the hunter for an answer, wondering how it could be that he knew an engraving would be there, and judging by the pen pressed firmly to a notebook in silent waiting, the blonde-haired writer standing between the two men was equally curious, if not more so.

The hunter grinned while stepping past them. "M.W.," he corrected, and watched out of the corner of his eye as the Sergeant rotated it so that the barrel pointed straight down to the floor, both for safety reasons, but also to satisfy the writer's interest in seeing even the obvious for herself. "It was mine," he confessed. "At least, until I gave it to a foolish man who foolishly sold it," he recollected, while beginning to glance around at the store's large inventory.

"What was his name?" Kimberly asked, wishing to know it for the completeness of her story.

"Ask Trinity," it was suggested. "Actually," he suddenly thought to say, as he moved around the corner of an aisle with the other two following, "if you would prefer a quality double-action revolver with even more stopping power, I would suggest that *you* take the Model 29, giving her the Python, instead."

"Where is that crazy girl, anyway?" Kimberly wondered out loud.

Holstering the Python that fit snugly into the old SAA's holster, intended to be kept as a memento, the retired Sergeant thought about the proposed swap as he followed after the persistent writer who could never seem to keep still, that is, unless her pen was eagerly awaiting the arrival of a new piece of information.

"Trinity?" Kimberly called out, as she stood on her tiptoes to peek above the top of the aisles, looking all around the store for the friend who was nowhere to be seen.

Practically singing her response to hearing her own name, *"O-ver he-ere,"* the young woman's voice answered, raising and lowering the pitch of each word with an upward and then downward inflecton.

The two most senior members of the party, themselves being several decades apart in age, followed the voice to the far western side of the store where the hats, shirts and pants were stocked and displayed on a few male and female manikins that faced one another across the aisle, Trinity suddenly popped out from behind the black curtain of one of two changing rooms, grabbing the writer's arm and giving her a little fright that came in the form of a slight jump accompanied by a feminine yelp.

"So, what do you think?"

"You *really* look like him," Kimberly said, to the smiling and posing young woman who turned herself toward the mirror on the wall, admiring the reflection of a bold outfit consisting of a black, long-tailed coat, a dark red vest over a gray, western style blouse, black leather cowgirl boots and a black cowgirl hat to complete the ensemble. "What do *you* think, Gramps?"

"Certainly a sight for sore eyes," Flynn admitted, feeling rather charmed by her feminine form in new, tight-fitting slacks. "And, as I said before, imitation is the highest form of flattery."

"Consider me flattered," Walther said from behind them, startling only Flynn and Kimberly with his sudden appearance. "It suits you," he complimented, as he stared at the reflection of his apprentice, setting his sights directly on her when she turned around to face him.

"Really?" she responded and smiled, no doubt happy that her appearance met with the approval of her great mentor.

"Come to think of it," he said, before smelling the inside of his shirt collar, "I suppose I could use a change of clothes, myself. I have been wearing these for far too long."

As he got started with selecting new apparel for himself, his fiery young apprentice went back into her chosen changing room to begin undressing, while the old Sergeant turned his attention to an open display of hunting knives that he began using in turn from top to bottom to test the CQC technique that had been taught to him the previous morning. Noticing that the fourth member of the party had returned to writing instead of using the opportunity to better equip herself, the hunter decided to intervene by employing what he knew to be the most effective method available. *"Trinity?!"* he called out to a half-dressed young woman.

"Yea-ah?" she answered back, in an amusing, high-pitched voice.

"Would you be so kind as to help Ms. Hunter choose a new look?!"

Though no one could see her in the dressing room, everyone suspected that the silence of a delayed response meant that she was smiling wide while restraining an outburst of excitement.

"Oh, I *suppose* I could do that," she soon replied, quite unable to conceal her almost giddy amusement.

The busy writer objected, of course, as the hunter fully expected her to. "I don't really need anything," she said, in an attempt to excuse herself from the annoying task of shopping with an obviously delighted Trinity, preferring instead to continue to focus on the development of her story.

"You most certainly do," Walther calmly insisted, as he rifled through a stack of folded pants in a hunt for the correct size. "You are presently ill-equipped to assist us, and in protecting yourself, as well."

"But, I have no experience or training with such things," Kimberly pointed out, motioning to the impressive guarded posture of the old Sergeant who was seen to be testing out the hunting knife that was most to his liking.

"Nothing that time and effort cannot remedy," Walther casually replied, after glancing at the battle-hardened old Sergeant. "Trinity will be more than happy to assist in the selection of your new attire."

"Yup!" came a response from the changing rooms.

"The Sergeant will select an appropriate blade for you."

"Aye," Flynn agreed, with his back to them, still testing knives.

"And, by then, I will have chosen a suitable firearm for you."

"...Fine," Kimberly reluctantly agreed, though she was blushing a little while defiantly tapping her pen on her own shoulder with her arms crossed, accepting that there was no sense in arguing with the man, so long as she wished to remain by his side and experience the adventure, firsthand.

Sensing apathy and a lack of proper motivation, the Dark Hunter, in intimidating fashion, moved into closer proximity to the Englishwoman, gaining her undivided attention. "We must make use of every possible advantage this time around," he boldly stated. "We were most fortunate to escape the previous encounters, absent even a single casualty, but, when a tactical retreat becomes tactically dangerous, that is the time to make a stand. The fate of the future rests on our collective shoulders."

Kimberly swallowed hard. "On mine, too?"

"Of course," he confirmed, with a slightly more relaxed demeanor, letting up on her somewhat. "You are here. You are alive. You *can* do something. After all, you are a true believer. More than that, you *know* that the stories are true. Right now, perhaps more than ever, this world needs those who dare to believe in the unbelievable. Plus," he said, further relaxing his demeanor and tone of voice, "it will be nice to have a clear and accurate record of everything that has transpired. Could prove to be invaluable in the future."

By the time he had picked out a new collared long sleeve shirt in the color of gunmetal gray, as it was written on the tag, a black vest and a new pair of black boots, since he had practically worn down to nothing the soles of his current pair, Trinity was brushing aside the curtain of the changing room she was in and stepped out with her new choice of outfit in her arms. "I'll be right back," she told Kimberly, as she strolled by her in a hurry, clearly worried that she might somehow lose her chance to makeover the bookish writer, who although was classically beautiful, could never be bothered to concern herself with her clothing or her looks in a fashion that went beyond the basics. "Stay right there, I'm just going to set these by the register."

The request being unnecessary, the writer wasn't going anywhere and continued to work right up until the moment the enthusiastic young woman returned to her.

"What's your favorite color?" Trinity asked, and waited for a response as she watched the blonde Englishwoman tuck her precious notebook back into her leather satchel.

"Care to wager a guess?" Kimberly responded.

Accepting the challenge, the younger woman tilted her head a little to the side and looked the writer up and down. *"Blue,"* she stated as fact.

"You say that as if you know for certain."

"I *do* know for certain," she boasted, while glancing around at the shirts on display in the women's section of the aisle.

"Uh huh, and how's that?" Kimberly asked, not at all believing her.

"Well, your car is blue, the pens in your bag are all blue, except for the red one that I really like, your nails are painted a dark blue, when they used to be light blue..."

The writer, up until around that point, had been nodding along with each statement, but in a mocking kind of fashion, wanting her to skip over the circumstantial evidence, knowing that any observant individual could be aware of such facts and still they could be explained away by mere chance or happenstance, alone, but she suddenly found herself stunned by the next level of accuracy that could not have been a guess nor an obvious, easily observed fact that could just as easily be dismissed as a random choice for that day.

"...and the bra and panties you have on are blue, too," she added, speaking under lower volume, removing the look of open-mouthed mockery from the writer's face.

"...I don't even want to know how you know that," Kimberly said, after crossing her arms out of embarrassment, feeling that her privacy had at some point been violated. "Wait, yes I do," she said in quick retraction, and stood in the way of the young woman's shopping, unable to ignore her own inquisitive mind. “Tell me how you knew that.”

“I'm not really sure if I can,” Trinity figured, doubting not her own ability to explain, but the ability of anyone other than her mentor to comprehend. “The world just seems different to me lately, that's all.”

“Go on,” Kimberly humorously said, wide-eyed with peaked interest, no longer engaging in mockery, wanting her friend to explain further as she tried to lock eyes with her.

“Well, colors are easily twice as vivid as they were before,” she began, as she softly touched an article of clothing that caught her eye. “They're all popping out at me in layers beneath layers of reality. Take this shirt, just for example. *Before,* like you and nearly everyone else, I could only see one layer. The outermost layer, I suppose,” she decided, no longer certain if the term *outer* or *inner* could even be applied to reality. “That's the way I used to see things. *Now,* I can see every layer of fabric and on through.”

“Hold on,” Kimberly said, quite taken aback by the casual admission. “You can see right through my clothes?” she whispered, partially correct in her interpretation of the strange explanation.

“Oh, I've been able to do that for awhile now,” Trinity confessed.

“You're joking.”

“No, I'm Trinity. Well, that's my name, anyhow. No, this is something different,” the fiery young woman seemed to say to herself, suddenly in her own world of thought while doing all the shopping for her friend, not even realizing that she was both embarrassing and boggling the somewhat prudish mind of the Englishwoman at the same time. “I think I'm just beginning to see the world the way it really is, beyond what I've always thought of as normal. Things aren't as separated as they once seemed to be. Everything is much more connected together than I ever would have imagined. If it weren't for him,” she said, glancing a good ways down the men's side of the clothing aisle, “I'd probably be losing my mind right now, but, it's actually pretty cool.”

“Him?” Kimberly repeated, ushering Trinity further toward the end of the aisle, just for the sake of additional privacy. “You're referring to Walther, yes?” she wished to clarify, not only for her own reasons that were still thought to be secretly kept, but for the integrity of her story and for those who might be reading at some point in the future.

"Yes and no," Trinity replied, since on one hand she was referring to her mentor, and on the other, to the Divine Light within him – the Spirit that had awoken her latent abilities, reigniting what was originally thought to be a broken link with her precious stolen Scarlet counterpart.

As the younger woman got on with browsing the women's side of the aisle, she began to detect a light, continuous scratching sound. Puzzled and listening intently to determine its origin, she soon whipped around with a pair of black slacks and a dark blue blouse draped over one arm arm, suddenly aware that the writer was no longer following her with great interest. "What are you *doing?"*

"Oh, come now," Kimberly responded, as if the other woman should not have been the least bit surprised to once again find her holding a pen. "You can't say such things and expect me not to write them down."

"Then I guess I'll just have to keep it all to myself from now on," Trinity teased, grabbing a pair of boots in midnight blue while on her way back to the dressing room that the writer would soon occupy.

"Please don't do that," Kimberly pleaded, as she followed after the wavy black hair of a rather remarkable young woman.

Meanwhile, on the other side of the store, the old Sergeant had decided on a unique curved-bladed weapon that featured an arched, hidden tang beneath a smooth mahogany handle that conformed well to the hand, chosen not only for its aesthetic appeal, but moreover because of its seamless, upended integration alongside a revolver in the close-quarters-combat stance. Two other blades of a more standard design, suitable for the smaller hands of the women in his company, he selected for their practical and more versatile usage.

Down the center aisle, on his way to the cash register, Walther and the Divine Light behind his eyes were pleasantly surprised to come across a pair of pure white leather gauntlets typically used for bull riding or calf roping, that he decidedly took down from a high shelf and set on top of the other selections he carried. After placing everything on the counter near the register, right next to another stack of clothes, he began moving along the front of the display cabinets that separated the storefront from the back area, scanning among the many handguns and revolvers for something suitable to one of the two laughing and joking females in the change room on his far right. Noticing an all-steel, short-barreled revolver that he had never before seen, the hunter leaned over the counter to look straight down at the information label that lay on the felt below it, seeing that it read: *Smith & Wesson M60 – .38 Special.* Another label that had been set below the first, read: *Waiting List.* He couldn't help but smirk at it through the glass.

"Since I'll be taking the M29," a raspy voice spoke, as footsteps approached the counter where three hunting knives would be set down atop a selection of women's clothing, "what are you thinking for a replacement? That is, if you even have a need for a sidearm, anymore."

"Well, I---"

"Your special order is ready," the sweet, redheaded shopkeeper suddenly announced, answering the old Sergeant's unheard question and cutting off the hunter's response to it as she returned from the stockroom with her bouncing red curls, setting a cloth-covered object down onto the glass counter top in front of the two highly interested men.

"*What* in holy hell is this?" Flynn asked her, just as Trinity and Kimberly showed up next to him with a selection of new clothes and accessories, all of them being for the writer.

"This is the new Super Blackhawk," Wendy answered, as the Dark Hunter assessed the weight of the weapon with a satisfying *hmm* and squeezed the grip that perfectly matched his hand while taking aim at the far wall through the sights of the big revolver. "Quite the powerhouse. It's a single-action forty-four magnum exceeding the design of what the lady is carrying," she said, not failing to notice the Smith and Wesson Model 29 holstered at Trinity's right hip. "It features adjustable sights and has been customized by my father to include several innovations you won't find on factory-standard guns. Safety bar to prevent accidental firing of the sixth chamber when fully loaded, non-fluted cylinder to ease recoil, and loading and unloading at half-cock is no longer a requirement," she explained. "Cobalt blue steel, large grip, ten-point-five inches for the barrel, and in addition to all of that, we've created a hand-load ammunition that far exceeds any factory load. With *these,"* she said, showing them one of the bullets she was talking about, held between her thumb and index finger, "this firearm will drop anything with a single shot," she boasted. "Well, *almost* anything."

"Can an M29..?" Flynn immediately thought to ask.

Taking in a breath in consideration before exhaling, the young shopkeeper and apprentice gunsmith answered the implied question by saying, "Theoretically, yes, however, I can't recommend it, nor do I suggest you even try without taking the necessary precautions for a standalone stress test. You could very seriously injure yourself if the increased pressure were to cause a structural failure. That being said, we *do* actually have a supply of hand-load forty-four that exceeds factory standard, but not nearly by the margin of these bad boys – what we've named the Super Forty-Four Magnum. I can safely recommend the other hand-load for the M29."

"We will take a hundred of each ammunition required," Walther said, before he set the gun that almost fully met with his approval down onto the white cloth that came with it, proceeding to tap twice on the glass surface of the counter with the index finger of his alternate hand. "This Model Sixty Smith and Wesson," he continued to point out. "Is that new?"

Everyone at the counter looked down through the glass at the revolver in question.

"It's fairly new," Wendy confirmed with a smile, apparently amused and not at all surprised by the attention the product was getting. "They've been very hard to get a hold of. They're so popular that the manufacturer can't keep up with demand and, as you can see, we've had to start a waiting list for them."

"Understandable," Walther acknowledged. "This would have been a good match for you, Ms. Hunter," he said, and ever-so-subtly winked at the redheaded shopkeeper.

"You think so?" Kimberly responded, already becoming interested in the designs of the small firearms. "Too bad there's a waiting list, and they probably don't want to sell that one," she correctly assumed.

"Quite right," Wendy said, "but, if this is what you want for her, it's no problem," she said, quickly unlocking the back of the display case to retrieve the revolver in question. "We just had a partial order arrive and I haven't telephoned anyone on the waiting list yet. Just say the word and one of them can be yours. This is the best straight-up thirty-eight special that a novice could ever hope to get," she said, prior to beginning a demonstration to showcase the weapon's features. "All-solid steel construction, comfortable grip, easy-load swing-out cylinder, three-point-five-inch barrel length, and it has surprisingly low recoil, even for a thirty-eight of this type. It's a can't miss," she summed up for the writer, in a pun that was both intended and unintended, as it was simultaneously a sales pitch as well as a joke.

Rather taken by its listed features and sleek appearance, the writer nodded in agreement with the young saleswoman who quite obviously knew her stuff. "Easy-load," Kimberly repeated, as it was the part that most appealed to her inexperience.

Walther blinked and subtly nodded at the apprentice gunsmith, who, using a pencil, immediately proceeded to add it to an ongoing list of the group's selections and additional requirements.

"The Python aside, I've taken the liberty of assuming that you'll be wanting belts and holsters for the new weapons," Wendy wisely stated. "Open-carry regulations and all. The Sheriff has put out orders to all law enforcement to seize anything hidden, *if* they happen to notice them, of course. They won't search you for no reason, after all. Probable cause, right?"

"Right," Kimberly acknowledged, remembering that Walther had previously been fined for his violation of open-carry regulations, as Scarletmere County was, to say the least, a bit of an oddball in comparison with all others.

"So, aside from all the clothing, we've got three hunting knives, one Colt Python, used, one Smith and Wesson M60 with belt and holster for the English lady, one custom Ruger Super Blackhawk with belt and barrel-through holster, one hundred rounds of ammunition in three-fifty-seven magnum, one hundred in thirty-eight special, one hundred in our forty-four magnum hand-load, and one hundred in our forty-four Super Magnum hand-load," the shopkeeper summarized. "Will you be requiring anything else today?"

On the opposite side of the register, the hunter patiently waited while the others glanced back and forth at each other with mixed reactions ranging from shrugged shoulders of apparent uncertainty up to shaken heads that told of genuine satisfaction before their eyes settled on him for a final decision. "That'll be all for now."

With instruction to remove the final total from a reported credit balance of two-thousand dollars, the shopkeeper began rifling through the clothes and accessories that were piled up along the counter, intermittently moving over to the cash register to punch down several of its heavy keys in order to tally everything up. "Well, Marcus," she eventually said, using the first name of the boy who had become the man standing before her, the others waiting in anticipation of the total, "with your discount extended to Mr. Flynn, that comes to just five-hundred and eighty-eight dollars and seventy cents, leaving a negative balance of one-thousand four-hundred twelve dollars and thirty cents. Would you like that as a check or in cash?" she asked, giving the Sergeant the option.

"That's quite the discount," Trinity quietly said, directing her comments to her bonny, light-haired friend. "There's easily a thousand dollars in weapons and merchandise there, and that's not even including the cost for all the ammo."

"Hold onto it for me," Flynn unexpectedly requested. "I'll come to collect it tomorrow. *If* there's a tomorrow."

Lacking an expression of confusion or even one of curiosity, the apprentice gunsmith nodded her understanding, much to the interest of the writer who glanced up from her work in expectation of a followup question. "According to my grandparents, if it wasn't for what I gather are the ongoing efforts of the Walther family and their allies, none of us would be standing here today," she said, and pressed her hands together in gratitude, making brief eye contact with each of the four heroes. "Darkstar is more than happy to continue supplying arms to the Dark Hunters."

Hearing such revelatory comments, the writer quickly returned to her pen and notebook, having been tipped off that there was more than likely a great deal of history between the two families whose youngest living members stood opposite one another – a history that went beyond the simplicity of a longstanding business relationship. This girl knew. She knew what was going on and she knew what was about to happen. She even knew that if it wasn't for the Walther family's efforts, everyone – literally *everyone* would already be dead.

After bagging a selection of clothing and packing up the guns in the original manufacturer's boxes, except for the used Python that had come in off the street, the redheaded, lightly freckled apprentice gunsmith wished the group Godspeed and sweetly said for them to come again.

Carrying the last of the shopping bags as he walked out of the store behind the others, the hunter flipped around the hanging sign on the inside of the door so that it once again read *OPEN* to anyone on the outside, and after handing over the last bag to be loaded into the trunk of the Ruby Red, he opted to slide into the passenger seat of the sky blue VW Beetle to ride along with his Silver counterpart and a charming Englishwoman.

With the midday sun shining down, the two cars soon turned in to a familiar gas station on the east end of town and pulled up alongside the two pumps, one behind the other. Being the first to step out, the old Sergeant adjusted his duster hat to block out the intense light of the sun before he unscrewed the Chevy's gas cap and retracted the fuel nozzle from the side of the nearest pump when the owner of the vehicle he intended to gas up snatched it away from him.

"I'm the only one who does this, remember?"

"Oh, that's right," Flynn retrospectively said, handing her the nozzle, and with nothing else to do, he followed Walther toward the concrete steps that led up to the store.

"Candy!" Kimberly hollered to the two men, as she gassed up her VW behind Trinity and her Ruby Red. *"What?"* she said, defensively, when she looked forward to find a bold young woman in a white blouse leaning against the side of her Chevy, staring back at her with a blank expression that gradually became a scarlet-lipped smirk.

Inside, all of the store's remaining pre-made, shrink-wrapped sandwiches, there being twelve in total, the hunter swiped into the shopping basket he carried in one continued motion while on his way by the cooler en route to a three-layered hanging basket of fruit that he would begin picking through with the compulsive desire to obtain only the apples that were in the best possible condition.

Meanwhile, in front of the counter and the store clerk, who happened to be a curious and heavyset woman of advanced age and who had a name tag on her shirt that revealed her name as *Gladys*, stood Master Sergeant Llewellyn Flynn, U.S. Army, retired, busy selecting from a variety of candy, chocolate and bubble gum that would be certain to appease the sweet tooth of the blonde woman seen through the store window to be filling up her VW's gas tank in line with a red Chevy and its dark-haired driver.

"One bill or two?" Gladys asked, when a shopping basket filled with sandwiches, apples and packages of beef jerky was set down beside the register along with everything Flynn had chosen in sweets.

"One," Walther replied.

"Is that all you want?" she asked, disguising well a refined sense of humor that age and experience tended to provide.

"And the gas."

"Which one and how much?"

"Where's the attendant?" Flynn sarcastically wondered, though it was impossible to tell, showing no sign of even a grin.

"Called in sick!"

"Both," Walther said, in answer to her question.

"Both?" she repeated, questioningly – one that the hunter and the Sergeant silently answered by looking up from the rows of candy and staring blankly back at her.

"Twenty ought to cover the gas," Flynn soon advised, as Walther counted out bills from a large wad of cash that the store clerk couldn't help but stare at, and then suddenly avert her eyes from, when the intimidating, dark-skinned man glanced up at her.

The clerk then began totaling everything up on the cash register and, during the process, glanced out the store window and asked, "How is it the two of you ended up in the company of those pretty young things?"

"Long story," Walther responded.

"Fate," Flynn offered up as a possibility, before biting down on and beginning to chew a piece of Kimberly's favorite bubble gum.

"Not including the fuel, it's twenty-one-eighty-seven for all this junk," she told them, and likely due to the fact that a whole twenty dollars was suggested as compensation for the gas, there was no need for her to go out to the pumps to confirm what was undoubtedly a lower amount. "Will there be anything else?" she hesitantly asked.

The Sergeant blew a bubble and loudly popped it between his tongue and the roof of his mouth, giving the store clerk a little fright as the hunter scanned the shelves behind the counter. “A box of those cigars,” he decided, after locking his eyes onto the $20 ticketed, unopened package and motioning to it with a subtle nod of his head.

“Matches,” Flynn stated, as the overweight Gladys stood on her tiptoes in order to reach the cigar box.

“Yes,” Walther agreed, with a snap of his fingers, remembering that he was fresh out. “And *lots* of matches,” he told the clerk, who proceeded to provide ten little boxes of matches at no additional cost. “God forbid I should ever run out again.”

“Taxes in, forty-three-fifty plus twenty gas comes to sixty-three-fifty,” was the new total given as Gladys bagged everything up with a speed that indicated how many untold times she must have done so over the years.

The hunter then smacked his hand down onto the counter and lifted it, revealing a small stack of dollar bills in an amount that was thought to be near to the total. “The remainder is yours, ma'am,” he said, and tipped his hat before taking his leave behind the retired Sergeant. “Thank you kindly,” he added, before the door closed.

Fanning out the paper bills and realizing the enormous tip she had been given, Gladys could only gawk through the store window at the unexpected kindness of the man she had only read about in the local newspaper, watching as he and his three companions, including the old attendant who had called in sick that day, got into their vehicles and drove off, heading north out of town.

Chapter 13

Starstruck Lover

12:15 hours.

The Ruby Red, occupied by Trinity and Flynn, led the way north out of town along a sunlit paved road, thirteen miles south of the closed down Camp Scarletmere and approximately fifteen miles away from their destination safe-haven beyond the Mere's north end. A short time later, traveling a safe distance behind them with the windows down, Kimberly depressed the brake pedal of her VW Beetle and came to a stop behind the lead car that had also come to a stop, due entirely to the unexpected presence of a patrol car and a road block with an orange sign that read, **ROAD CLOSED**, in bold, black lettering. Beyond the wooden barricade and the patrol car that read *Sheriff's Department* on the driver's side door, and, presumably, on the other side as well, was a sudden and dramatic difference in the condition of the forest on just one side of the road, representing the outer limits of the Dark Demon's Lifeless Zone of influence. Soon after sunrise, people had begun to take notice of the alarming change occurring within Scarlet Forest, and understandably so.

"Wait here," Walther instructed Kimberly, as he began to exit the Blue Bug – the writer's inspired, recently-thought-of, though hardly original name for her car.

"What are you going to do?"

"Just wait here," he reiterated, and shut the door from the outside while bent over at the waist to give the driver a stern look that suggested he really meant it. "Let me borrow those sunglasses," he then requested, suddenly noticing them on top of the dash, resting up against the windshield.

"I forgot I even had these," Kimberly said, as she picked them up, quickly dusting them off on her blouse and handing them over.

As the Dark Hunter approached the Sheriff's Deputy, who appeared to be a young man who was losing his patience standing beside the driver's side door of the red Chevy, attempting to signal to and convince its stunningly attractive, scarlet-lipped, wavy-haired driver to roll her window down, he reached into the lining of his cowboy hat and withdrew a small object held casually between two fingers that were then extended to the jittery new officer of the law. When the Deputy relaxed his grip on a holstered sidearm and accepted the identification card that was strangely volunteered to him, he flipped its dark side around to white to read it, and down came the driver's side window of the red Chevy, more clearly revealing the attractive female driver whose expressionless face suddenly turned into a beautiful smile and back again the moment his eyes returned to the black and white card in his hand. "United States Secret Service?" Deputy Greene read out loud. "Why would they send *you* for a dead forest?" he asked, as he returned the card to the man who, thanks to a pair of dark sunglasses, definitely looked the part of Secret Serviceman. "And who are these girls driving you?"

Trinity was about to provide the Deputy with an honest answer when Walther held up a hand to silence her from potentially skewing what he had planned. Then, like a good student, she put her hands on the steering wheel and stared forward through the windshield in silence.

"They...know the area," Walther answered, with a brief pause that allowed him time to choose his words carefully. "They were contracted as civilian escorts to drive us."

"Who's *us?"* the young lawman next asked, and bent down to have a look at the older man in the Chevy's passenger seat, who stared forward and maintained a silent poker face.

"That is...Lieutenant-Colonel Flynn...United States Army," Walther replied, with a little added class to support the story being sold.

"A Secret Serviceman and a U.S. Army Officer?" the confused Deputy said. "Just what in the hell is going on here?"

"We think...that it might be the Russians," Walther quietly theorized, using the Cold War to the group's advantage without breaking his slightly modified persona.

Deputy Greene shifted his eyes from side to side as if suddenly wary of the presence of actual Russian spies in the vicinity. With an alarmed expression, he then stepped closer to the dark-skinned man from the Secret Service to speak very quietly in close proximity, perhaps in case *they* were listening. “You mean, like some kinda chemical weapons attack?”

Keeping up the facade that the Deputy himself was actually helping to create, Walther slowly nodded a very serious confirmation.

“My God,” Greene whispered in exasperation, and placed a hand over his mouth in shock. “Is it safe to be out here?”

“That is what...we are here to ascertain,” the Dark Hunter informed him. “In the meantime, I have to suggest that you move aside these roadblocks so that people can drive through without stopping and potentially exposing themselves to danger. It is unfortunate that you have been out here...for some time, so be certain to check yourself into a hospital if you begin to feel the onset of any...unusual symptoms.”

“O-Okay,” Greene agreed, and immediately began moving aside the two wooden barricades on his own by lifting one end and swinging them from the middle of the road and out to the shoulder. “What about *you* people?! Aren't you worried about exposure?!”

“Part of the job!” Walther quite truthfully answered, as he back-stepped to the VW. “Goes with the territory! Radio the Sheriff on your way out of here!” he added. “Tell him a Federal investigation is underway, but say nothing of a Russian attack!”

“O-Okay, but, why not?!”

“Mass panic and hysteria!”

“Right!”

Trinity and Kimberly both rolled up their driver's side windows as the inexperienced and gullible Deputy Greene left in a hurry, heading south, driving in the opposite direction from the way the other cars were facing. When the two pairs looked at one another and then through either the front or rear windshields of their respective cars in order to gauge the reaction of the other members of the party, the overall hilarity of the situation took effect, with shared laughter breaking out within the two vehicles.

On the right side of the road, the daunting, misty, petrified Scarlet

Forest defied even bright sunlight in the halted state of advance of its life-draining circumference, constantly reminding the travelers that the one responsible for it all had receded into the safety of her dark domain. Luckily, with the sun beaming down through a cloudless sky, forcing at least some degree of light through the mist and down to the road, the remainder of the drive proved to be uneventful and consisted mainly of filling up on the food and snacks that were mostly divided between the four weary travelers.

As they neared their blessed destination, the treeline that was expected to be just as petrified as the rest of the forest in the area was surprisingly showing signs of life once more. The closer they approached, the more dramatic the restoration of the flora and fauna within the isolated area seemed to be, reminding the travelers that the blessing cast upon the house now bathed in unveiled sunlight, slowly coming into view as hanging branches passed overhead, was not only in full effect, but really could not be disenchanted by anyone or anything other than the original enchanter.

Two cars rolling along a gravel driveway produced a rumbling sound under eight tires until they simultaneously came to a stop in front of the sunlit safe-haven not long after midday. The Looms' house looked and felt very different in the light of day, but even when blanketed by nightfall, no force of darkness could corrupt the land on which it stood so long as the indestructible Scarlet Starsword remained in existence.

Having safely arrived, the two pairs consisting each of a man and woman began unloading the supplies they'd brought along from Darkstar G&H. Upon opening the trunk of the Ruby Red, Trinity's focus was on gathering up as many of the shopping bags, all of which contained the group's new clothes, that she could possibly hook onto the fingers of both hands. Flynn, being the ex-soldier who quite unofficially answered the call of a return to duty, took to carrying in the new weapons and the boxes upon boxes of revolver ammunition. While eating an apple, Walther, being the only one among them who could manage the mass and weight of the cloaked item angled across the floor of the VW, carried only that across his shoulders, finally relieving the vehicle's compressed shocks. Kimberly, however, stuck to carrying her satchel along with her remaining candy and the group's other, less important food items.

With an apple pinned between his teeth in mid bite, the hunter somehow managed to use his lock pick one-handed, unlocking and opening up the solid wood door before he put away the handy tool and bit the rest of the way through the Golden Delicious piece of fruit in his mouth. Chewing away on one of his favorite juicy varieties, he stood aside and waited for the others to enter first before he began moving through the entryway at a slight angle to avoid damaging the walls with the Relic he carried, and would quite cautiously set down on an area rug that covered part of the ebony hardwood floor under the piano in the living room.

"I really need to take a shower," Trinity said, after setting down several shopping bags of clothes onto the big blue sofa.

"I will go and get the generator running again," Walther responded, feeling rather exhausted, yet managing to avoid falling for the living room's lure of comfort in order to take care of one last chore before he would allow himself to finally take a well deserved rest.

With the hunter taking his leave, the old Sergeant placed the new revolver boxes and a carton of ammo for each one out on the coffee table while the candy-loving writer began to once again focus her attention on adding more information to her notebook, leaving the youngest member of the group with nothing to do but to remove her belt along with Ol' Loudmouth before resting herself down in the oversize chair that was most to her liking.

"I can't help but wonder how this is going to end," Kimberly said, voicing her written concern from her seat in the living room's gold-colored, oversize chair, while Flynn sat on the sofa inspecting a single chambered round as it was rotated around in the Python's clicking cylinder to be sure it was in proper alignment. "It could occur any number of ways. Will we be successful with relative ease, or will the goal be achieved with great difficulty? Will we survive the inevitable encounter with death, herself, or die during the effort ourselves? Perhaps we will make it through to claim victory unscathed, or perhaps we will suffer a tragic loss in the process. Part of me fears that victory cannot be achieved without sacrifice, while another part simultaneously hopes that that won't be the case, even while knowing that our dark foe is driven by neither fear nor hope."

"She *just is,"* Flynn stated, as the simplest and most rational way of understanding her motives, or lack thereof.

"Well, what do *you* think, Trinity?" Kimberly asked, seeking an alternate perspective, with her eyes and pen still down on her notebook.

The sound of gentle snoring provided the only answer she would receive from the exhausted young woman who had very cutely fallen fast asleep between the arms of a scarlet-colored chair. A soothing voice echoed in the dream world of her mind – a voice responsible for lulling her directly into a state of rapid eye movement wherein she dreamed of reuniting with the ancient weapon she was once too terrified to touch.

Sleep... Sleep...

Looking up at the sound of snoring, seeing who the culprit was, though saying nothing to awaken her, the writer switched to her sketchbook and quietly took a seat on the floor, directly in front of a darkly-dressed sleeping beauty whose lovely scarlet lips beneath her tipped-down cowgirl hat could truly shame the red, red rose.

Not long after that, the hunter returned to the house and made his way directly to the living room, rubbing his tired eyes, only to find a certain blonde Englishwoman sitting cross-legged on the floor, staring up at his apprentice, sketching the shape of her beautiful face and the outline of the chair she had fallen asleep in. Walking around to the busy artist's back, "Get some rest," he quietly suggested, and gave her shoulder a squeeze before continuing on his way to the west end of the ground floor, disappearing into the darkness of an unlit hallway.

Completing enough of the rough sketch to finish it from a more comfortable seat, the Englishwoman turned her head to look toward the sofa behind her, seeing that the old Sergeant was still sitting there, though he'd moved on to running a small wire brush through each of the six empty chambers in the rotating cylinder of Walther's old Colt Python.

"Would you like to sleep on the sofa or in one of the rooms upstairs?" Flynn preemptively asked her, detecting her looking at him by no means other than his peripheral vision, keeping his usually raspy voice to a minimum and, in that moment, his natural tone of voice managed to come through.

“No way I'm going back up there,” she quietly responded, as she got back on her feet while looking at the sleeping young woman in the chair, having not at all forgotten about the traumatizing experience of the second floor that would prove to be incomparable to the experience of what was soon to come.

~

In the lower west-end guest room, the tired hunter removed his jacket, kicked off his boots, unbuttoned his vest and shirt and stripped them off together, and finally walked straight across the hall and into the guest bathroom wearing nothing more than a pair of gray socks and a pair of underwear to match. After closing and locking the door, he leaned up against it bearing no small amount of anxiety and fatigue in both body and mind.

You need not suffer this on your own. Allow me to---

“No!” he said aloud, in response to the Great Voice within.

In the living room, the attention of the writer and the old Sergeant were suddenly drawn toward the hallway and then to each other before they both shrugged their shoulders at nearly the same time.

The offer is appreciated, the hunter internally voiced in response, *but I must deal with this in my own way,* he reasoned, while removing the last of his clothes. *I trust that you will continue to augment and advise me in other ways,* he internalized, as he reached into the shower to turn it on, knowing and not really caring that the generator had not been on long enough to make the water even somewhat warm.

Yes, Young Master.

Why do you call me that? Oh, never mind. I am sure I already know, he realized, as he stepped into the standalone shower and shut the frosted glass door to begin washing away the dirt and the doubt.

~

13:30 hours.

After finishing the pencil sketch that was shaded in red to highlight the chair, Trinity's scarlet lips, and a subtle amount of color within the hard-pressed graphite shading that the artist curiously detected to be mysteriously showing in the hair of the young woman who slept unknowing of the additional alterations to her physical appearance, Kimberly kindly tucked a blanket around her sleeping friend and curled up on the sofa as Flynn headed up the cobweb-covered staircase. Thankfully, the house was clear of spiders, and the webs, themselves, were mere remnants of the previous occupants that had been dispatched by scarlet fire.

Upon reaching the second floor, the old Sergeant faced the decision of choosing a bedroom, and rather than entertain the idea of going down the still dark and ominous western hallway, he turned away to the right and walked to the end of the eastern hall where he discovered the master bedroom. Entirely at odds with the military man, the room was lit only by the veiled sunlight that made it through the sugar pink curtains that were drawn shut in front of the windows. The framed floral paintings that hung on the walls had been collecting dust for a year, as were the bedside tables and the dresser featuring an attached mirror that the Sergeant sat in front of on a lone wooden chair. Looking through the smallest drawers on the end, just out of curiosity, he discovered a hair brush and a bottle of sweet smelling perfume in the first, a bottle of disinfectant in the second, and a Zippo lighter, an intricately designed brass key, and several packages of incense in the third. Knowing that everything had belonged to Leona, the recently departed Caretaker, as the hunter had referred to her, he withdrew one of the incense sticks from the only opened package and held it horizontally under his nose. Deciding he liked it, and as a way of honoring the deceased, he set it into the dusty incense holder that had been left on top of the dresser and lit the tip using the silver lighter he claimed as his own. After watching the flame grow in intensity for a few seconds, he blew it out and then stood up from the chair, staring at the rising smoke as he removed his duster hat and trench coat, both of which blended with the olive drab of his underlying army fatigues, serving to camouflage him well – in forested environments, anyway. In the Caretaker's bedroom, all things being considered, he didn't exactly blend in. Practically every color, other than the one he was wearing, was featured in at least one of the floral paintings that decorated the walls. And so, enjoying the jasmine scent that quickly permeated throughout the room, the old Sergeant yawned as he retired to the comfort of the raised bed that had been protected from the accumulation of dust by the privacy curtain that had been drawn shut around it.

The Looms' house was dead silent as the four took respite within, protected by an enchantment that kept the unnatural darkness at bay beyond the edge of the property. A few hours passed by in the sleepy old home when the two women in the living room were sharply awoken by a loud banging.

"I'm awake," Kimberly said, defensively, right before she rolled off the sofa in a daze and fell onto the floor amid the banging that repeated again and again. "What *is* that? What's going on?" she asked Trinity, who was still seated in her chair, but wide awake with her head turned toward the front of the house.

"Oh, jeez, he found me," she said, as she stared right through the walls with the aid of her new ability to easily ascertain the cause of the banging on the front door.

"Who?" Kimberly immediately thought to ask.

"My boyfriend," Trinity replied. "What should I do?" she asked the writer, who was by that time peering around the curtain and through the window at the man on the doorstep.

"Oh, my God..." Kimberly slowly spoke, upon realizing who it was that was so impatiently pounding on the door. *"He's* your boyfriend?"

"Yeah..?" she confirmed from her chair.

"What are the chances?" Kimberly mumbled to herself, as she continued looking between the curtains at the casually dressed man sporting tan cargo shorts and a plain brown t-shirt.

"I'll hide," Trinity suggested as an idea, while seated on her knees in a reverse position, peeking over the top of the chair at her English friend before quickly lowering herself just out of sight.

"What are you on about? He *knows* we're in here."

"How?" the hidden young woman asked, as if she was genuinely surprised by the writer's statement.

"The cars are out front," it was suggested, being that they were the most blatantly obvious reason that someone was sure to be home.

"Dammit..."

The pounding continued as they quickly moved through the house and down the hall to the entryway, not at all knowing that Walther would not be a happy hunter to have been disturbed so soon after going to sleep. Opening up the door, “You're *waking* everybody *up!”* Kimberly exclaimed, harshly scolding the man.

“You!” he angrily responded, upon gaining confirmation to what he suspected. “You couldn't leave well enough alone, could you? Where is she!? *Trinity!?”* he shouted into the house, as he attempted to push the door all the way open to get by the blonde writer, who, to his complete surprise, produced a small revolver at her waist, aimed at his midsection.

“Ah, ah, ah,” she quickly said, vocalizing her discouragement, causing the physically fit, dirty-blonde-haired young man to back off. “I didn't say you could come in. We're in the middle of a very important mission and can't be disturbed.”

“What, *sleeping?”* he mockingly responded, and received a confirmation from the armed Englishwoman in the form of a thoughtful expression followed by a nod with raised eyebrows. “Look, lady...” he began to say.

“Kimberly,” she interrupted, “but, it's Ms. Hunter, to *you.”*

He scoffed, saying, “...Whatever. I don't believe for a second that you convinced her to come back here, and I have half a mind to get the Sheriff involved,” he threatened. “How do you think he'll react when I tell him you're holding my girl here, at gunpoint, all for the sake of your so-called story?”

The writer couldn't help but scoff, herself, and laugh in mockery of the preposterous accusation. “You assume she's here not of her own free will.”

“Well, isn't she?”

“Actually, that's an interesting psychological question,” she realized, her attention wandering away from the moment, until she made a mental note to explore the idea in future writings.

“Don't you know that she's afraid of this place?”

“Not anymore she isn't.”

“Will you just let me see her, already?”

“That's not such a good idea.”

“And why not?”

“...I can't even begin to answer that,” Kimberly admitted, after trying and failing to formulate even a semi-plausible explanation.

"Who else is here, anyway?" the young man asked, in pursuit of answers along a different line of questioning, accepting that he would continue to get nowhere in asking about his girlfriend.

"Why should I tell *you?"*

"What possible harm could it do?"

"...One whom you refused to help."

"You're lying," he incorrectly assumed. "Walther's in jail."

"Not anymore he isn't."

"If that's true then bring him to the door and let me talk to him."

"That won't be necessary," Kimberly plainly responded, after Trinity whispered in her ear from just out of sight behind the door.

"God... And why is that?" he asked, doing his best to conceal a great deal of frustration.

"Because he's right behind you."

After turning around and looking straight back from where he was standing, the curly-haired, dirty-blonde young man with a light beard saw nothing but the cars parked in the driveway. "Nice try, but I don't see---"

At that very moment, the Dark Hunter stepped forward and disenchanted the shield of rending light from around his body, making it seem as if he had slowly and fractionally materialized from entirely out of nowhere to angrily stand face-to-face with an unwelcome guest who was then too scared stiff to move.

---Walther."

The Dark Hunter scowled and firmly gestured for him to head on into the house, and when he turned around to do so in acceptance of the darkly-dressed man's demand, he again froze in place at the sight of the most strikingly beautiful, darkly-dressed woman he'd ever set his eyes on.

"Hi, John," a sweetly timid, familiar voice said to him.

That was the last thing he heard before passing out due to shock.

Chapter 14

Looking Back

17:30 hours.

Having caught the unwelcome visitor from behind before he fell to the stone walkway, the hunter stood there on the doorstep in the presence of two female onlookers with his hands under John's arms, unimpressed by the young man's reaction and fairly annoyed by the fact that they had to assume responsibility for his unconscious state.

“What are we going to do with him?” Kimberly asked.

“We could always bury him in the back yard,” Walther suggested.

“Very funny,” Trinity responded, as she took hold of her boyfriend's legs and, together with her mentor, carried him into the house. “That man *was* my father, you know.”

“Apologies,” Walther said, with a bit of a grunt, feeling that Camp Scarletmere's manager had put on some muscle since he last saw him. “I had forgotten about that.”

Feeling anxious as a result of what was surely a suspicious-looking situation, the writer instinctively poked her head outside and glanced from side to side, though the chances of anyone seeing their suspicious activities were practically nonexistent. The one thing she took notice of was a brown Studebaker parked on the other side of the Ruby Red before she closed and locked the heavy door to follow behind the hunter, forming several questions she wished to ask him about his newly revealed ability that shed light on how he always managed to appear from out of the blue. “How did you *do* that?!” she called out, as she fast-walked down the corridor beyond the entryway.

“Later!” Walther responded, feeling a little preoccupied as he and his apprentice turned left in front of the grand staircase, moving through the open double doors of the living room.

After dumping the man's unconscious body onto the sofa, the

hunter immediately proceeded to pick up his new belt and holster from atop the coffee table, strapping it securely around his waist. “Now would be an appropriate time for the two of you to get prepared,” he suggested, while glancing between the two women. “Take all of the weapons with you,” he instructed, as he quickly unboxed and began to load the customized Super Blackhawk.

“Don't hurt him,” Trinity requested, feeling a tad bit nervous.

“I need to be here to document this,” Kimberly said in objection, feeling that what was going to happen next would surely be noteworthy.

“No, you do not,” Walther insisted, as he took a seat in the gold-colored chair facing the sofa, where he continued to load to capacity the hunting revolver resting across his lap. “I can recall every single detail for you at a later time, no matter *how* obscure,” he assured her, sounding enigmatic, until she remembered that his apprentice had made a similar claim once before. *“Trinity,”* he boldly said, and without having to speak another word to his trusting apprentice, he watched as she picked up the new belt and holster containing his old Colt Python with one hand, and two brand new, sheathed hunting knives with the other, before forcing them into the arms of the writer.

Trinity then glanced around the living room for the Smith and Wesson M29 she removed prior to falling asleep. “Where's mine?”

“Flynn has it,” her mentor answered, quite appreciating the safety bar that prevented accidental firing of the loaded sixth chamber. “Take the Python, instead,” he advised, and motioned with a nod to the gun that hung down in its secured holster, attached to the belt that was haphazardly draped over the shoulder of the writer. “It is much more suited to you. Plenty of stopping power if you load with .357, and not as much kickback.”

“So, this is really the same gun that you used to save her that night. I don't know how I feel about this.”

The Dark Hunter glanced up at them and back to his own weapon before he nodded, remembering the fateful night from one year prior that served as a catalyst for the rebirth of an ancient ally. “If things had not unfolded in just the way that they did, the sword would most likely never have come to you.”

With her hands free, Trinity sadly nodded and picked up a few of the shopping bags containing their new clothes and ushered the stubborn writer back through the open double doors and up the grand staircase, leaving her mentor sitting in an oversize living room chair with a loaded gun in his lap, patiently awaiting the awakening of John.

Shutting his eyes for awhile, the hunter soon detected movement in the room by way of the sound of someone tossing and turning on the sofa, though even with his eyes shut tight he could still see everything as if illuminated using an unseen third eye if he chose to. Not long after that, John suddenly burst awake, sitting up straight on the sofa.

"Welcome back," a deep, familiar voice said to him, immediately drawing his attention toward the center of the room.

"Walther..." he said in acknowledgment. "How did I get in here?" he wondered, having no recollection of his fainting spell on the doorstep. "Where is she? What did you do to her?" he impatiently asked, leaving no time for a response in between each question.

The hunter looked toward the top of the staircase and beyond. "Taking a bath with Ms. Hunter."

"Huh?" John responded, as he turned himself around to face the darkly-dressed man whose grin as a match was struck to light the cigar in his mouth suggested that he must have been joking, and so he began to stand up to seek out his altered girlfriend when the unmistakable sound of a clicking gun hammer forced him to reconsider.

"Well," Walther said, as he puffed on and rotated the cigar to ensure that it evenly lit before shaking the flame of the match out, "here we are again," he stated, in reminiscence of one night in particular.

"What are you going to teach me about *this* time?" John quite mockingly asked, as indicated by his chosen tone of voice and an accompanying demeanor that included the crossing of his arms.

"What is it you wish to know?" Walther openly offered, as a trail of smoke slowly swirled upward and faded away into the air.

"Everything," John demanded. "How you appeared from out of nowhere, for one thing. I want to know how you got out of jail. I want to know how you convinced Trinity to go with you and why she looks the way she does. I want to know what you're doing with that blonde

writer who thinks she's got some grand story to tell, and I want to know what the hell the three of you are doing in the Looms' house, which, by the way, is technically my father's house, ever since the Caretaker disappeared last year."

"Four of us," Walther corrected, singling out an incorrect assumption. "Well, five at this present time, including yourself."

"Who's the other?"

"That would be Sergeant Flynn."

"M-Misery Flynn?" said John, sounding more than surprised, practically choking on his words. "That crazy old man from town?"

"That crazy old man..." Walther said, pausing only to exhale a plume of smoke, "...was a Master Sergeant in the United States Army, and a man twice decorated for valor during World War Two. He has taken it upon himself to further assist the world in its time of need."

"I don't understand," John admitted. "What time of need?"

Slightly annoyed, the hunter stared at him and retro-haled a little of the cigar smoke before quickly exhaling through his nose, quite like an angry bull, wondering how the man could possibly witness so many telltale signs and still remain ignorant and unaware.

Show him.

The Dark Hunter glanced at the covered object on the floor below the piano and remembered what his father had told him many a time. Accepting that the man seated across from him would not and could not believe the unbelievable yet truthful explanations for everything he wanted to know, and thus, in the interest of sparing time, he agreed with the unexpected suggestion that only he could detect and fathom the meaning of. While standing up from the cushioned, golden chair, he turned it to the right so that it faced the direction of the matching chair in the favorite color of his apprentice, and *vice versa,* making it so that the two chairs of nearly identical styles faced the other.

"What are you doing?" John asked, having already become highly suspicious and leery of the altered arrangement of the furniture.

"Sit," Walther nicely requested, returning to his chair, motioning for the young man to take over the vacant golden chair that had been realigned first and foremost.

Resisting the offer at first, John remained seated on the sofa with his arms crossed and his feet planted flat on the floor. "You're playing the part of psychiatrist, now?" he prodded, referencing the fact that the hunter had cleverly deceived him and many others a year prior. "Why don't you just have me lay on the couch, doc?"

"Is it your wish to know the truth, or not? This is by far the most effective method."

"Fine," he reluctantly agreed, and made his way over to the chair in the color he actually liked most of all. "I'll play your little game."

The hunter subtly shook his head from side to side. "If this is a game, it is the most deadly game of all. There will be no unknowing of what you will soon come to learn," he warned, before scooting his chair much closer to the other so that they were seated directly in front of one another. "Are you prepared?"

"For what?"

"Look into my eyes. Look into my eyes. Seriously, now, I need you to look directly into my eyes if this is going to work."

"Is this some sort of hypnosis?"

"In a manner of speaking," Walther replied, and the moment John begrudgingly leaned forward and locked eyes with his, the eyes of the Spirit of Light came through as an opaque silver-white, paralyzing the body of the ensnared young man in order to isolate his spirit and take it on a wild ride through recent history.

~

The process of memory integration began with the soul-crushing event of a stormy night and the death of Walther's father, who lay at home in a soft bed with his teenage son at his side, issuing the boy his final charge. Tears streamed down the younger Dark Hunter's face as he sat at the deathbed of the great man, the wandering preacher in disguise, who had taught his son everything he knew. As strength faded from his body and his voice, the continuing, undying mission of the Walther family came to rest on the shoulders of young Marcus.

With the streaking of stars that moved his consciousness forward in time, John suddenly found himself standing on a grassy hillside overlooking a body of water that was quite familiar to him. The sun was already shining bright from a perceived low-rising angle of morning, causing him to hold up his hand to shield his eyes, and just as he did, so did another man who lowered himself down to the ground to balance on his toes and take in the incredible view. Attempts to speak to the hunter and gain his attention yielded no response, and with a furrowing of his brow, a rapid blinking of his eyes and a thoughtful moment, he realized that he could neither be seen nor heard.

Hearing the faint sound of footsteps rustling against the grass behind them, Walther rose up from the ground as John turned around to find a beautiful, long-haired brunette approaching only one of them, with a smile and a summer dress so lovely in combination that she undoubtedly possessed the power to melt even the most bold and steadfast man. The woman, of course, was Leona, the Caretaker, who, before he could speak to her, instantly forgetting that he wasn't really there, disappeared down a forest path with a dark-haired girl in a white dress leading the way home.

With his vision suddenly going black, John went into a panic, and even more so when his sight was restored to the red, gruesome horror of blood-soaked floors and putrid guts of animal remains in the room of an old cabin. Knives, machetes and other blood-soaked blades hung from a wall of death, causing him to turn away in fear and disgust only to be further shocked by the presence of the distracted hunter, who stood unaware that a larger man was silently approaching him with a knife drawn and held in murderous fashion, about to deliver a killing strike. Before he could intervene, his vision cut to black and slowly began to return with each blink of his eyes, and all the while the heavy, labored breaths and groans of an injured man could be heard nearby. By the time his sight was clear again, the wounded man, whom he determined to be none other than Walther, was gone. On the floor where he had been standing lay the body of his burly attacker, left for dead in a widening pool of blood that, much to his dismay, suddenly began receding inward at the very moment his vision began fading to black.

Feeling a pull on his consciousness and its subsequent injection into what he accepted was another past event in which he had no control, John found himself staring into his own reflection, listening to a conversation already well underway in what he recognized was the master bedroom of the Looms' house. Seated in a chair facing the attached mirror of a dresser, he stood to his feet and turned around to observe the lovely Leona attending to the well-stitched shoulder wound of a shirtless, dark-skinned hunter. With the sweet, floral smell of incense in the air, he watched the Caretaker hold a cloth to a bottle of disinfectant and tip it upside down for a moment, allowing the cloth to absorb some of the clear liquid. Leaning his back against the dark wood wall that ran parallel with the side of the bed, John crossed his arms in front of his chest and got as comfortable as he could while enjoying the fact that as tough as Walther was, he nonetheless winced and growled from the stinging pain of the disinfectant.

I told you, now hold still.

Looking around the room at the floral paintings that decorated the walls, he began to wonder why he was being shown that particular moment in time when he suddenly heard Leona make a request that recaptured and held his undivided attention.

Why don't you finish telling me what you and John know about the Mere?

As Walther spoke, John began to put it all together in conjunction with his own experiences that, until that time, could not be explained rationally. According to the hunter, who sat shirtless, hat-less and uncharacteristically nervous as a gorgeous woman attended to him on her bed, the body of water known as Scarletmere had been cursed long ago, in ancient times. Anyone who came into contact with it was subject to being influenced or even controlled altogether, especially during the time of a full moon, as it was somehow able to hijack their senses and emotions.

Human emotion is a target. A source of power. Control human emotions and you control ***them****; their desires and their actions, circumventing natural will.*

With neither Leona nor John able to comprehend the point of it all, Walther attempted to make it perfectly clear to one of them in stating that to become immortal, the Mere must acquire human souls for itself – a statement so disturbing that the lovely host and Caretaker flinched and caused the hunter to experience some amount of unnecessary pain. Already on edge, John was suddenly startled into correcting his seemingly relaxed posture when he heard Walther yell out in pain, only to return to leaning up against the wall with a shake of his head when Leona apologized for unintentionally hurting her patient, and the unsettling story continued.

The next statement that John took in as he listened and watched the two seated on the bed, was that the mere longed for a vessel to ease the process of soul collection – *vessel* being a word that Leona correctly interpreted to mean *body*. With occult sacrifice and enough blood in the water – an expression normally used to explain causality – the Mere developed a dark life force within itself. A consciousness, to which the duality of good and evil did not apply, emerged when enough soul energy was gathered together.

As the Caretaker and the Dark Hunter began to ease their obvious sexual tension and attraction to one another with laughter and levity, all of which John found to be highly amusing, the light bulbs of the lamps in the room suddenly went out, throwing the room into darkness. A dim light was detected out of the corner of his eye to be emanating slightly to his right, and moving toward the bedroom door, he discovered the source in the form of a brass candelabra bearing three lit candles atop a corner table in the hallway. More than that, in the foreground of the candlelight was the hunter, knelt down on one knee, embracing and consoling a familiar dark-haired girl.

There, there, girl. Everything will be okay from now on.

As Walther continued to comfort her, she turned her head toward the dark bedroom where John stood watching the memory of the scarred, sweet girl he recognized as Lydia. It was when her gaze lowered to the floor and her expression of comfort and security in the arms of the hunter dramatically shifted to one of anger that John hesitantly turned around to follow her line of sight, knowing what he was going to find. Though he was sure it wasn't there a moment ago, a body with a masked face – a large, horrific tribal mask that was burned into his memory, weakly illuminated by the glow of the candles, bearing an expression of anger that nearly matched the girl's own – lay twitching on the floor, apparently still alive after suffering what he already knew to be multiple gunshot wounds. With the aid of his own memory, the next occurrence was somewhat anticipated, with Lydia passing right through him and dropping to her knees, brandishing a dagger that she began to violently thrust into the chest of the man who was her father, again and again and again, producing more and more blood to stain her pretty, white dress. Disturbed by what he was seeing and knowing there was nothing he could do to stop her, he backed away and averted his eyes at the final thrust's moment of impact before Walther, having failed in his first attempt, intervened for a second time by forcibly picking up the oddly satisfied girl from around the waist. As John stood in the glow of candlelight with his back to the hall, nearly traumatized from actually seeing the gruesome details of what happened that night, frozen in both shock and sadness for Lydia, he found that the smile on her face as she was carried away was nearly as disturbing as the bloody incident itself.

Right after that, suddenly and completely without warning, the ceiling, floors and walls of the bedroom cracked and split apart as if the entire house was being torn asunder by an unseen force, and as the structure seemed to be collapsing all around him, John instinctively shut his eyes and raised an arm up to his head, bracing himself for the fall and to protect himself from injury. There was no fall, however, as the sensation of wind and raindrops on his skin caused him to reopen his eyes. Instead, he found himself unharmed, standing in a grassy, rainy clearing below a darkened sky. Hearing voices behind him, he whipped around to find Walther and a younger, cute-faced, unaltered version of Trinity – the one he was then used to seeing on a daily basis – standing out in the storm, facing one another in a heated confrontation he remembered witnessing from afar. As the two were visibly seen to be arguing back and forth, John turned around, shielding his eyes from the rain with his arm, looking toward the lighted cabins in the camp where he saw himself standing with a similar posture, trying to get a view of what was happening through the pouring rain. After a year of wondering what could have happened to set Trinity off that night, he realized that he would soon know the truth for himself, as she had evaded the subject time and time again.

With the sound of the storm dying down, though it did not actually let up, while the sound of their distant location increased so that he could hear what was happening, oddly enough, what Walther had told him a year ago turned out to be true, though the explanation that was reduced to its most basic yet still unbelievable form fell utterly short of capturing the stunning event that began with a series of visible sparks and auditory snaps in his girlfriend's hand. In the blink of an eye, the object she recovered from the ground was transformed into an otherworldly sword that momentarily burned a bright, blazing red aura until it fell from the hand of its unprepared counterpart.

John found himself transported, staring directly at the upended, scarlet red sword stuck in the wet ground by a long and thin triangular blade that together with its hilt and cross guard gave it a sleek, four-point-star-shaped appearance – details that were taken in with astonishment and bewilderment as he moved around it in a fearful semi-circle in order to keep his distance and get closer to the ensuing conversation. Knowing what was seconds away from happening, he sat on the ground next to the distraught girl who would become his significant other in time and took in the hard to swallow truth about her relationship to Lydia – a fact he was not privy to until that very moment – along with the disturbing fact of the then-recently-deceased girl's resurrection. Not long after that, shaking his head well in advance of what he knew from experience to be a deception, John watched as Trinity calmly headed to the driver's side door of her car while telling the hunter that the passenger side was already unlocked. Of course, it wasn't, and despite the many pleas from the darkly-dressed hunter who remained alongside the Chevy for as long as he could, Trinity frantically drove off into the night, desperate to get away from a situation she couldn't handle and a mission she did not want to accept.

When the taillights of the Ruby Red disappeared beyond the treeline of the forest – the forest that in the present was no longer lush and healthy in the area of the camp – John's attention turned to the hunter who appeared to be headed directly toward him with a rather intense glare. Remembering that he couldn't be seen, and though he wasn't actually there, he instinctively sidestepped out of the hunter's path and turned to follow him when his eyes locked onto the fading glow of a sword that would be pulled out of the earth by the time it and his vision together went dark.

The last event he would be shown came in the form of a viewpoint looking down the dock that extended out onto the Mere from the shore of the camp, and at the end of the furthest platform, standing in the moonlight, was the Dark Hunter, who slowly unsheathed a most unique sword at his waist, exposing it to the light of the moon that rendered its silver-colored blade the deepest red.

Hold it right there!

~

Hearing the rumbling sound of an iron jail cell door closing and slamming shut, John's consciousness returned to his body in natural time, released from the captive and captivating experience of Walther's memories. With the overwhelming process of memory integration completed, the glow of the hunter's silver eyes slowly faded away, leaving John in a state of emotional shock. Tears welled up in his eyes as he sat motionless while the furniture was moved back into position, and still as the other man in the room resumed smoking the still-lit cigar tasting of coffee and cream that had been set down on the very same plate that was left right there in the living room over one year ago, used once again as an ashtray. In silence, they remained below the light of the chandelier that hung down from the high ceiling, with the Dark Hunter standing, smoking and patiently staring down at the changed man, giving him ample time to process the life-changing experience while awaiting his first words spoken thereafter.

"You aim to kill her," John concluded.

"She is already dead," Walther sadly corrected. "We intend to destroy her before *she* destroys *us.* Do not mistake the memory of sweet Lydia with the darkness that has overtaken her body. To do so would be a grave mistake, and I mean that both metaphorically and in the literal sense. The ancient demon in her youthful skin will stop at nothing to get what it wants, and what it wants is to acquire life energy to the point where no single force will be of any threat to its dark dominion over the world."

"Not even..."

Knowing what he was going to ask, the Dark Hunter had already begun shaking his head, indicating negative.

"...you and Trinity..?"

"At *that* point, there exists only one remaining chance for victory. However, it has never happened before, much less even attempted. The degree of difficulty is beyond exceptional."

"What would you have to do?"

Walther slowly blinked his eyes and gave his head a quick double shake, knowing and somewhat signifying that the question asked was at least partially out of context with the answer.

Having trouble reconciling the new truths given to him, the camp owner's son drew in a deep breath through his nose as he rested his head back against the golden fabric of the chair, shutting his eyes. "This is insane," he plainly admitted. "More so because it actually *is* all true. I mean, what happened to Bennett, Leona and Lydia, even Shane and Maggie...they're all dead because of the moon's affect on the Mere."

"Now you know what the town and the Mere were actually named after," Walther pointed out, as a slow-moving, wispy trail of cigar smoke floated around his hat. "A long time ago, Native Americans of the Cree tribe lived all over the State before most of them relocated to what is now Canada. They called the Mere, *mihkwâkamiw,* meaning, *the red water.* They learned to steer clear of it, though I am certain, now, that the lesson came to them at a significant cost."

"What makes you certain of *that?"* John wondered.

"My counterpart," Walther answered, nodding his head in the direction of the piano.

Wide-eyed, John stared at the covered object laying across the floor in front of the piano bench, by that time having some understanding of what the word *counterpart* actually suggested. "There are *two* of them!?" he exclaimed, and gripped the arms of his chair as a result of a memory that flashed in his mind – a memory originally not his own – suddenly remembering how afraid of the fire sword he had been and still was. "How can there be *two* of them?" he asked, a question born out of the strange feeling of being scared and curious at the same time.

"Six."

"Huh?"

"There are *six* Divine Relics," Walther corrected, as he tapped the top of his cigar with his index finger to clear the ashes from the tip. "Wherever the other four are, I do not know," he said, as he, too, stared across the living room at the cloak-covered weapon. "It is exceedingly rare for two of them to be active at the same time. We are most fortunate to have them as allies."

"Fortunate?" John repeated in disbelief. "You call this insanity *fortunate?"*

Ignoring the man's apparent pessimism, Walther began moving toward the piano, setting John even more on edge than he already was. "This one came to the aid of my grandfather in the year 1900, and long before that, to one of the Cree whose tribe was being massacred by the very same demon overtaking this land once again," he explained, before he crouched down and began uncovering the weapon. "Do not worry, I have no intention of evoking it here."

With that said, apprehension gave way to curiosity, and John at last stood up from his chair to look over the hunter's shoulder and see the relic for himself. What he witnessed in the few moments that it was exposed was a sleek, silver-colored object of approximately five feet in length by no more than ten inches in height at its largest end, very much resembling a long rifle, only larger. What might be called the weapon's barrel had a unique oval shape, though the relic's design was thoroughly unique, for certain. Its smooth, contoured underside was undoubtedly shaped to accommodate the hands of one strong enough to wield it. Along the right side that was facing the ceiling and, presumably on the other, in keeping with the symmetrical design of what looked to him to be an otherworldly creation, was a row of horizontally cut vents for what he figured was airflow and heat distribution purposes, though he would eventually find out that he couldn't have been more wrong in that regard. Though the relic resembled the shape of a firearm, there was no apparent action and no working parts that were externally visible. There was no hammer to cock, no trigger to pull, and no place to insert ammunition, at least, not in any caliber or form he was familiar with.

"I suppose there was a bit more that you wanted to know," Walther acknowledged, as he covered up the weapon. "I would have simply shown you, myself, but the aftereffects are quite draining. Something tells me you might be willing to listen to words, now, so you might want to sit down again," he suggested, as he took a seat on the sofa and rubbed his tired eyes before he began with explaining that it was Kimberly and Flynn who together convinced the Sheriff to set him free. After that, he knew that finding Trinity was first on his list of next-to-impossible things to accomplish and, uncertain where to begin his search again, it was the writer who suggested that it would be easiest to look for the last name *Ryder* in the phone books of surrounding towns and cities and to systematically call each number asking for her, as her family name was somewhat uncommon and there was a reasonable chance of success in the lowest amount of time. Of course, the hunter knew that the wily young woman would never agree to meet with them, but, lo and behold, on attempt number seven, a woman with a Japanese accent answered the phone. Upon hearing the name of her adopted daughter, she responded to the caller's polite inquiry and charming accent by simply informing her that Trinity had moved in with her boyfriend. Playing the made-up-on-the-spot role of a friend from last summer, the clever and persistent writer even managed to acquire an address that was only a moderate drive away. With some initially delicate conversation followed by an evocation and immediate convincing on the part of the Fire Spirit that awakened within the Starsword, Trinity finally agreed to play her fated part.

"Scarlet, as she agreed to be called, cast a Great Blessing on the area surrounding this house," Walther said, in between puffs of his expiring cigar, "but you should be aware that the petrified forest is now Lydia's territory. We managed to survive several encounters with her and her minions thus far, but she continues to surprise with abilities I can only describe as...disturbing. Thankfully, I have a surprise of my own, though I cannot help but be aware that something is being kept hidden from me."

Appearing to him to be having further, or, in the very least, continued difficulty processing everything that had transpired over the last year or so, the hunter opted to leave the overwhelmed man alone for awhile, but not without offering to make him something warm to drink, helping to ease the process of settling-in to the new knowledge. "Best you just sit there for awhile and let it all sink in. Can I offer you some coffee, or perhaps a cup of tea?"

Not even bothering to ask which of the two he would prefer, due to the fact that John was sitting there nodding and mumbling to himself about the events of the past, the hunter headed for the kitchen to ready a pot of each, knowing that the others would very likely be requiring a pick-me-up as well.

~

On the second floor, Flynn slept soundly in a very comfortable bed, entirely undisturbed by the commotion that had taken place at the front door and in the bathroom as well, just down the hall from the master bedroom where two beautiful women were toweling dry.

"I didn't think we'd have time to do a wash, so I commandeered some of Leona's underthings," Trinity explained. "They've been in a dresser drawer for a year, but knowing her, I'm sure they're clean."

"She had great taste," Kimberly commented, allowing her towel to fall to the floor so she could slip into a matching pair of icy-blue-colored undergarments, having already accepted that it no longer mattered if her friend saw her in the nude, because, truth be told, she already had and could, anytime she wanted, now that it was within her ability to control.

Trinity, of course, had chosen the closest set to red: A matching pair of bra and panties in burgundy that she slipped into after rubbing her hair mostly dry using the cottony-soft, pink towel she'd previously tied around herself. "You should've seen the old timer. He was snoring with his mouth wide open, like this," she said, and proceeded to mimic what she'd just heard and seen in the master bedroom.

For a good thirty seconds, the women couldn't stop laughing at the impression the writer was reasonably sure was dead-on. When the laughter between them subsided, they could finally focus enough to brush their hair apart from one another, in full-frontal privacy.

"I hate to say it," said Trinity, while brushing her dual-tone hair, "but, that might've been the last bath either of us will ever take. It'd be a shame if we all died so soon after meeting each other."

The writer paused, mid-stroke, while brushing her blonde hair that was nearly twice as long as the red and black hair in the other mirror. "Are you afraid..?"

"Of her, or of death?"

"Either one, I suppose."

"Flynn thinks they might be the same thing, but, yes," the fiery young apprentice seemed to have no trouble admitting. "However, fear can be controlled, especially where the two of us are concerned. I'm just as scared of Walther as anything else I've seen. If the Dark Demon could feel fear, she would be afraid of him, too. Of course, she should really be more concerned about *me,* don't you think?" she asked the writer, while posing for herself in the full-body mirror.

Behind her, Kimberly stopped brushing her hair to adjust the mirrored door of the medicine cabinet. Looking at a reflection of a reflection of her developing friend, whose wavy hair had grown out significantly and had become a dark shade of red on one side and an even amount of natural black on the other, she nodded in complete agreement before tying her long blonde hair back into a ponytail.

~

A short time later, while on his way back to the living room from the kitchen, carrying a fully-loaded brass serving tray with a stack of teacups, a brewed pot of coffee, and a white ceramic teapot full of steeping Earl Grey, Walther came to a brief stop near the foot of the staircase to direct his hearing up to the second floor. Detecting nothing other than feminine laughter emerging and approaching from the bathroom, he smiled and continued ahead on his way, setting the tray down on the coffee table next to several boxes of bullets just as Trinity and Kimberly reached the top of the stairs to begin a side by side descent sporting new outfits and weapons.

Seated in thought with a great deal on his mind, John glanced to his right upon hearing the sound of footsteps on the bare hardwood floor and did a double take, watching the ladies on second glance in a stunned awe of their physical beauty coupled with the dark, southern charm of their new clothes. Dressed nearly the same in appealing style with the obvious difference being their chosen color of blouse, they were equipped with matching boots, slacks, vests, and long coats – all in a matte black. Around their waists were dark brown leather belts with attached holsters for the firearms that hung from their right hips where one side of their coats were tucked behind, out of respect for the County and State's open carry regulations that aimed to deter the criminal use of concealed weapons with a responsible, armed citizenry. And so, the pony-tailed, blonde-haired Kimberly, in a dark blue blouse, and Trinity, wearing the dark red that matched the subtle color emerging in her hair, together entered the living room, getting a descending whistle of approval from even the Dark Hunter.

"You've changed so much in two days, I hardly recognize you," John said, when he stood up to greet one whom he loved, staring the fiery young woman in the eyes with no small amount of love and affection. "You really look amazing."

"You both do," Walther said from the sofa, failing in that moment to conceal his attraction toward one of them in particular.

Able to see into her man's body and soul to gain insight into the truth of his words and feelings, Trinity felt a rekindling of romantic emotions and desires that Scarlet had purposely blocked in order to keep the mind of her young host focused on their mission of vital importance. Since the Starsword was no longer in present company to reinforce such an emotional blockade, it melted away with relative ease, sending her straight into his loving arms.

As their lips united in a fiery passion, the eyes of the other man and woman briefly met and averted with a smirk and blushing embarrassment, respectively, while John felt an unusual, amazing, heated sensation on his tongue. *"Wow,"* he said, when they separated. "What *was* that?"

"Huh?" Trinity said, just before the writer blew a bubble and loudly popped it. "Oh, *that.* Cinnamon bubblegum."

With slight disappointment in his voice, "Oh..." he responded, since the answer he was expecting to hear had nothing to do with gum, candy, or even toothpaste or mouthwash.

"You don't seem all that surprised by her condition anymore," Kimberly commented, taking notice of his drastically different demeanor and attitude compared to that of what it was no more than an hour ago, going right for the notebook in her satchel so that she could make note of the observation.

"I've been brought up to speed," he explained, though, at the time, it wasn't much of an explanation for the detail-oriented writer who glanced over at the hunter for a better one and was waved off until some time later.

Choosing a cup of tea for herself, that her mentor had just filled to the rim with aromatic Earl Grey, Trinity sat in her favorite chair near to John's golden chair, somehow managing not to spill a drop, and watched the hunter pour two cups of black coffee – one for himself and one for the Englishwoman who sat down next to him on the sofa while still writing.

"Thank you," Kimberly said, taking a moment to look up from her work to acknowledge the hunter's correct anticipation of her choice and of how many lumps of sugar and, at the same time, to covertly eye him and how handsome he looked in his new black vest and silver shirt in addition to then being freshly shaven, having gotten rid of a five o'clock shadow that had been looking like the next days' six.

"Coffee or tea, Sergeant?!" Walther loudly asked, raising his voice before anyone else among them even heard the sound of footsteps that began descending the stairs from above.

"Let's start with some coffee," the spry, aging man responded, as he took hold of the dark banister and quickly made his way down to ground level in his full olive drab army fatigues, showing no sign of slowing down for a man of his advancing years. "Ah, young Mr. Donovan," he said, as both a friendly greeting and in simple recognition of the camp owner's son. "What brings you into the fray? No pun intended."

"I was looking all over for *her*, trying to get some kind of a lead," John informed the group, as Flynn walked around the coffee table to take the only remaining seat on the sofa. "I tried all the places I thought she might go, asking if anyone had seen her, though I'm pretty sure if they saw her, now, they wouldn't even know it. The bakery, the flower shop, the grocery store, the antique store," he listed off, at the end of which Trinity smiled and nodded. "Nobody had seen her in days. Finally, I bumped into a Scarletmere Deputy outside of the restaurant I like to go to, way south of here. Naturally, I asked what he was doing out of his jurisdiction and he got to talking about how he needed to get his mother out of town. When I asked him what he meant, he asked if I had seen the forest around the Mere lately. Of course, I told him that I hadn't because the camp is closed. That was when he told me to stay far away from the Mere. I thought he was only repeating the words of the locals until he mentioned that some people from the government were investigating. His last comment was about wishing he could get another look at the sexy driver of a red Chevy 210, which sent me racing up here, much to my horror that the forest was dead. It didn't seem to have an effect on this area, but, at least now I know why, as hard as the reason is to believe."

"So, you *do believe?"* Kimberly asked him.

"Well, *now,* I do," John confirmed, before taking a drink of the calming tea that had been sweetened with honey by his honey, who knew just the way he liked it.

In the early hours of the evening, the party of five finished their coffee and tea and, following the hunter's suggestion, made their way toward the back door for what he termed *a test of new hardware.* Facing north on the overgrown lawn in the back yard, Walther began with Trinity at his side, who loaded the new-to-her Colt Python with six rounds of .357 magnum ammunition, having her take aim at the first of two large archery targets that had been set approximately twenty yards away, at the edge of the property. Squeezing off a fairly loud round that echoed in the distance, the fiery young woman instantly decided that she was in love with the gun that was far more comfortable in her hand than the Smith and Wesson M29 in the old Sergeant's possession. After but a few more seconds, the cylinder was spent, and the satisfied young apprentice stepped back next to her rather impressed boyfriend to make room for the next shooter in line – "Lightning" Llewellyn Flynn.

Having been trained as a heavy weapons expert during his time in the army, the Master Sergeant handled the recoil of the powerful .44 magnum with steadfast control and accuracy, sending round after round in and around the bulls-eye of the damaged target until the cylinder was empty.

"Nice shooting there, Sergeant," Walther sincerely complimented. "How do you like her?"

"She fires true," Flynn answered, in his raspy voice.

"Ms. Hunter," Walther next said, calling for the nervous writer who hesitantly responded to the summons by slowly moving forward toward the assumed target line where the Dark Hunter stood waiting for her reluctant participation. "Draw and load."

"O-Okay," she replied.

"Do you know how to eject the cylinder? Yours swings out, unlike most others."

"Yup," she replied, and proceeded to slide each bullet, taken one by one from her jacket pocket, into the brand new, all-steel revolver for the first time.

Behind them, John crossed his arms in front of his chest upon realizing that the weapon that had earlier been drawn against him to prevent his entry into the house was not even loaded. "She tricked me," he commented to his girlfriend, who stood next to him smiling and watching the writer with pleasant anticipation.

"Pull the hammer back with your thumb," Walther instructed, and tapped the part of the gun he meant with his index finger to be certain she understood. "Best to keep your index finger away from the trigger until you are set to fire," he advised, as a precautionary measure to safeguard himself from her nervousness.

"Like that?" she asked, referring to a half-cocked position.

"Not quite," he told her. "Bring it all the way back," he said, demonstrating patience toward a total novice in firearms. "Now, take aim at the target and hold your position while I take a look at you."

"A-Alright."

"Are you nervous?" he asked, as he positioned himself behind her.

"Ah...a little..."

The experienced hunter then took the time to correct the Englishwoman's posture, instructing her to look down the sight in line with the bullseye, told her to exhale and slowly squeeze rather than sharply pull the trigger in order to fire true, and to keep both eyes open rather than develop the treacherous habit of always closing one of them.

"Why can't I close my other eye?" she naturally wondered.

"Doing so will naturally alter your perception and, with your left eye shut, you will not be able to take notice of any enemies that may be advancing on you from that very direction," he explained, during which he held up an index finger and advanced it toward the writer's left cheek without her noticing until he made gentle contact with her skin, causing her to suddenly open her left eye in reaction to his touch. "See what I mean? Never do that. There is nothing to gain and everything to lose," he summarized. "Fire when ready," he said, stepping one pace backward so as not to be breathing down her neck.

Though not as loud as the two weapons that were previously fired, her aim was nevertheless more accurate, as the bullet had impacted the second archery target at the very center of its red bullseye.

"Beginner's luck?" John figured.

"Tell me, Ms. Hunter," Walther said, "do you believe in luck?"

"Certainly not," Kimberly replied, giving her head a stern shake. "There's no such thing as luck. There is only chance."

Loving her answer, subtle though the difference may be, the hunter couldn't help but grin. "Well, then," he said, right before he struck a match to relight the remains of one of his cigars, "fire at will."

With a brief pause between each of the remaining rounds of .38 Special ammunition, during which her companions became more and more interested in the next result, the M60's cylinder was soon expended, much to the amazement of all who were in attendance, included the shooter, herself, who had only become more and more confident with each passing squeeze of the trigger. Upon completing and passing the hunter's test with flying colors, light applause came from behind the writer, who looked down at her right hip in order to properly holster the new firearm she thought she could never learn to like and had just fallen in love with, not mentioning the other.

"Well done," Walther complimented.

"You *must* have fired a gun before," John figured, as the group began to slowly walk back along the lightly trampled path through the tall grass leading up to the house.

Kimberly shook her head, indicating negative. "I'm a fast learner."

"No doubt," he agreed, "but, all in a row? At that range, you'd think it was impossible for a novice."

"Improbable," Walther corrected, from behind the others.

"You're a natural, Ms. Hunter," Flynn said over his own shoulder, in compliment of the feat, knowing that he probably couldn't do better even if he took his time and tried his absolute best.

"I'm just glad she's on *our* side," Trinity casually joked, though there was certainly an amount of truth in that statement – an amount that would be exponentially greater in the future, as it would be for all of them, unbeknownst though it was at the time.

Being up to speed but feeling useless in the way of lending any assistance to the group and the mission, John began to wonder what he was going to do when the imminent time came. Staying at the house would all but assure his death if the unthinkable were to happen – or perhaps he just didn't want to think about it. The protection cast over the property would be instantaneously disenchanted if Trinity's Spiritual Link were to be, in one way or another, permanently severed. "It's too bad you don't have another gun, or I'd volunteer to go along," he decided, surprising the others with his sudden offer.

"You really want to come with us?" Trinity asked him, with an expression that was more or less neutral.

He then took her by the hand, stopping her from advancing along behind the two in front who continued onward. "I want to come with *you,*" he both clarified and confessed to the woman he loved.

"Oh, John," she said, hooking her arms around his left before they continued walking, having become a bit emotional when she realized that the offer to risk his life solely came about because he didn't want to be without her.

Puffing on the last remains of one of his cigars while walking behind the young lovers, "Do you really mean that?" Walther asked John, as he began rummaging through the inner pockets of his jacket, looking like he was searching for a replacement to light up. "It will be exceedingly dangerous, though I suppose you know that, now."

He nodded, understanding enough of what was going on to know that the situation was dire. "If the mission fails, everyone will eventually die, anyway. I'd rather die trying to make a difference than to live out the rest of my days in fear knowing that I could have done something about it, even if that something is likely to be small."

"I'd rather die on my feet than live on my knees," Kimberly quoted, having stopped to look back from a short distance away, near the back door of the house alongside the old Sergeant, who was seen scraping the side of his thumb across the edge of a blade to determine its sharpness.

"Well said," Flynn complimented.

The writer shrugged. "Wasn't me."

"As you wish," Walther said to John, withdrawing from his pocket a cigar to replace the remaining harsh taste of another, which he smelled and tossed away out of apparent disgust. "Ms. Hunter," he casually said, right before striking a match that popped and ignited using nothing more than the roughness of his thumbnail.

Knowing what he was calling for, the writer reached into her leather satchel and withdrew an object wrapped in a white cloth. Holding it in her hands for everyone to see, she unfolded the layers to expose a rare item that four of the five had seen at least once before.

Being the last to look up and take notice of what it actually was, the old Sergeant alarmingly asked, “Why do you have that?!” as he glanced between those whom he suspected to be in on it.

“We planned on giving it back to you afterward, assuming we'd still be alive, of course,” Trinity offered as an explanation.

“With your permission,” Walther said to the gun's rightful owner, “Mr. Donovan will use it in order to accompany us. That is,” he added, turning his attention toward John, “if you are still willing.”

The camp owner's son, feeling strong in his decision, answered by saying, “Whatever role you can plan for me, I'll play it as best I can.”

“You know, I don't think I have any ammo left for it,” Flynn realized, through a search of the pockets of his camouflage fatigues.

As the group headed toward the door, the old Sergeant stood still and looked at the last remaining bullet in his possession for the somewhat uniquely chambered Colt. Holding it up at eye level between his thumb and forefinger, he soon flicked it into the air as John passed by, allowing him to catch it as it came falling down from the darkening sky.

Just as they reached the back door of the house, a thought crossed Kimberly's busy mind. “Hold on a tick,” she said, as she turned around to glance down at the hunting revolver that extended along the outside of Walther's left thigh. “What about *that?”*

The others turned around with the shared interest in what the writer was talking about, and so, walking back to a fair distance of approximately thirty yards, the Dark Hunter drew the Super Blackhawk from its barrel-through style holster, took aim from his hip and fan-fired four booming rounds in the blink of an eye, destroying all that remained of the red paint in the bulls-eye of the first far-off archery target. The remaining two rounds in the weapon's cylinder were then fired with the hunter staring down the gun's sights, sending a pair of bullets straight on through the two wooden ground supports on either side of the target, sending splinters of wood flying in all directions and the target itself falling straight down to the ground.

“Showoff,” Kimberly mumbled.

Chapter 15

Confronting Darkness

19:00 hours.

The party of five once again gathered in the living room of the Looms' house to discuss strategy and what the Dark Hunter felt was the best course of action to achieve victory and hopefully remain alive, though he stressed that millions of lives were at stake and had to be regarded as more important than their own, and that if an opportunity to remove the threat or to turn the tide of battle should present itself, it may never come again and therefore should be acted upon without hesitation.

When sunset was well underway, four split into two pair and armed themselves with plenty of what was hoped to be spare ammunition within the interior of Kimberly's sky blue '62 VW Beetle and Trinity's Ruby Red '57 Chevy 210. Accompanying the writer from the back seat was the ex-soldier, Master Sergeant "Lightning" Llewellyn Flynn, U.S. Army, retired, yet in all the ways that mattered, the old man was still on active duty – no longer in service to his country, but rather to the world.

Accompanying his fiery-spirited girlfriend, John Donovan, Junior, perhaps the least experienced one among them when it came to matters of darkness, had already decided that not only did he have everything to lose in the matter at hand, he had everything to gain, for literally everything that mattered was at risk of being lost.

One at a time, the cars reversed to turn around and were soon rolling down the gravel driveway, one behind the other, with the license plate that read RUBYRED clearly visible through the windshield of the trailing VW. Leaving the safety of the area they had recently begun to refer to as Scarlet's Blessing, and not knowing what to expect when they ventured yet again into dark territory, the four heroes were locked, loaded and ready to encounter the expected and the unexpected.

Before long, while fast-traveling down the paved road between the twisted, petrified trees near the west edge of Lydia's Lifeless Zone, the two cars came to a familiar crossroads and stopped. From their vantage point, the left side of the intersecting road had a small wooden sign with an arrow that was reversed from its cross-road counterpart, with painted red letters that read:

<—— ***Camp Scarletmere***

When facing south, the bold arrow pointed to the left, that being east along the lone dirt road to the camp. Looking through the rear windshield of the Chevy in front, John mouthed and signaled an *okay* with his hand by joining together the tips of his thumb and index finger to make a circle as he extended the three remaining digits. Above the steering wheel of the VW behind him, Kimberly responded with a single thumbs up and so the two vehicles turned left, slowly rolling onward toward their fate.

Hearts pounded as they drove along the gloomy and misty winding road that was, in the past, quite inviting and tranquil. On either side, pair after pair of glowing, indigo eyes, both large and small, watched and stared as the group of four progressed along – eyes that awaited the full setting of the sun and the falling of the shroud of night. Headlights shone on the large, painted sign of the Mere, illuminating the great artistry that no longer resembled the grim reality around the next turn. The water had become a foreboding and forbidden jet black, and when the last light of day faded from the gloom of the sky, the side windows of the cars that had come to a stop in line with one another in the clearing of the vacant camp were rolled down just enough for a revolver and an accompanying hand to fit through, and then all hell broke loose from the forest.

Countless numbers of reflective eyes were exposed in the cold light of the moon that took the place of the vanished sun, revealing the dark-furred animals to which they belonged. Charging madly toward the center of camp, caring not for the usual taste of one another, but only for the tasty flesh of human, came all manner of the Dark Demon's corrupted and most threatening beasts of the forest. Roaring bears, snarling mountain lions, growling wolves, gnashing foxes, and even enormous, bellowing, snorting moose – all corrupted by a reestablished growing and widening sphere of influence that had been termed *Lydia's Lifeless Zone* – obeyed the command of their dark master to kill the one who posed the greatest known threat to its reign of darkness. In the night sky above, ravens, hawks and eagles circled menacingly, awaiting the order to dive-bomb their unsuspecting prey.

Round after round of varying calibers of ammunition were expended from three revolvers that were quickly reloaded and fired dry once again, dropping many of the creatures whose dark brethren were nearing too close for anyone's non-existent comfort.

"Roll 'em up!" the old Sergeant ordered, from the back of the VW, as loud as his raspy voice could go.

"Now!" John said, a second after Trinity rolled up her window.

Placing the expended Python in her lap and closing her eyes, the young symbiont to the Spirit of Fire concentrated on the space around the two vehicles, reached deep down into the depths of her fiery soul and visualized the symbol for infinity in her minds eye. Rising from the ground and shooting up over the height of the cars, a wall of fire in the shape of a figure-eight sprang to life from the moment she opened her scarlet eyes, isolating everyone from the onslaught of the ground-treading beasts that were unfortunate enough to stumble into a blaze that disintegrated them in a matter of moments. Those left on the outside that attempted to jump the wall of scarlet fire would suffer a fate no different than the others who came into contact with the barrier, as the flames seemed to have a life of their own, flaring up at just the right time to prevent any of the corrupted creatures from crossing over to the other side.

Feeling protected enough to roll their windows down, Flynn, Kimberly, and even John, who reloaded and made use of the Colt Python taken from his girlfriend's lap, began firing at will in a heated effort to eliminate the remaining few animal minions that stalked around them on the other side of the barrier that Trinity actively maintained while gripping the steering wheel in concentration. With the threat seemingly at an end, and just when she thought it was safe to let the barrier down, a combined flock of ravenous birds descended on the vehicles from above, biting and clawing from each roof at the gun-wielding hands of the others. Each of her brave comrades suffered damage to their hands, but no one more so than the old Sergeant who took an eagle's talon straight through his left hand before the bird's head was blasted off at close range by the loud pop of Kimberly's M60, causing their ears to ring, as it was a shot fired from within the VW.

"Your knife!" Flynn shouted in reaction. *"Use your knife!"*

Another bird, a raven, was stabbed in its breast and, at the same time, was shoved away from the driver's door of the VW as it flapped its wings and fell to the ground where it twitched and died what looked to be a painful death. With the windows rolled back up to prevent the crazed birds from getting to them, though they clawed, beak-bashed and dive-bombed the front and back windshields of both vehicles, Trinity gradually became so enraged by the ensuing damage to her cherished possession that she let out a shrill scream more deafening than any gunshot, resulting in a burning-hot heat wave that expanded upward, setting all of the winged animals ablaze at once in the blink of an eye.

Time seemed to stand still in the moments after that, until Trinity glanced around at the forest and then at the sky, directly through the roof of the car using heat vision. Detecting nothing, she determined that the coast was clear. However, with everyone's combined attention placed only to one side of the vehicles – the side facing the petrified forest – they had been distracted and hadn't looked back to take notice of a black mist that floated out of and atop the Mere, remaining low to the ground as it traveled through the air and collected on the other side of the parked cars where it swirled upward to form the shape of a girl with skin as black as the darkest of nights. Extending her arm for the mist to follow along, she materialized a deadly, black-bladed weapon in her right hand.

The second person to notice Lydia's dark cohesion was Flynn, who, from the back seat of the VW, sat momentarily stunned with his gaze affixed on the moonlit form that suddenly opened a pair of demonic, dark purple eyes and readied herself to strike down with a sword that ignited in a pulsing energy of the very same color as the opaque windows into a dark soul. *"Get out of the car!!"* he yelled out.

On reflex, the writer looked in the rear view mirror just as a metallic object loudly impacted the back of the car. Horrified by what her eyes beheld, she pushed open the driver's side door and dove out along with the Sergeant, barely avoiding being caught up in the melting, bubbling pool of black sludge that used to be a sky blue '62 VW Beetle.

"Move! Move! Move!" Flynn quickly ordered, just as a drill Sergeant would, as he, himself, crawled along the ground on his elbows before quickly turning over onto his back to begin firing his weapon at the head and upper body of the demonic girl who was seen to be walking them down in the moonlight, rendering her temporarily sightless and buying not more than a few seconds that allowed he and the writer to return to their feet.

"Get in!" Trinity yelled from the driver's seat of the only remaining vehicle, right before John began firing the reloaded Colt Python at the advancing Dark Demon, who, in her unrelenting desire to eliminate those who might challenge her, took the most direct route forward and through the smoldering, tar-like remains of the car she had just destroyed, unintentionally providing those who were fleeing from her very presence with more time to get away.

Even before the Sergeant and the writer were completely aboard, the fiery young driver stepped on the Chevy's gas pedal, tearing up the ground as its tires spun around until they gripped and sent the car rocketing forward at an increasing speed. While the Python and the M29 were being cleared of empty bullet casings in the back seat for a reload, Kimberly, with all the courage she could summon, leaned out the passenger window and began firing her .38 Special at their dark pursuer, doing minor, temporary damage to the sword-wielding demon who had abandoned the use of legs in favor of riding on a black cloud that propelled her forward at a steadily rising velocity.

Coming off the bare ground in the clearing where there was once a field of neatly mowed grass, Trinity turned onto the dirt road near the camp's counselors' cabins and floored the Ruby Red toward the exit as the Englishwoman beside her frantically reloaded with nervous hands, losing a bullet or two between the seat and the floor in the process. Thankfully, the men took over in the nick of time, firing loud, flashing rounds of .367 and .44 magnum bullets while leaning out of the windows from the back seat on either side of the speeding car, dealing an extreme amount of damage that no human could possibly survive, slowing the Dark Demon's advance with each and every violent impact that made it past the captive sword being used as a shield. Nevertheless, red wounds that constituted the bullet damage on the girl's petite body were healed one by one, in mere seconds.

In the Chevy's rear view mirror, Trinity witnessed the specific movement and cross-motioning pattern of her stolen counterpart that was to her unmistakable, telling her of the Recitation that was being enunciated to trap the car within the confines of the camp. Directly ahead, right where the dirt road met with the petrified forest to begin its winding exit, headlights illuminated a pillar of fiery dark energy that suddenly expanded to form the shape of a cross with five interconnected points, taller than the car and as wide as the road.

"Hold onto something!" Kimberly shouted from the passenger seat, when she realized that the driver had no intention of stopping.

Though the roaring Chevy was significantly slowed on contact, the trap ultimately failed and dissipated due to the counteraction of a blessing that had been casually and unnoticeably bestowed upon the car days ago by none other than the graceful touch of Scarlet, herself, via Trinity, of course, allowing for the possibility of escape. The moments during which the vehicle was slowed, however, was all time the Dark Demon needed in order to close the distance. Just as she caught up to them and death seemed unavoidable, a beam of bright, sparkling silver tore through the air across the water of the Mere at the speed of light, enveloping the car and its passengers. At the same moment, by any observable measure of time, the right arm of Lydia, caught by the outer left edge of the focused blast, was vaporized in a searing instant. The Relic she carried – her instrument of destruction – was violently repelled high into the moonlit sky. Though it blanketed everything around them for several seconds, preventing them from seeing anything outside of its area of effect, the beam of silvery white light wasn't painful to look at, nor was it harmful to anyone other than the one who bore a twisted and dark soul, who let out a horrific, otherworldly, demonic scream until the light suddenly blinked out, revealing once again the dark figure of a girl who stood in waiting on two legs. Where her sword-arm once was, a throbbing and wriggling collective of blood red tentacles grew outwardly from her torso and, in very little time, began to show signs of a rejuvenating appendage. That was when Trinity turned around in her seat and took back the Colt Python from the hands of her disturbed, paralyzed-with-fear boyfriend, who immediately called her name and yelled for her to come back as she ran off into the forest while expertly reloading the revolver with bullets taken from an outer pocket of her long coat.

From entirely different areas of the forest – one that was quite close to the Ruby Red and the other being far off in the east – the loud boom and corresponding echo of gunshots could be heard ringing out in the night as the weakened Dark Demon focused only on reconstructing her damaged body. The unanswered gunshots of Flynn's M29 appeared to do significant damage, blowing hole after hole through the girl's dark body that somehow retained its red fluids, closing up the gaping wounds in a bloody sequence of events that provided enough time for John to climb into the driver's seat under protest of hollered orders from the old Sergeant to drive them the hell out of there.

Immediately upon healing, the Dark Demon, in the silhouette-like form of Lydia, opened her opaque purple eyes to find no one and nothing in her sights. Aware of the approximate direction from which the Silver Nova that she knew all too well had come, she demonically bared her black-toothed, gritted teeth and whipped herself around in a fury to gaze in the direction of the far-off eastern forest beyond the Mere, where she knew her ancient enemy was hiding. Standing still with her lifeless eyes open and her head tilted slightly downward, she stared through her wavy black hair across the water in unflinching silence, awaiting the causality of shadow casting away from the light.

Action was preceded only by the caw of a lone raven perched atop the highest peak of a petrified tree near the shore of the Mere, below which an empty swing hung from the lowest branch extending out above the black water that uniquely bore no reflection whatsoever of the veiled moon and the stars in the sky above it. Every time a concentrated beam of silver light approached at unfathomable speed, a moving shadow of the girl's form was created in conjunction with the light from the moon. The demon in Lydia's shell bent over backward, twisted and contorted her youthful body in horrific and unthinkable ways, dancing like a spider, suddenly shifting into her own halted shadow again and again in order to avoid being hit by the silver streaks that were being fired by a stealthy sniper whose location was ultimately detected.

Ceasing the attack to once again charge and replenish the drained supply of light energy within the ancient weapon to which he was bonded for life, the Dark Hunter vanished to move to a new location as his highly evasive target steadily walked toward the shore in anticipation of her enemy's next move. When she reached the decline of the dirt road that led down to the boat launch, a single round was fired from Flynn's old Colt SAA in the hands of John Donovan, Junior, who had gotten out of the Ruby Red a ways up the road to approach his target from behind and in silence. Instead of passing all the way through her, the low-caliber silver bullet burned and sizzled away inside of the back of her head, driving her to whip around and extrude the annoyance in order to deal with the one who had dared to come back to challenge her.

"Don't you remember me, Lydia?" he said, after swallowing the intense fear he was feeling. "It's *me. John."*

Though a series of memories leading up to the death of young Lydia were unconsciously triggered in her hijacked mind, they apparently did nothing to sway the Dark Demon's intention to quickly kill the man standing before her and be done with it. Just as she was about to attack him and absorb his life force, a fully-charged, unavoidable blast of whirring silver light overcame them both, severing the dark entity from its host and sending the light-skinned body of the girl falling forward. Before she could hit the ground, John dove forward out of an instinct to protect her, managing to at least prevent the young girl's body from violently crashing down. Looking up from the lifeless ground, what remained where the black-skinned Lydia once stood was beyond a nightmarish creature. Possessing a true form far more haunting and alien to the senses than any of those prior, it continuously let out the most deeply resonant and terrifying sound of agony imaginable as the damaging light sapped its accumulated power. Desperately desiring to return to its host body, it reformed into the Shadow of Lydia and lunged forward from the very moment the silver nova dissipated, but found itself overcome by a hail of bullets that halted its advance and knocked it backward with each devastating round.

Scooping up Lydia's body in the presence of her wailing Shadow that was suddenly silenced by another wave of silver light, John turned around and ran past the others as fast as he could, up the road toward the Ruby Red that had been left idling just around the first bend. Running not far behind him, the old Sergeant and the writer shook the empty bullet casings from the cylinders of the two Smith and Wesson revolvers and began reloading in case they were pursued by God knows what. Speeding up to get to the car first, the old Sergeant opened up the back door in advance of John's imminent arrival, and they proceeded to slide Lydia's half-naked, petite body into the back seat before quickly closing her inside the protected vehicle and looking back the way they came.

"It would be prudent to get her away from here!" Kimberly strongly advised, as soon as she detected thoughts and accompanying expressions on the faces of her male companions that suggested they were thinking about heading toward danger yet again.

The two men looked back at the car, entirely uncertain which move to make until it was revealed to them through its emitting of a darker, bolder shade of red in the form of a fractal energy shield that the protection of the body held within its enchantment was all but guaranteed to be kept safe and sound.

"Something tells me she can't be gotten to," Flynn surmised, from the unusual visual cue that lasted only a few seconds until it returned to being invisible to the naked eye.

Near the shore of the Mere, the thin, hairless, faceless and featureless loathing-of-life Shadow had but one instinct: to return to a body with which it was compatible. Destabilized and no longer able to sense the presence of its former host, it lurched forward, moving step by step in the direction of the Mere, intent on taking refuge within the safety of its watery domain in order to restore its fading power. Far too slow to evade its eternal nemesis still in hiding across the water, it took a low-powered but well-placed narrow beam to the chest, having no ability or even the intention of avoiding the searing precision of Silver's light that blasted through its dark body, right where the heart of a human would have been. Without a mouth to vocalize its pain and anguish, it could only shudder violently; the action itself generating a strange sound opposite the high frequency of the focused beam until the silver light blinked out, leaving a gaping, oval-shaped wound that would not be regenerated as it struggled to continue forward, damaged and desperate to reach its blackened sanctuary.

The low boom of a powerful revolver then rang out into the night, momentarily dropping the fleeing Shadow to one knee until it rose up from the ground, ignoring the three life forms it detected to be fast approaching from behind. The next two bullets missed their marks, but the follow-up rounds fired from the Smith and Wesson models 29 and 60 hit the thin legs of the retreating alien-like creature at the same time, dropping it to both knees to suffer additional shots to the back until it could heal only the wounds necessary to mobilize itself and rise up once again.

On the eastern shore of the Mere, the Dark Hunter phased back into the visible spectrum of light and took aim at the ancient darkness that was nearing ever closer to the point of escape, where it would remain unreachable, and would in short time begin to wreak unforgettable havoc upon the outside world.

"Lyth..."

Summoning all available moonlight and starlight in the sky to its noble cause, the environment became pitch black in every direction until sight was suddenly restored to all by a silvery-white flash and an accompanying voice sounding of God in Heaven.

"...nüvah!!"

A wide and powerful beam of silver light boomed, pulsed, and enveloped everything and everyone in its brilliant path, healing the injuries of some while at the same time reducing its primary target to a steaming pile of a tar-like substance. Oozing across the ground toward the shoreline, it resisted the barrage of bullets that passed through and into the ground as it continued along at a snail's pace, intent on reaching its immortalizing safe-haven in any state of being.

Believing their failure to be imminent, the Sergeant and the writer reloaded and continued firing as *they* walked the black monster down, when, from above, a cross-shaped star of burning red fire descended and multiplied by five to surround and immobilize the remains of the Shadow on all sides. To the ears of the onlookers, the sound of blazing fire slowly increased in volume until they realized that a tone unlike any natural fire was actually originating from behind them. Beginning with John, the group of three turned around to bear jaw-dropping witness to an emblazoned warrior who carried with her a Divine Relic, together yet to be known in both legend and myth, alike, as *the Scarlet Star* – one of the Seven Saviors to safeguard Earth's dawning of the next Age of the Great Year.

"Trinity..." John said under his breath, as he stared at a young Goddess whose hair and eyes beneath her black cowgirl hat had become as a liquid-like scarlet red that blended with an upwardly flowing aura all around her body, that for its divine intellect did not affect the condition of her new apparel.

As the sword-bearer walked straight toward her comrades with no intention of stopping, John, Kimberly and Flynn moved aside, one after the other, to allow the Goddess of Fire to pass through to her target: her ancient enemy, still held helpless and motionless on the shore but a few meters from the water of the Mere.

"Get back," Scarlet's Divine Voice commanded, echoing through the night in otherworldly unison, and with a quick and strong jerk of her arm, the blade of the sword yielded a melting hot, liquid plasma, forming a continuously flowing blend of vibrant color beginning with a dark red center that became a dark pink stretching to hot pink and culminating in a white double-edge to contain the power of a compressed red dwarf star.

As the others ran back up the road out of fear of what was to follow, a burst of heat beneath the feet of a Goddess propelled her high into the sky, and as her radiant sword was raised high above her head, crossing over the moon, the writer looked back to bear witness to the ancient weapon that was swung violently downward, launching its destructive energy as a spinning projectile in the star-cross shape of its blade. Upon impact with the trap containing a lingering remnant of the Dark Demon, an eruption of fiery liquids and gases completely enveloped the containment area and evenly expanded in all directions, forming a much larger version, remaining geometrically perfect in its shape. When the burning star collapsed inward and faded away into nothingness, the steaming water that was held at bay began flowing in, filling up the deep void that remained, altering the landscape forever with a Sign of the Divine.

Riding on the hot air beneath her feet, Trinity gently floated down from the sky and softly set herself down at the end of the dock. Drawing a deep breath of fresh air into her lungs and exhaling, she allowed the sword's radiant aura, and then her own, to fade away, sending the area into the darkness of dim moonlight. Looking to the far off eastern shore on the opposite side of the Mere, her unique, layered vision picked up the heat signature of a lone gunman who quickly vanished in a refractory white and silver light.

"Is it over?" Kimberly wondered, as she holstered her revolver while staring down from the hilltop at the young woman facing the water from the dock, who quite nearly matched her own appearance if it weren't for the differences in color of both hair and blouse.

"It would appear so," Flynn answered, while reloading his weapon.

That was when John spotted something out of the corner of his eye, far to the left of the boat launch, near to the big tree with the swing that he, himself, had tied to its largest branch over a year ago. "Um...you guys..." he said, in a concerned tone of voice, upon more or less realizing what it was that he was looking at. *"Trinity!"* he called out, quite alarmingly.

Flynn, John and Kimberly gathered near the base of the petrified tree, their eyes transfixed on downward angle as they waited for the sword-bearing young woman to take her time in coming to them. "Stay back," the old Sergeant's raspy voice warned as he tugged on the curious, pony-tailed blonde's arm, pulling her away from that which was so concerning. "Don't get too close."

John handed over the empty Single Action Army he carried, returning it to its rightful owner. "Roger that, Sarge," he confirmed in agreement, wiping dry his sweat-covered brow by pulling up the bottom of his very plain, sandy brown t-shirt that was totally at odds with the getup of any of the others, unintentionally revealing the abs and pectorals he'd clearly been working on.

"I can't fathom..." Kimberly commented, glancing back and forth between the base of the tree and toward the double-wide dock that stretched out over the reflective water on the group's collective right. "What does this mean?" she wondered out loud, receiving only a shrug and a plain look of uncertainty from the two men who wouldn't so much as break their gaze while standing there. They soon made way for Trinity, giving the changed young woman plenty of space to conduct her business regarding the very strange matter at hand.

Stuck into the earth in front of the big tree and its skeletal-like branches that extended out over the water, having fallen down from the sky, was a sword – a sword that looked almost identical to the ancient weapon in Trinity's gloved right hand. Not long after laying eyes it, the young apprentice took off her long black jacket and tossed it over the inert sword, cloaking it so that she could pull it out of the ground without so much as risking direct contact.

"What does it mean?" the writer asked her scarlet-haired friend, who, with both weapons, began leading the way back up the incline of the hill at the camp's boat launch.

"One of two possibilities," she offered as a vague response, using her own natural voice, though she was actually speaking aloud the response that Scarlet had internally provided for her.

Just up the road and around the first turn – or the final turn if one was crazy enough to be arriving at Camp Scarletmere – the Ruby Red was idling where it had been parked and left to protect the priceless treasure that lay within. Staring down through the rear window at the raven-haired girl with the aid of her improved sight, Trinity fully expected to find the cold, lifeless body of her younger half-sister laying dead in the back seat, yet the overwhelming emotion brought on by the experience was so difficult to control that her divine passenger had to numb the initial shock to allow her the fortitude to even open the door. Sitting down on the seat next to the girl's legs as the Sergeant thoughtfully offered his camouflaged coat as a blanket to cover her with, the cold light of the moon was enough to illuminate the interior of the car, revealing the flawless condition of a youthful body to those watching. Even the burn scars that had marred the right half of her face in life were gone, replaced with naturally soft skin that was lovingly touched in fond memory of a joyous time together. Much to the group's collective shock, with the exception of she who could already see, that was when Lydia's chest began to slowly rise and fall.

Awakening to a gentle caress of her cheek, the raven-haired girl, thought to have been forever lost, turned her head into the comforting warmth of her sister's hand and slowly opened her natural eyes.

Epilogue

Signs & Wonders

Three days later, in the kitchen of the Looms' house, the whistle of a kettle on the stove was interrupted upon being picked up by a young blonde girl of thirteen years – fourteen, in a way – who proceeded to pour hot water into her mother's favorite teapot that, sadly, now belonged to her. Seated all around the leftover food atop the dinette behind her was the old man, Sergeant Flynn, drinking from a cup of coffee; the dedicated English writer and artist, Kimberly, adjusting her glasses while sketching what she intended to be a final work of art for her project; Trinity, her scarlet-haired half-sister who was still enjoying seconds of the hearty meal on the plate in front of her; the camp owner's son, John, enjoying watching his fiery-spirited girlfriend indulge herself in southern-style cooking; and lastly, there was Walther, the Dark Hunter, puffing on one of his smelly cigars in silent contemplation of who knows what.

Everyone who wanted tea in turn thanked the young blonde who sweetly went around the table filling their cups before she returned to the only empty chair. Seated at the head of the table opposite from her, was Walther, whose gaze remained bold and serious until the girl made eye contact with him, prompting a wink that was cutely returned before she eagerly resumed eating the rest of what was on her plate. Glancing down the length of the table to her right and left, sat John and Trinity in their respective seats, facing one another, and beyond them was Flynn and Kimberly, seated to the hunter's left and right, likewise facing one another. When her glance returned to the closest seat on her left, she returned a smile from the one she knew to be her half-sister, though words of that fact had in fact not been exchanged between the two.

"Mm," Trinity said, after biting into another piece of fried chicken.

"This is fantastic."

The blonde girl seated to her right nodded in agreement while spooning more mashed potatoes onto her own empty plate.

"How can you possibly eat that much?" Kimberly wondered, having looked up from her sketchbook and down to the other end of the table.

"Give her a break," Trinity said in the girl's defense. "She hasn't eaten in a year."

The old Sergeant took another drink from his coffee cup and set it down. "I think she was talking about *you,"* his raspy voice clarified for the writer, and for the amusement of the rest of the table, who all shared a laugh upon hearing it.

When the combined sound of six laughing voices died down, Walther stood up from his seat and indicated with a flashing gaze that he wished to speak privately with one of them, and so John followed the hunter's smokey trail through the swinging door, out of the kitchen and toward the living room where he found him propping up the top of the piano.

"We will start at the low end and work our way up, soldier," Walther announced, enlisting the man to help him with the task of tuning it, which, compared to the job of constructing a funeral pyre and transporting a dead body in an old, unbalanced wheelbarrow, was going to be a piece of cake.

"Yes, Sir!" John answered, deciding to play the hunter's game. "But, ah, don't you need one of those tuning forks or something?"

The hunter shook his head. "Perfect pitch," he stated, briefly pointing a finger toward his own ear. "Say, did you know the piano is both a string instrument as well as percussive?"

"What are we going to do about her?" John asked, evading a subject he knew nothing about. "It's not as if she can stay here alone, and besides, this house is up for sale. Not that anyone from around here would ever buy it. The rumors flying around town will continue to see to that, I'm sure."

The hunter briefly raised his eyebrows and puffed on his cigar. "Press the key every three seconds," he instructed, before setting the corona down so that the smoldering end extended harmlessly over the edge of a shelf on the wall behind him, right next to a framed family photo that, for more than one reason, no longer matched reality. *"Good,"* he said, when the tension and tone was just right. "Next."

"Does she remember anything?" John asked.

The hunter nodded. "Yes. It is both sad and fortunate that she remembers all of it," he enigmatically answered. "Everything single thing. Next key. So, you wish to find a buyer?"

"Well, *I* don't," John confessed, in the middle of pressing an out-of-tune key again and again, hearing an altered pitch each time he did so. "I've grown fond of this house. Dad has been trying to sell it for a year and, well, for awhile I didn't care, but, I'd hate to see it go to some random person who wouldn't cherish it."

"Next," Walther said again. "What are you looking to get for it?"

"Minus the piano," John said, glancing around at the furnishings in the living room, "the asking price is fifty thousand, though I can't imagine a wandering hunter like yourself being able to afford it."

The Dark Hunter looked up from the task of tuning the expensive instrument and locked eyes with the owner's son, who ceased pressing the lowest sharp in the upper row of black keys.

"Though, from what I gather, you're no ordinary hunter."

Grinning, Walther was the first to break eye contact and looked back down at his hands as his recruit resumed striking the key they were working on. "I can pay you fifty-four thousand."

"...You're kidding."

"If I can keep the piano."

"You wanna live here..?"

"The girl needs someone to look after her, and I promised her mother I would," he recalled, as he picked up his cigar and puffed on it until its ember became hot again, all while he stared in memory of the beautiful, smiling woman in the photo on the shelf. "That one is fine," he confirmed, meaning the next piano key he heard sounding a note, before setting the cigar back down in the same place in order to free up his hands for the tuning of the next string that quite clearly sounded flat.

"Dad will be thrilled," John responded, "but, are you sure about keeping Lydia around here? I mean, what if someone recognizes her?"

"They won't," Walther assured him, letting a contraction slip into his speech, confident that the girl's altered appearance would provide her with plenty of cover and plausible deniability in the days ahead.

In not too much time at all, the piano was tuned, and hearing the sound of sequential chords played in arpeggio, brightly ringing and then darkly sustaining throughout the house, everyone was compelled to gather in the living room under the magic of a musical spell. Rifling through a limited selection of sheet music on a nearby book shelf, the hunter soon found the name of a composition that he knew well. “Ah,” he pleasantly said, upon reading the title of the work. “Clair de Lune,” he announced for the others. “Perfect.”

Just as it was described in a single word, perfect droplets of sound reverberated throughout the house, bouncing off of the dark wood walls that aided the acoustic quality of every note. So wonderful was the tone and the performance of such an enchanting piece of music that all who were in attendance became misty-eyed from the complex emotions of love and of gratitude toward one another, though none were more teary-eyed than young lady Lydia, who felt glad to be alive and free from the clutches of death, happy to be experiencing the joy of music as one of her life's most powerful moments.

After saying goodnight to one another, the saviors of the world – though they were as yet unsung and unhonored – retired to their separate quarters in agreement to get some much needed and well-deserved rest before parting ways in the morning. And so, on the second floor, Flynn took the master bedroom without complaint, Kimberly agreed to take the spare room once Trinity and Scarlet together agreed to exercise their power in burning up the spiderwebs on the ceiling and walls of the western hallway, and the wavy blonde-haired Lydia was tucked into bed in her old room by her fiery half-sister, strangely having no apparent fear of anything, as the Dark Hunter looked on from the doorway with concealed concern for a young lady's well-being.

The light of a crescent moon shone down on the sanctuary of Walther's soon-to-be-purchased house as he returned to the ground floor with his apprentice at his side. Offering to take the sofa, he gave up the remaining guest room to the two lovers, John and Trinity, with one of them insisting that they bring along a certain deadly weapon on the grounds that Scarlet hated sleeping alone.

Hours passed in blissful silence as those who dwelt within Scarlet's Blessing slept the night away. And then it began.

Lydia...

Awakened by the sound of a familiar voice – one that had the effect of instantly bringing tears to the young lady's eyes – Lydia, in her pure white nightgown, sat up in bed.

"Mama..."

Lydia...

Staring at the mysterious sounding, glowing Siren in the shape of a star-cross that had appeared at the foot of her bed near the open window, the bleached-blonde-haired girl was compelled to follow the small, enchanting object as it moved through the unnaturally lit, dark purple bedroom, disappearing from sight upon moving directly into the closed door. Caught in a trance, she slowly opened the door wide, revealing the dark, little star that had been waiting for her in the hallway before it once again disappeared beyond a closed door on the right, sending the area into near darkness but for the strange light in deep purple that emanated around the frame.

The sixth door of the hallway, once opened, revealed a staircase leading up to the attic. Climbing the stairs one at a time, with both feet being brought to rest on each step before ascending to the next, the attic door very slowly closed under its own weight behind her, its old hinges producing a slight creaking sound as she continued to advance forward and upward.

Illuminating the entire attic with the effect of a black light, the purple-sparkling Dark Star magically hovered, humming and shimmering through the air above the entranced girl's head, capturing her undivided attention until it directly descended and disappeared into a wooden footlocker that was laying flat on the floor. Moonlight shone in through a lone, circular window, faintly illuminating the chest in the place of dark starlight. Lowering herself directly onto her knees in front of the padlocked chest, the young lady reached out to cradle the steel in her hand, and without making direct contact, the lock physically warped and came apart at the molecular level, having lost cohesion, allowing her to open the lid with but a subtle gesture of a delicate hand. Squinting her eyes to look down through the rays of purple and black light still being eerily generated by the little Dark

Star that so entranced her, she discovered something else, entirely. Never before existing, having no known name at that time, lay an ebony sword of the blackest night – *the Scarlet Shadow* – longing to return to the hand of its dark master.

Lydia.

When she granted its wish by making direct contact with it, grasping the hilt with her left hand, her fingernails, her eyes, as well as all the strands of her bleached-blonde hair smoothly alternated over to a purple so dark that they were nearly back to being black.

The End

www.ingramcontent.com/pod-product-compliance
Lightning Source LLC
LaVergne TN
LVHW041201150826
845673LV00001B/246

* 9 7 8 1 7 7 7 7 2 3 5 8 3 *